Praise for the authors of
It Happened One Christmas

CARLA KELLY

"Kelly is a master at emotional, uplifting romances."
—*RT Book Reviews* on *The Wedding Ring Quest*

"A powerful and wonderfully perceptive author."
—*New York Times* bestselling author Mary Jo Putney

GEORGIE LEE

"Lee takes readers on [a]...sexy romp."
—*RT Book Reviews* on *A Debt Paid in Marriage*

"Lee's novel hits the sweet spot."
—*RT Book Reviews* on *Engagement of Convenience*

ANN LETHBRIDGE

"Adventure, sensuality and romance are beautifully blended."
—*RT Book Reviews* on *Captured Countess*

"Dangerous excitement blended with poignancy and passion."
—*RT Book Reviews* on *Falling for the Highland Rogue*

D1024053

JAN 2 2 2016

Carla Kelly started writing Regency romances because of her interest in the Napoleonic Wars, and she enjoys writing about warfare at sea and the ordinary people of the British Isles rather than lords and ladies. In her spare time she reads British crime fiction and history—particularly books about the US Indian Wars. Carla lives in Utah and is a former park ranger and double RITA® Award and Spur Award winner. She has five children and four grandchildren.

A lifelong history buff, **Georgie Lee** hasn't given up hope that she will one day inherit a title and a manor house. Until then, she fulfills her dreams of lords, ladies and a Season in London through her stories. When not writing, she can be found reading nonfiction history or watching any movie with a costume and an accent. Please visit georgie-lee.com to learn more about Georgie and her books.

In her youth, award-winning author **Ann Lethbridge** reimagined the Regency romances she read—and now she loves writing her own. Now living in Canada, Ann visits Britain every year, where family members understand—or so they say—her need to poke around every antiquity within a hundred miles. Learn more about Ann or contact her at annlethbridge.com. She loves hearing from readers.

Carla Kelly
Georgie Lee
Ann Lethbridge

It Happened One Christmas

SAN DIEGO PUBLIC LIBRARY
LA JOLLA BRANCH

3 1336 09938 0330

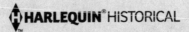 **HARLEQUIN** HISTORICAL

If you purchased this book without a cover you should be aware that this book is stolen property. It was reported as "unsold and destroyed" to the publisher, and neither the author nor the publisher has received any payment for this "stripped book."

ISBN-13: 978-0-373-29855-6

It Happened One Christmas

Copyright © 2015 by Harlequin Books S.A.

The publisher acknowledges the copyright holders of the individual works as follows:

Christmas Eve Proposal
Copyright © 2015 by Carla Kelly

The Viscount's Christmas Kiss
Copyright © 2015 by Georgie Reinstein

Wallflower, Widow…Wife!
Copyright © 2015 by Michèle Ann Young

All rights reserved. Except for use in any review, the reproduction or utilization of this work in whole or in part in any form by any electronic, mechanical or other means, now known or hereinafter invented, including xerography, photocopying and recording, or in any information storage or retrieval system, is forbidden without the written permission of the publisher, Harlequin Enterprises Limited, 225 Duncan Mill Road, Don Mills, Ontario M3B 3K9, Canada.

This is a work of fiction. Names, characters, places and incidents are either the product of the author's imagination or are used fictitiously, and any resemblance to actual persons, living or dead, business establishments, events or locales is entirely coincidental.

This edition published by arrangement with Harlequin Books S.A.

For questions and comments about the quality of this book, please contact us at CustomerService@Harlequin.com.

® and TM are trademarks of Harlequin Enterprises Limited or its corporate affiliates. Trademarks indicated with ® are registered in the United States Patent and Trademark Office, the Canadian Intellectual Property Office and in other countries.

Recycling programs for this product may not exist in your area.

Printed in U.S.A.

www.Harlequin.com

CONTENTS

Christmas Eve Proposal

Carla Kelly

To the people of Kirkcudbright, Scotland. Although my own relatives left your environs in 1867 to find a new life in the United States, you will always have a place in my heart.

Dear Reader,

Throughout my Regency-writing years, I've become a specialist in "Dukeless Regencies." My stories and novels are, more often than not, devoted to the ordinary folk of the early nineteenth century. I often write about the Royal Navy, whose wooden walls truly kept England from invasion by Napoleon.

What better time than Christmas to focus on two such common people, one a specialist in the Royal Navy—a sailing master—and the other an ordinary woman who works in a tearoom. Christmas brings a special grace to us all. For a few moments in a world growing more complex by the minute, we step back and relish the wonderful story of other ordinary people, a carpenter and his wife, who are touched by grace, and the great promise of a very special baby.

Christmas is a believing time. We believe we can become better; we believe in mercy; we believe in ourselves. We have hope again, and we look kindly on loved ones, acquaintances and even strangers. And that is the magic of Christmas, of Hanukkah, of other holiday worship: if we will let it, the season can change our lives, too.

Merry Christmas to all of us ordinary people.

Carla Kelly

Chapter One

'Surely you never expected to stay at Walthan Manor, Master Muir?'

What a self-righteous prig Midshipman Tommy Walthan is, Sailing Master Benneit Muir said to himself. *He's a pipsqueak, a lump of lard and an earl's son. God spare me.*

'Oh? I assumed that since you commissioned me to drill you in navigation methods, that I would be more useful close by.' That was the right touch. Ben didn't hold out much hope that any amount of tutoring would improve the wretched youth's chances of passing his lieutenancy exams next year in 1811, but it was nearly Christmas and the sailing master had no plans.

There wasn't time to go home to Scotland, or much reason. The girls Ben had yearned for years ago were all married and mothers many times over. His mother was gone, his father too old to travel and his brothers in Canada.

Walthan gave that stupid, octave-defying titter of his that felt like fingernails on slate. It had driven other midshipmen nearly to distraction, Ben knew, but at least it was one of the irritants that spurred others to pass their exams and exit the HMS *Albemarle* as quickly as possible. Even the captain, an amazingly patient man, had remarked that nothing short of the loss of his ship would ever rid them of Tom Walthan. No other captain wanted him, no matter how well connected his family.

'*Stay* at Walthan? Lord, no, Master Muir! I can't imagine what my mama would say, if you stepped from this post-chaise with your duffel. Better find a place in the village, sir.' The midshipman coughed delicately into his sleeve. 'You know, amongst people more of your own inclination.'

Ben decided that the village would be far enough away from Walthan's laugh, but he didn't intend to sink without a struggle.

'You'll shout my room and board?' Ben gave the midshipman the full force of the gallows glare he usually reserved for the quarterdeck. It wasn't that he couldn't afford to pay his own whack, but he was tired of being cooped up in the post-chaise all the way from Plymouth with Tom Walthan, the midshipman from Hades.

'If I must,' Walthan said, after a lengthy sigh, that made Ben feel sorry for the lad's nanny, gone now. He had no doubt that Walthan's mother had long since given up on him.

'I fear you *must* pay,' Ben said. 'Do you know of lodgings in Venable?'

'How would I?' Walthan waved his hand vaguely at the cliff edges and sea glimpses that formed the Devon coast. 'Venable has a posting house. Try that.'

Ben gave an inward sigh, nothing nearly as dramatic as Tom Walthan's massive exhalation of breath, because he was not a show pony. He had hoped to find a quiet place to finally slit the pages on *The Science of Nautical Mathematics* and settle down to a cosy read. Posting houses were not known as repositories of silence.

'Besides, I still must explain why I have asked you here

to help me study for my exams,' Walthan said. 'The last time I wrote Mama, I was pretty sure I would pass.' Another delicate cough. 'And so I informed her.'

'That attempt in Malta?' Ben asked. He remembered the barge carrying four hopeful midshipmen into the harbour where an examination board of four captains sat. Three had returned excited and making plans, Walthan not among them. The laggard's disappointment was felt by everyone in the *Albemarle*'s wardroom, who wanted him gone.

'Those were trick questions,' Walthan said, with all the hurt dignity he could muster.

Ben swallowed his smile. 'Oh? You don't see the need of knowing how to plot a course from the Bight of Australia to Batavia?'

'I, sir, would have a sailing master do that for me,' Walthan said. 'You, fr'instance. It's your job to know the winds and tides, and chart the courses.'

Hmm. Get the idiot out of his lowly place on the Albemarle *and he becomes almost rude*, Ben thought. 'And if I dropped dead, where would you be?' The little nuisance was fun to bait, but the matter was hardly dignified, Ben decided. 'Enough of this. I will do my best to tutor some mathematics into you. Stop here. I'll see you tomorrow at four bells in the forenoon watch at Walthan Manor.' Ben shook his head mentally over the blank look on the midshipman's face. 'Ten o'clock, you nincompoop,' he said as he left the post-chaise and shouldered his duffel.

Now where? Ben stood in front of the public house and mail-coach stop, if the muddy vehicle visible in the ostler's yard was any proof of that. He peered through the open door to see riders standing shoulder to shoulder, hopeful of something to eat before two blasts on a yard of tin reminded the riders to bolt their food or remain behind. Surely Venable had more to offer.

As he stared north and then south, Ben noticed a small sign in the distance. He walked in that direction until he could make out the words, Mandy's Rose. Some village artist had drawn a rose in bud. Underneath he read, 'Tea and good victuals.'

'Victuals,' he said out loud. 'Victuals.' It was a funny word and he liked the sound of it. He saw the word often enough on bills of lading requiring his signature, as food in kegs was lowered into the hold, another of his duties. Oh, hang it all—he ran the ship. Victuals. On land, the word sounded quaint.

'Good victuals, it is,' he said out loud as he got a better grip on his duffel. He tried to walk in a straight line without the hip roll that was part of frigate life. Well balanced aboard ship, he felt an eighteen-year awkwardness on land that never entirely went away, thanks to Napoleon and his dreams of world domination.

A bell tinkled when he opened the door to Mandy's Rose. He hesitated, ready to rethink the matter. This was a far more genteel crowd than jostled and scowled in the public house. He doubted the ale was any good at Mandy's Rose, but the fragrance of victuals overcame any shyness he felt, even though well-dressed ladies and gentlemen gazed back at him in surprise. Obviously posting-house habitués rarely came this far.

His embarrassment increased as his duffel seemed to grow from its familiar dimensions into a bag larger than the width of the door. That was nonsense; he had the wherewithal to claim a place at any table in a public domain. He leaned his duffel in the corner, suddenly wishing that the shabby thing would crawl away.

The diners had returned to their meals and there he stood, a good-enough-looking specimen of the male sex, if he could believe soft whisperings from the sloe-eyed, dark-skinned women who hung about exotic wharves. He put his hand on the doorknob, ready to stage a retreat. He would have, if the swinging door to what must be the kitchen hadn't opened then to disclose a smallish sort of female struggling under a large tray.

He would never have interfered with her duties, except that a cat had followed her from the kitchen and threatened to weave between her feet.

Years of battle at sea had conditioned Ben Muir to react. Without giving the matter a thought, he crossed the room fast and lifted the tray from her just before the cat succeeded in tripping her. Two bowls shivered, but nothing spilled.

'Gracious me, that was a close call,' the woman said as she picked up the cat, tucked it under her arm and returned it to the kitchen, while he stood there looking at her, wondering if this was Mandy's rose.

She was back in a moment, her colour heightened, a shy look on her face as she tried to take the tray from him. He resisted.

'Nay, lass, it's too heavy,' he said, which earned him a smile. Thank the Lord she wasn't angry at him for disrupting what was obviously a genteel dining room by standing his ground with the tray.

'I do tend to pile on the food,' she said. Her accent was the lovely burr of Devon. He could have held the tray for hours, just to listen to her. 'Stand here, then, sir, and I'll lighten the load.'

He did as she said, content to watch her move so gracefully from table to table, dispensing what was starting to make his mouth water. A touch of a shoulder here, a little laugh there, and he knew she was well acquainted with the diners she served. Small villages were like that. He remembered his own in Scotland and felt the sudden pang of a man too long away.

And all this because he was holding a tray getting lighter with every stop at another table. In a moment there would be nothing for him to do, but he didn't want to leave.

'There now.' She took the tray from him. 'Thank you.'

He nodded to her and started for the door. He didn't belong there.

She never lost her dignity, but she beat him to the door and put her hand in the knob. 'It's your turn now, sir. What would you like?'

'I don't belong here,' he whispered.

'Are you hungry?'

'Aye. Who wouldn't be after breathing the fragrance in here?'

'Then you belong here.'

It was more than the words. Her eyes were so frank and kind. He felt the tension leave his shoulders. The little miss wanted him to sit down in a café that far outranked the usual grub houses and dockside pubs where he could be sure of hot food served quickly and nothing more. Mandy's Rose was worlds away from his usual haunts, but he had no desire to leave.

She escorted him to a table by the window. The wind was blowing billy-be-damned outside. He thought a window view might be cold, but he could see it was well caulked. No one seemed to have cut a single corner at Mandy's Rose.

'Would you like to see the bill of fare?' she asked.

'No need. Just bring me whatever you have a lot of,' he told her.

He blushed like a maiden when she frowned and leaned closer, watching his lips. 'I'm not certain I understood you, sir,' she said, equally red-faced.

He repeated himself, irritated that even after years away from old Galloway, his accent could be impenetrable. He gave her a hopeful look, ready to bolt if she still couldn't understand him. A man had his pride, after all.

'We have a majestic beef roast and gravy and mounds of dripping pudding, and that's only the beginning.'

Damn his eyes if he didn't have to wipe his mouth. Gravy. He thought about asking her to bring a bowlful and a spoon, but refrained.

'And to drink?'

'Water and lots of it. We've been a long time on blockade.'

She nodded and went to the kitchen, pausing for another shoulder pat and a laugh with a diner. He watched her, captivated, because when she laughed, her eyes shrank into little blue chips. The effect was so cheerful he couldn't help but smile.

She paused at the door and looked back at him. Her hair was smooth, dark and drawn back in a ribbon, much as his was. He had stood close enough to her to know that she had freckles on her nose. That she had looked back touched him, making him wonder if there was something she saw that she liked. He knew that couldn't be the case. He was worn out and shabby and ready to leave the blockade behind, if only for a few weeks. The ship would be in dry dock for at least six weeks, but he was the sailing master and every inch of rope, rigging, ballast and cargo was his responsibility.

He had agreed—what was he thinking?—to devote three weeks to cram enough navigational education into Thomas Walthan's empty head for him to pass his lieutenancy exams. Whether or not he succeeded, Ben had to report to Plymouth's docks in three weeks, because duty called. He glanced out the window, where sleet scoured the cobblestones now. At least he would go back well fed and with the lingering memory of a kitchen girl who looked back at him. That was about all a man could ask for in perilous times.

'Auntie, we have the most amazing man seated by the window,' Mandy said. 'He's in a uniform, but I don't know what kind. He's not a common seaman. He's from Scotland. He wants whatever we have the most of and lots of water. And, Auntie, he has the most amazing tattoo on his neck. It looks like little dots.'

'Mandy's Rose doesn't see too many tattoos,' Aunt Sal said. 'Earrings?'

'Heavens, no!'

Aunt Sal smiled over the gravy she stirred, then set it on a trivet. She turned to carve the beef roast, poising her knife over the roast. 'Here?'

'Another inch or two. There. And lots of gravy. You should have seen his eyes follow the gravy I served Vicar Winslow. And your largest dripping pudding. That one. We have some carrots left, don't we?'

'Slow down, child!' Sal admonished as she sliced a generous hunk of beef and slathered gravy on it. She poured more gravy in a small bowl while Mandy selected the biggest dripping pudding and set it on a plate all its own. She slid the bowl on, too, added cutlery and took it into the dining room.

She stopped a moment, just to look at the Navy man. Palm on chin, he was looking out the window at the driving sleet. He had taken off his bicorn hat and his hair was a handsome dark red, further staking his claim as a son of Scotland. He looked capable in every way, but he also looked tired. *The blockade must be a terrible place*, she thought, as she moved forward.

'Dripping pudding first and lots of gravy,' she said to get his attention. 'I'll bring some water and then there will be beef roast with carrots. Will that do?'

'You can't imagine,' he said, tucking his napkin into the neck of his uniform.

She set down the plate and smiled as he poured a flood of gravy over the pudding. A cut and a bite was followed by a beatific expression. Nothing made Mandy happier than to see pleasure writ so large on a diner's face. She wanted to sit down and ask him some questions, but Aunt Sal had raised her better.

Or had she? Before she realised what had happened, she was sitting across from him at the small table. She made to rise, astounded at her brazen impulse, but he waved her back down with his knife and gave her an enquiring look.

'Where are my manners, you are likely wondering?' she said.

'I could see a question in your eyes,' he said. 'Ask away, as long as you don't mind if I keep eating. I'm used to questions at sea.'

He had a lovely accent, Mandy decided, and she could understand him now. How that had happened in ten minutes, she didn't know. 'It's this, sir—I was wondering about your uniform. I know you're not a common seaman, but I don't see an overabundance of gold and folderol on your blue coat.' She smiled, which for some reason made him smile. 'Are you a Quaker officer of some sort and must be plain?'

He set down his knife and fork, threw back his head and laughed. Mandy put her hands to her mouth and laughed along with him, because it was contagious.

'Oh, my,' he said finally. 'I'll have to share that in the wardroom, miss…miss.'

'Mandy Mathison,' she said.

'You're Mandy's Rose?' he asked, as he returned to the dripping pudding.

'I am! My name is Amanda, but Aunt Sal has always called me Mandy. She scolded me one day when I was two and pulled up a handful of roses, then cried because of the thorns.'

'An early lesson, lass, is that roses have thorns.'

'So true. When she leased this building and started the tea room, she named it for me. But, sir, you haven't answered my question.'

'I'm hungry,' he said and Mandy knew she had overstepped her courtesy. She started to rise again and he waved her down again. 'I'm senior warrant officer on the *Albemarle*, a forty-five frigate. Forty-five guns,' he explained, interpreting her look. 'It's only been in the last three years that we masters have had uniforms.' He held up one arm. 'This is the 1807 model. I hear the newer ones have a bit of that folderol on the sleeves now.'

'I shouldn't have called it that,' she said. 'What do you do?'

He chewed and swallowed, looking around. Mandy leaped up and hurried into the kitchen again, returning with the pitcher of water and a glass.

'I forgot.' She poured him a drink.

He drank it down without stopping. He held out the glass again and he did the same. He let out a most satisfied sound, somewhere between a sigh and a burp, which made the vicar turn around.

'We drink such poor water on blockade.' He picked up his knife and fork again and made short work of the dripping pudding. Mandy returned to the kitchen with empty plates from other diners and came back with that healthy slab of roast and more gravy, setting it before him with a flourish, because Aunt Sal had arranged the carrots just so.

'Sit,' he said, as he tackled the roast beef. After a few bites, he took another drink. 'I'm in charge of all navigation, from the sails and rigging, to how the cargo is placed in the hold, to ballast. Everything that affects the ship's trim is my business.'

'I'm amazed you can get away from your ship at all,' Mandy said. She hesitated and he gave her that enquiring look. 'Are you going home for Christmas?'

'Too far, lass.' He leaned back and gave her an appraising look. 'Do you know Venable well?'

'Lived here all my life.'

'In a weak, weak moment, I agreed to help Thomas Walthan cram for his lieutenancy examinations.' He lowered his voice. 'He's a fool, is Tommy, and this will be his fourth try. I'll be here three weeks, then it's back to Plymouth and those sails and riggings I mentioned. Do you know the Walthans?'

Oh, did she. Mandy decided that after this meal she would probably never see the sailing master again, but he didn't need to know everything. 'They're the gentry around here. His father is Lord Kelso, an earl.' She couldn't help her smile. 'Thomas can't pass his tests?'

The master shook his head. 'I fear there's a small brain careening around in that head. My captain wants him to pass and promote himself right out of the *Albemarle*.'

He returned to his meal and she cleared away the dishes from the last group of diners, the vicar and his wife, who came in every day at noon.

'I believe you're flirting with him,' the vicar's wife whispered, as Mandy helped the old dear into her coat. 'You'll recall any number of sermons from the pulpit about navy men.'

Mandy nodded, hoping the master hadn't overheard. She glanced at him and saw how merry his eyes were. He had overheard.

'I'll be so careful,' Mandy whispered in her ear as she opened the door.

Reverend Winslow took a long look at the master and frowned.

Now the dining room was empty, except for the sailing master, who worked his way steadily through the roast, saving the carrots for last. When he thought she wasn't looking, he spooned down the last of the gravy.

'Is there anything else I can get you?' she asked, determined to wrap herself in what shreds of professionalism remained, after her battery of questions.

'What else is in your kitchen?' he asked.

'Just a custard and my Aunt Sal,' she replied, which made him laugh.

'How about some custard? Maybe I can chat with your aunt later.'

She returned to the kitchen, just in time to see Aunt Sal step back from the door.

'I've been peeking. He's a fine-looking fellow and that *is* an odd tattoo,' Sal whispered. 'He certainly can pack away food.'

'I don't think life on the blockade is blessed with anything resembling cuisine. He'd like some custard.'

Aunt Sal spooned out another massive portion, thought a moment, then a more dainty one. 'You haven't eaten yet, Mandy. From the looks of things, he wouldn't mind if you sat down again.'

'Auntie! When I think of all your lectures on…' she lowered her voice '…the dangers of men, and here you are, suggesting I sit with him?'

Aunt Sal surprised Mandy with a wistful smile, making

her wonder if there had been a seafaring man in Sal's life at some point. 'It's nearly Christmas and we are at war, Mandy,' she said simply.

'That we are,' Mandy said. 'I suppose a little kindness never goes amiss.'

'My thought precisely,' Sal told her. 'I reared you properly.'

Mandy backed out of the swinging door with the custard. The master formally indicated the chair opposite him and she sat down, suddenly shy. And sat there.

'See here, Miss Mathison. Despite what that old fellow thought, I have enough manners not to eat first. Pick up your fork.'

She did as he said, enjoying just the hint of rum that her aunt always added to her custard. In a week, they would spend an afternoon making Christmas rum balls and the tea room would smell like Percival Bartle's brewery on the next street.

He ate with obvious appreciation, showing no signs of being stuffed beyond capacity. Then he removed the napkin from his uniform front and set down his fork.

'I have a dilemma, Miss Mathison…' he began.

'Most customers call me Mandy,' she said.

'I've only known you about an hour,' he replied, 'but if you like, Mandy it is. By the way, I am Benneit Muir.' He wiped his mouth. 'My dilemma is this—Thomas Walthan won't hear of my staying at Walthan Manor. Apparently I am not high bred enough.' He chuckled. 'Well, of course I am not.'

Mandy sighed. 'That would be the Walthans.'

'I can probably find a room at the public house, but more than anything, I'd like some peace and quiet to read. Can you suggest a place?'

'Venable doesn't...' she began, then stopped. 'Let me ask my aunt.'

Aunt Sal was putting away the beef roast. Mandy slid the dishes into the soapy water where soon she would be working, now that luncheon was over.

'Aunt, his name is Benneit Muir and he has a dilemma.'

Aunt Sal gave her an arch, all-knowing look. 'Mandy, you have never been so interested in a diner before.'

'You said it—he's interesting. Besides, you as much as suggested I be pleasant to him, because it is Christmas.' She took a good look at her aunt, a pretty woman faded beyond any bloom of youth, but kind, so kind. 'Apparently he has agreed to tutor Thomas Walthan in mathematics, but you know the Walthans—they won't allow him to stay there.'

'No surprise,' Aunt Sal said as she removed her apron.

'The posting house is too noisy and he wants quiet to read, when he's not tutoring. We have that extra room upstairs. What do you think?'

'A room inches deep in dust.' Aunt Sal took another peek out the door. 'We don't even know him.'

Mandy considered the situation. She had never been one to cajole and beg for things, mainly because she had everything she needed. She didn't intend to start now, but there was something about the master that she liked.

'No, we don't know him,' Mandy said, picking her way through uncharted water. 'Maybe he would murder us in our beds. Or shinny down the drainpipe and leave us with a bill.'

'That seems doubtful, dearest. He just wants peace and quiet? There's plenty of that here.'

Mandy said no more; she knew her aunt. After a moment in thought, Aunt Sal gave her another long look.

'On an hour's acquaintance, you think you know him?'

'No,' Mandy replied. She had been raised to be honest. 'But you always say I am a good judge of character. And besides, didn't you just encourage me?'

Aunt Sal folded her arms. '*That* chicken is coming home to roost,' she said. 'Remind me not to be so soft-hearted in future.'

'It could also be that I am tired of my half-brother riding roughly over everyone,' Mandy said softly.

Aunt Sal put her hands on Mandy's shoulders and they touched foreheads. 'Should I have started Mandy's Rose in another village?'

'No, Aunt. This is our home, too.'

Aunt Sal kissed Mandy's forehead. 'Let's go chat with the sailing master.'

Here comes the delegation, Ben thought, as the door to the kitchen swung open. *At least I'm not on a lee shore yet.*

This could only be Aunt Sal. He took her in at a glance, a woman past her prime, but lively still and obviously concerned about her niece. He knew he was looking at a careful parent. He got to his feet, swaying a little because he still didn't have the hang of decks—no, floors—that remained stationary.

She came closer and gave a little nod of her head, which he returned with a slight bow. She moved one of the chairs closer from the nearest table, but Mandy sat at the same table where he had eaten that enormous lunch. That gesture told him whose side Mandy was on and he thought he might win this. It was a game he had never played before, not with war and eighteen years at sea.

'I am Sally Mathison, proprietor of this tea room. My niece tells me you are looking for quiet lodgings for a few weeks.'

'Aye,' he replied. 'I am Benneit Muir, sailing master of

the *Albemarle*, in dry dock near Plymouth. I'll be here three weeks, trying to cram mathematics into young Thomas Walthan's brainbox. It will be a thankless task, I fear, and I would most appreciate a quiet place at night, the better to endure my days.'

'Is he paying you?' Sal Mathison asked.

'Aunt!' Mandy whispered.

'No, it's a good question,' he said, quietly amused. 'He is paying me fifty pounds.'

He could tell from the lady's expression that the tide wasn't running in his favour, despite Mandy's soft admonition. Honesty meant more honesty.

'I'm tired, Miss Mathison. I often just stay with the ship during dry dock, because I am invariably needed because my ship's duties are heavy. Scotland is too far to go for Christmas, and besides, my mother is dead and my brothers live in Canada. I… I wanted something different. And, no, I do not need the money. I bank regularly with Brustein and Carter in Plymouth.' *That should be enough financial soundness, even for a careful aunt*, he thought.

'I was rude to ask,' Sal Mathison said.

'I rather believe you are careful,' he replied, then put his hands palm up on the table, petitioning her. 'Just a quiet place. I don't even know if you have a room to let.'

Hands in her lap, Aunt Sal looked him in the eye for a long moment and he looked back. This wasn't a lady to bamboozle, not that he had any skill along those lines. He could only state his case.

'I don't drink, beyond a daily issue of grog on board. I don't smoke, because that is dangerous on a ship. I mind my own business. I am what you see before you and, by God, I *am* tired.'

He knew without looking that Mandy's eyes would soften at that, because he was a good study of character, a valuable trait in a master. It was Sal Mathison he had to convince.

Her face softened. 'Right now, the room is thick in dust. It used to be my mother's room, Mandy's grandmama.' Her eyes narrowed and he knew the matter hinged on the next few seconds. She nodded, and he knew he had won. 'Two shillings a week—that includes your board—paid in advance.'

Happy for the first time in a long while, he withdrew six shillings from his pocket. He handed them to her. 'I can dust and clean, Miss Mathison.'

'I'll let you. Mandy can help. I have to start the evening meal.' She stood up and he got to his feet as well. She indicated that he follow them into the kitchen.

'Go upstairs, Mandy, and open those windows. We need to air it out.'

Mandy did as she was bid. Curious, he watched her go to an inside door which must lead to stairs. There it was again—she looked back at him for the briefest moment. He felt another care slide from his shoulders. He looked at Miss Mathison, knowing what was coming.

'Under no circumstances are you to take advantage of my niece, Master Muir,' she told him. 'She is my most precious treasure. Do you understand?'

'I do.'

'Then follow me. I have a broom and dustpan.'

He reported upstairs with said broom and accoutrements, left them with Mandy after a courtly bow, then went below deck again for mop and bucket. Mandy's hair was tied back in a scarf that displayed the even planes of her face. He thought she was past her first bloom, but she still radiated youth. On another day, it might have made him sour to think of his own missed opportunities, thanks to the Beast from Corsica. Today, he felt a little younger than he knew he was. Maybe he could blame such good tidings on the season.

But there she stood, broom in hand, lips pursed.

'Uh, I paid six shillings for this room,' he teased, which made her laugh.

'Master Muir...' she began.

'I am Ben if you are Mandy.'

'Very well, sir.'

'Ben.'

'Ben! I'll dust and then you sweep.'

She dipped the cloth in the mop water, wringing it out well. He watched her tackle the nightstand by the bed, so he did the same to the much taller bureau. He took off his uniform coat and loosened his neckcloth, then tackled the clothes press.

'Why haven't you let out this excellent room before?' he asked, dusting the top of the window sill. He looked out. God be praised, there was a view of the ocean.

'Auntie and I rattle along quite well without lodgers,' she told him. 'Besides, it was Grandmama's only two years ago, when she died.' Mandy stopped dusting and caressed the headboard. 'What a lovely gram she was.'

She started dusting again, whistling under her breath, which Ben found utterly charming. She laughed and said, 'It's "Deck the Halls". You may whistle along, too.'

To his astonishment, he did precisely that. When she sang the last verse in a pretty soprano, complete with a retard on the final *la-la-la-la*, he sang, too. 'Do you know "The Boar's Head" carol?' he asked.

She did and he mopped through that carol, too, with an extra flourish of the mop on the last *'Reddens laudes Domino'*.

'We have some talent,' she said, which made him sit

on the bed and laugh. 'Move now,' she said, her eyes still bright with fun. 'The dusty sheets go downstairs.'

He waited in the room until she came back up with clean sheets and they made the bed together.

'Aunt Sal thinks we're too noisy,' Mandy said and she squeezed the pillow into a pillow slip with delicate embroidery, nothing he had ever seen in a public house before. 'I told her that you will come with me to choir practice tomorrow night at St Luke's.' She peered around the pillow, her eyes small again, which he knew meant she was ready to laugh. 'You will, won't you? Our choir needs another low tenor in the worst way.' She plumped the pillow on the bed. 'Come to think of it, most of what our choir does is in the worst way.'

'I will be honoured to escort you to St Luke's,' Ben replied and meant every syllable.

She gave a little curtsy, and her eyes lingered on his neck, more visible now with the neckcloth loose. He knew she was too polite to ask. He pointed to the blue dots that started below his ear and circled around his neck.

'The result of standing too close to gunpowder,' he told her.

'I hope you never do that again,' she said. It touched him that she worried about an injury he knew was a decade old.

'No choice, Mandy. We were boarding a French frigate. As a result, I don't hear too well out of this ear and my blue tattoo goes down my back.'

She coloured at that bit of information, and Ben knew he should have stopped with the deaf ear.

'I pinched my finger in the door once,' she said. 'I believe we have led different lives.'

'I know we have,' he agreed, 'but I'm ready for Christmas on land.'

'That we can furnish,' she assured him, obviously

happy to change the subject, which he found endearing. 'Help me with the coverlet now.'

After the addition of towels and a pitcher and bowl, Mandy declared the room done. 'Your duffel awaits you downstairs, Master Muir,' she said, 'and I had better help with dinner. We'll eat at six of the clock.'

He followed her down the stairs, retrieved his duffel and walked back upstairs alone. He opened the door and looked around, vaguely dissatisfied. The room was empty without Mandy.

'You sucked all the air out of the place,' he said out loud. 'For six shillings, I should get air.'

Chapter Two

'Mandy, you're moping,' Aunt Sal observed in a tiny break in the busy routine of dinner, made busier tonight because the vicar and his wife and half of St Luke's congregation seemed to have found their way to Mandy's Rose.

'Am not,' she replied, with her usual cheery cheekiness. 'It's this way, Aunt Sal—when have we ever had a guest as interesting as Master Muir?'

'I can't recall.' Aunt Sal nudged her niece. 'The shepherd's pie to table four.'

Mandy delivered as directed, charmed to discover that Vicar Winslow had put two tables together to include the sailing master. Ben Muir was the centre of attention now, with parishioners demanding sea stories. She wanted to stay and listen.

Empty tray in hand, she felt a twinge of pride that the sailing master was their lodger. His uniform looked shabby, but he was tidy and his hair nicely pulled back into an old-fashioned queue. He had a straight nose and eyelashes twice as long as hers.

But this wool-gathering was not getting food in front of paying guests. Mandy scurried into the kitchen and did her duty.

* * *

By the time the last patron had set the doorbell tinkling on the way out, Mandy's feet hurt and she wanted to sit down to her own dinner.

Aunt Sal helped her gather the dishes from the dining room. 'This was a good night for us,' Sal said as she stacked the dishes in the sink. 'I wonder what could have been going on at St Luke's to merit so many parishioners. Mandy, gather up the tablecloths.'

She did as her aunt said, ready to eat, but feeling out of sorts because the sailing master must have gone right to his room. She had gathered the linens into a bundle when the doorbell tinkled and in walked Ben Muir.

'I was going to help you, but Vicar Winslow wanted to show me where St Luke's is.'

'St Luke's would be hard to miss. It's the biggest building in town.'

'He expects me there tomorrow night at seven of the clock, and you, too. I said I would oblige. Now, is there anything I can do for you?'

Mandy surprised herself by thinking that he could kiss her, if he wanted, then shoved that little imp of an idea down to the cellar of her mind. 'I've done my work for the night. Martha comes in tomorrow morning to wash the linens and iron them. It's my turn to eat.'

Dismiss him, while you're at it, she scolded herself, wondering why she cared, hoping he would ignore her rudeness.

'Could you use some company?' he asked. '*The Science of Nautical Mathematics* is calling, but not as loudly as I had thought it might.'

'It would never call to me,' she said honestly, which made him laugh.

'Then praise God it falls to my lot and not yours. D'ye think your aunt has some dinner pudding left?'

'More than likely. I can always use company, if you don't mind the kitchen.'

'Never.' He opened the swinging door for her. 'Mandy, my father was a fisherman in a little village about the size of Venable. All I know is kitchens.'

Now what? Mandy asked herself, as Aunt Sal set her long-awaited dinner before her. She could put on airs in front of this man and nibble a little, then push the plate away, but she was hungry. She glanced at him, and saw the deep-down humour in his eyes. *He knows what I'm thinking.*

'I could be missish and eat just a tiny dab, but that will never do,' she found herself telling him.

'And I would think you supremely silly, which I believe you are not,' he replied. 'Fall to, Amanda, handsomely now,' he ordered, in his best sailing master voice.

She ate with no more hesitation, nodding when he pushed the bread plate in her direction. Aunt Sal delivered the rest of the dinner pudding to Ben and he wielded his fork again, happy to fill up with good food that didn't come out of kegs and barrels, as he said between mouthfuls.

When the edge was gone from her hunger, she made the decision not to stand on ceremony, even if he was a sailing master. Nothing prompted her to do so except her own interest.

'You called me Amanda,' she said. 'No one else does.'

'Mandy is fine, but I like Amanda,' he said. He finished the pudding and eyed the bread, which she pushed back in his direction.

'Well then,' was all she said.

He loosened his neckcloth, then looked at her. 'D'ye mind?'

'Heavens, no,' Mandy said. 'I'm going to take off my shoes because I have been on my feet all day.'

'Tell me something about the Walthans,' Ben said. 'I have known that dense midshipman for three long years. What is his family like? I mean, I wasn't good enough to stay at the manor. Are they all like Thomas?'

What do I say? Mandy asked herself. She glanced at her aunt at the sink, who had turned around to look at her. 'Aunt Sal?'

'Mandy and Thomas are half-brother and sister,' Aunt Sal said. She returned to her task. 'My dear, you carry on.'

Mandy doubted that the master had been caught by surprise on any topic in a long while. He stared at her, eyes wide.

'I find that…'

'…difficult to believe?' she finished. 'We share some resemblance.'

He gave her a look so arch that she nearly laughed. Aunt Sally set down a glass beside his hand and poured from a bottle Mandy knew she reserved for amazing occasions. Was this a special occasion? Mandy thought it must be, to see the Madeira on the table.

'You need this,' was all her aunt said.

Ben picked up the glass and admired the amber liquid. 'Smuggler's Madeira?' he asked.

'It's a sordid tale,' Mandy teased. 'No! Not the Madeira!' She sighed. 'My half-brother.'

It wasn't a tale she had told before, because everyone in Venable already knew it, with the sole exception of Thomas and his sister Violet. As Mandy told him of her mother and the current Lord Kelso falling in love, Mandy looked for some distaste in his expression, but saw nothing but interest.

'They were both eighteen,' Mandy said. 'They eloped

all the way to Gretna Green and married over the anvil. Old Lord Kelso was furious and that ended that. The marriage was promptly annulled, but by then...' He was a man grown; let him figure it out.

'Ah, well,' he said, twirling the stem of the empty glass between thumb and forefinger. 'And here you are, neither fish nor fowl, eh?'

No one had ever put the matter like that, but he was right. 'I would probably be even less welcome at Walthan Manor than you,' she said. 'My mother died when I was born and my dearest aunt had the raising of me.'

'You did a lovely job,' he said, with a slight bow in the direction of the sink, which made Mandy's face grow warm.

'I believe I did,' Aunt Sal said, sitting with them. 'She is my treasure.' She touched Mandy's cheek with damp fingers. 'I can take up the story here. Old Lord Kelso gave me a small sum, which I was supposed to use to disappear into another village with his granddaughter. I chose to lease this building and open a tea room, instead.'

'Was Lord Kelso angry?' Ben asked.

From his expression, Mandy thought he was imagining the squall that must have broken over one woman and an infant, just trying to make their way in the world.

'Outraged,' Sal said, her eyes clouding over. She grasped Mandy's hand now. 'He mellowed through the years, especially after James—the current Lord Kelso—made a better match a year later with a Gorgon who gave him two irritating children—Thomas...'

'The ignorant midshipman,' Ben teased, his eyes lively.

'And Violet, who has endured two London Seasons without a single offer,' Sal said in some triumph. Her face fell. 'I shouldn't be so uncharitable about that, but if it had been my Mandy...'

'Life can bruise us,' he said.

'Only if we choose to let it,' Mandy said. 'What on earth would I have done with a London Season?'

'Find a title, at the very least,' Ben said promptly.

'How? You said it yourself, Master Muir—I am neither fish nor fowl.'

'I didn't mean...'

'I know,' she said, her eyes so kind. 'Old Lord Kelso did mellow. He came in here now and then for tea and Aunt Sal's hot-cross buns at Easter.'

'And mulled cider and Christmas date pudding,' Sal said. She inclined her head towards Mandy's. 'We even missed him when he died two years ago.'

Mandy nodded, remembering how odd it felt to experience genuine sorrow, but with no leave to declare it to the world. 'I... I even wanted to tell the new Lord Kelso—my father—how sorry I was, but he would only have laughed. But I miss old Lord Kelso,' she said simply.

She stood up, gathering her plate and his. 'It's late, sir, and morning comes early at Mandy's Rose. Let me take a can of hot water to your room.'

'I'll take my own and yours, too,' the master said. 'I don't have to be at Walthan Manor until four bells in the forenoon watch.' He bowed to her. 'Ten o'clock. After years at sea, this is dissipation, indeed.'

'I dare say you've earned it,' she said as she filled a can of hot water for Ben and another for herself.

Shy, she went up the stairs first as courtesy dictated, knowing that when she raised her skirts to keep from tripping, he would see her ankles. *They're nice ankles*, she thought, wondering if he would notice.

He had carried up both cans of hot water while she managed the candlestick, so he told her to go into her room first. He followed her in with the hot water and set it on the washstand. She lit her own candle by her bed, then handed him the candlestick, shy again.

'Thank you,' she said.

'For what?' he asked, with that pleasing humour in his eyes.

'For coming to Mandy's Rose,' she said, feeling brazen and honest at the same time. 'We'll show you a merry Christmas.'

'I already feel it,' he said, as he closed her door.

She lay in bed a long time that night, wondering how far down his back those blue dots ran.

If that had been Amanda's London Season, she'd be married and a mother by now, Ben thought, *and I'd be eating alone with* Nautical Mathematics *propped in front of me.* Of course, if it had been her Season, she never would have given a sailing master a glance.

The mystery of life seemed a fitting topic to consider the next morning, as Ben lay with his hands behind his head, stretched out in total comfort. *Nautical Mathematics* still remained unopened on the bedside table. He contemplated the pleasure of a bed that didn't move. Because he had paid his six shillings, he let his mind wander and contemplated what it might feel like for Amanda Mathison to curl up next to him with her head on his chest.

There had been other women curled up so, but after he paid them, they left. How would it be to have a wife who didn't go anywhere after making love? A wife to admire across the breakfast table? A wife to have a bulge and a baby moving inside her? A wife to scold a child or two, then grab them close, kiss and start over? A wife he could tease and tickle? A wife to tell him to behave when he needed it? A wife to open the door to him on a snowy evening, his duffel slung over his shoulder, home from the sea?

* * *

He couldn't imagine it, except that he could, so he felt more grumpy than usual as he set out for Walthan Manor after breakfast. He tipped his hat to Amanda at the door to the tea room and had the most wonderful intuition that if he looked back, she would still be standing in the open door. He resisted the urge to look because he was an adult, after all. Not until he was nearly at the end of the street did he look back, and there she was, still in the doorway. He doffed his hat with some drama. He saw her put her hand to her mouth, so he knew she was laughing. He was too far away, but he just knew her pretty eyes were squinting and small because she was laughing. Did he know her so well in one day?

'I am turning into a fool,' he said out loud, after looking around to make sure there was no one within earshot. He thought of his resolution through the years never to burden a wife with a navy man always at sea. As the war ground on, he had considered the matter less and less, mainly because he knew no woman in her right mind would marry a sailor. He decided to blame his uncustomary thoughts on the tug and pull of the season. He knew nothing would come of it.

The thought kept him warm through the village, then down the long row of trees bare of leaves that ended in a handsome three-storey manor with a gravel half-moon drive in front.

A butler ushered him in from the cold, gave a bow so brief as to be nearly non-existent, then led him directly into what was the library. What a magnificent manor this was, worlds beyond what a sailing master could ever hope for. Ben looked around with real pleasure when he entered the library, inhaling the fragrance of old leather and paper. He set his charts on a table and took out tablet, compass and protractor, confident that Tom Walthan hadn't thought to bring along his own from the frigate.

The butler was replaced by a maid bearing a tea service. She set it on the table, curtsied and started to scurry away until he stopped her to hand off his boat cloak and bicorn. Funny that the butler hadn't seen to the matter.

Then it struck Ben that the inmates of Walthan Manor, probably on that little prig's advice, considered him a sailor with only slightly more seniority than an earthworm. It was a humbling thought. Maybe he needed such a snub; a man could get so used to deference that he forgot he was just a sailing master, and no earl.

Four bells in the forenoon watch came and went as Ben cooled his heels in the library. The clock struck eleven before Thomas Walthan appeared, surly and sullen. The wretched youth had evidently forgotten how he had importuned and begged the sailing master to throw him an academic line with some badly needed tutelage. The sooner they began, the sooner...

The sooner what? Master Ben Muir realised that he had no desire to go anywhere other than directly back to Mandy's Rose. If an imp had suddenly collided with his shoulder, perched there and demanded, 'Where away?', Ben probably could not have remembered the name of his frigate. He just wanted to sit in Amanda Mathison's vicinity and moon away an hour or two. But Ben was a lifelong realist and such was not his lot.

'Sit down, Walthan,' he snapped. 'You're an hour late. Let us begin.'

Mandy started watching for the sailing master as four o'clock came and darkness gathered. She had wanted to start watching sooner, but couldn't think of a single excuse to offer Aunt Sal why the dining room, tables already set, needed her attention. That the dining room windows boasted the only view of the road had suddenly become her cross to bear.

In her matter-of-fact way, Aunt Sal had commissioned Mandy to tidy the master's room after he left that morning. For no reason—she knew he was gone—Mandy had hesitated before the closed door, shy for no particular purpose.

The room was already tidy. Ben's bed was made, his shaving gear neatly arranged, his hairbrush squared away on the bureau. Nothing was out of place, right down to that daunting book on his bedside table. She looked at it, shaking her head to see that he hadn't even begun to read it. *I'm wasting your time*, she thought, then reminded herself that she had not forced him to sit with her while she ate last night. He had seemed genuinely pleased to while away an hour in the kitchen.

Mandy had straightened out imaginary wrinkles from the bed. She did the homely tasks the room required, dumping the night jar, emptying out the wash water, sniffing his strongly scented lemon soap, wondering if he slept on his back or his side. Exasperated with herself, Mandy had swept out the room, closed the door behind her and resolved not to think of the sailing master, a man she barely knew.

Her resolve lasted to four o'clock. Were the dreadful Walthans going to keep him slaving there until dark? Didn't they have a Christmas party to attend somewhere? And so she pouted, earning her a glare from Aunt Sal.

To her relief, one of the tea room's patrons of long standing came early for dinner, so Mandy could linger in the dining room. Never in the history of serving guests had one patron received such attention. She was pouring the old gentleman his second cup of tea when she saw the sailing master out the window.

He walked with purpose, still with that pleasant rolling stride that would probably brand him forever as a navy man. And, no, it wasn't her imagination that he started walking faster, the closer he came to Mandy's Rose.

'Have a care, Mandy,' her patron cautioned. 'Don't need tea in the saucer, too.'

She stopped pouring, hoping he wouldn't mind bending closer to the table to sip from the cup before trying to lift it. Mandy gave what she hoped was a repentant smile, ready for a scold.

The scold never came. Dear Mr Cleverly just nodded as if she drowned his saucer every day.

'Where's your fine-looking fellow with the blue neck?' he asked.

'*My* fellow?' she asked, puzzled. 'Whatever could you mean? Oh, he's not my…' she started, then stopped as the doorbell tinkled and that fellow with the blue neck came into the dining room.

He looked like a man with a headache: frown lines between his eyes, a droop to his shoulders. He smiled at her, but it was a tired smile. Wordless, she held out her arms for his hat and cloak, which he relinquished with a sigh.

'Long day,' was all he said as he nodded to her, winced as though the movement hurt and headed for the stairs. In another moment, she heard the door close to his room.

'*I'd* never willingly spend a day at Walthan Manor,' Mr Cleverly said.

After he left, Mandy cleared the table and went into the kitchen, where Aunt Sal took one practised look and asked her what was the matter.

'I think Ben has the headache. Must have been a wretched day,' Mandy said.

'You can take him some…'

Aunt Sal stopped. They heard footsteps on the stairs.

Please just come in the kitchen, Mandy thought, then sighed when the kitchen door opened after a quiet knock.

He looked at Mandy, at Aunt Sal, then back to Mandy. 'If you have something for a headache, give it to me now.'

Aunt Sal hurried to the shelf where she kept various remedies, some of a female nature, others not, while Mandy took Ben by the arm and sat him down at the kitchen table. Some mysterious leaves in the tea strainer, a little hot water, then honey, and her aunt set it before the sailing master. Like a dutiful child, he drank it down, then made such a face that Mandy almost laughed.

'Good God, that must be effective,' he managed to gasp.

'Dinner might help,' Mandy said. 'Mr Cleverly just left, but he wanted to remind you about choir practice tonight.'

'Mandy, I don't believe our guest is up to singing and certainly not listening to St Luke's choir,' her aunt said.

'I am made of sterner stuff than that,' Ben assured them. 'Believe me, it will be the highlight of an otherwise wretched day. Sit down, Amanda.'

She sat while Aunt Sal served him consommé and toast. When the line between his eyes grew less pronounced, Mandy followed soup with a little of last night's beef roast mixed in with potatoes and turnips. He shook his head over anything else and leaned back in his chair.

'Amanda, what a day…' he began and told her about the late start, and Thomas Walthan's vast dislike of all things mathematical. 'This is a hopeless task. I despair of teaching him anything, particularly when he has no willingness to *try*.'

She listened to him, imagining that he was her husband, or at least her fiancé, who had come home after a trying day and just needed a listening ear. Although she knew she would never do it, she wondered what he would do if she took her turn with complaints about a late poultry delivery, and a soufflé that refused to rise to the occasion. She knew he would listen. How she knew, she could not have told a jury of twelve men; she just knew and the thought was a comfort.

With an embarrassed sigh, he told her about the humiliation of being served luncheon on a tray in the library, instead of at least in the breakfast room.

'You're not used to such Turkish treatment, are you?' she asked. 'I mean, if I were in charge of the sails and rigging and all that business that keeps a ship afloat, I'd expect a little deference.'

She saw the embarrassment in his eyes.

'Am I too proud?'

'Maybe a little,' she told him, because he *had* asked. 'You know what will be the outcome of this—my ignorant half-brother will still be a midshipman when he is my age and blame it on you.'

'You, my dear Amanda, are a mighty judge of character,' he said, which made her blush. 'At your advanced age of...'

'Twenty-six.'

He made a monumentally faked show of amazement, which suggested that his headache had receded. 'Foot in the grave,' he teased. He grew more serious almost at once. 'Perhaps my continued incarceration in the library might prove useful to someone.'

'How?'

'I had finished a sandwich and had another half hour before Thomas told me he would leave his luncheon—must've been more than a sandwich for him.'

'Poor man,' she teased. 'I dare say you have gone days and days without food.'

'Aye to that. Anyway, I thought I might look around

in what I was informed was *old* Lord Kelso's library—apparently your father barely reads—and I sought out Euclid's *Elements*.'

She made a face and Ben's lips twitched. 'I have noticed that you're a bit of a reluctant school miss when I mention mathematics.'

'I see no evidence that you have delved into that forbidding text on your night table,' she retorted, then blushed. 'I tidied your room, so I noticed. The pages aren't slit.'

He put a hand to his chest. 'Forbidding? I happen to enjoy the subject, for which everyone on the *Albemarle*, except your nincompoop half-brother, is supremely grateful.' He leaned closer. 'My cabin is invariably tidy. That is a consequence of close quarters at sea.'

She rose to clear away his dishes and he took her wrist in his light grasp. 'It can wait, Amanda. I just like you to sit with me.'

'Euclid's *Elements*,' she reminded him. 'And?'

'Sure enough, the old boy had a copy of that esteemed work. I opened it and look what was marking Chapter Eight.'

He pulled out a folded paper sealed with the merest dab of wax and held it out to her. 'Behold.'

'My goodness.' She read, '"Codicil. In the event of my death, to be given to my solicitor."' She handed back the sheet as though it burned.

He took it. '"In the event", indeed,' he said. 'We of the Royal Navy know death to be more of a certainty than an earl, evidently.'

'It's a turn of phrase,' she said, happy to defend the old man who had always treated her kindly, once he overcame the initial shock of her birth.

'I know,' he said. 'You have told me he was a good sort.' He ducked his head like a little boy. 'Should I apologise?'

'Don't be silly.' She looked at the folded paper. 'His so-licitor is Mr Cooper and you'll see him tonight, if you feel brave enough to chance the choir practice.'

'My dear, I served at Trafalgar. I can manage a choir practice, headache or not.'

He gave her such a look then, the kind of look she thought she always wanted some day from a man.

'If I may escort you?'

She nodded, suddenly too shy to speak.

'Should I ask your aunt's permission?'

'Master Muir, you already know that I am six and twenty. No need for permission.'

'You'll point out Mr Cooper, will you?'

'Certainly. I wonder, sir, were you tempted to break the seal and take a peak?'

'Tempted, but I wouldn't. I hope it's good news for someone.'

'Lord Kelso died two years ago. I assume the will was read at the time.'

'Maybe there is a new wrinkle. I do like a mystery,' the master said as he rubbed his hands together.

Mandy hurried through the rest of dinner, a model of efficiency and speed. She thought Aunt Sal must be hav-ing a silent chuckle over her niece's obvious excitement over something as simple as a walk to the church for choir practice, but she kindly kept her own council.

Mandy hurried up the stairs for one look in front of the mirror, even though she knew the face peering back at her too well. She mourned over her freckles and nose that no poet would ever rhapsodise about, then dismissed the matter. Her figure was tidy, teetering just slightly on the edge of abundance, and Aunt Sal had always seen to a modest wardrobe of good material. 'You will never shame anyone,' Mandy said out loud, but softly.

She sat on her bed, thinking about the mother she had never known, but fully aware that without the love, generosity and courage of her maiden aunt, her life would have taken a difficult turn. She owed the Walthans nothing and that knowledge made her wink back tears and know that in church tonight, she could spend a minute just sitting in the pew, thinking of the Babe of Bethlehem and His lucky blessing of two parents—no, three—who loved Him.

'Some day, dear Lord,' she whispered, more vow than prayer, 'some day the same for me.'

She looked up at a slight tap on her door. She opened it to see the sailing master, smelling nicely of the lemon soap she had sniffed that morning. She had no mother or father to give her advice or admonition, but Aunt Sal had raised her to think for herself. No one had to tell her she was putting herself into capable hands, even for something as prosaic as a saunter to St Luke's. She just knew it.

One thing she could certainly say for this navy man: whatever his years at sea, he had a fine instinct for how to treat a lady, if such she could call herself. He helped her into her overcoat, even while she wished, for the first time ever, that the utilitarian garment was more *à la mode*. He swung on his boat cloak with a certain flair, even though he had probably done just that for years. How else did one don a cloak without flinging it about? But the hat, oh, my. It made him look a foot taller than he already was and more than twice as capable. Did navy men have any idea what dashing figures they cut? Mandy doubted it, especially since Ben seemed so unconcerned.

As usual, the winter mist was in plentiful supply. Years of experience with salt air and mist had trained Mandy to negotiate even the slickest cobblestones. The sailing master had no idea of her ability, evidently. Without a word, he took her arm and tucked it close to his body, until she couldn't fall down. She almost told him she didn't require such solicitation, but discovered that she liked being close to him.

'It gets icy on the blockade,' he said. 'You should see the lubbers slip across the deck.'

'We haven't seen snow in several years,' she said, wondering when she had ever resorted to talking about the weather with anyone. Perhaps after the master left, she would have to broaden her acquaintance beyond the poulterer, the butcher and the dairyman. How, she wasn't sure, but other females did and she could, too.

'Is Mandy's Rose open on Christmas Day?' he asked, slowing down so she could match his stride, a nicety she enjoyed.

'No, but we'll fix you a fine dinner,' she said, surprised at how breathless she felt. Before she realised what she was doing, Mandy leaned into his arm. Her footing was firm and she had no particular reason for her action, except that she wanted to lean. The experience was comforting and she liked it. He offered no objection, except she thought she heard him sigh. Hopefully, she wasn't pressing on an old wound.

Maybe there was mist, but she thought it highly unfair of St Luke's Church to loom so quickly out of the dark and fog. She slowed down and the sailing master slowed down, too.

'Girding your loins for an entrance?' he teased. 'Is it that kind of choir?'

She could laugh and tease, but why? He was here three weeks, then gone. 'The choir is good enough. I just like walking with you.'

He was silent for a long moment and Mandy wondered if she had offended him.

'Amanda, you need to get out more.'

'Happen you're right,' she replied, honest to the core.

The other choir members were already gathered in the chapel. To a person, they all turned to look at Mandy and her escort. She smiled—these were her friends—and wondered at their uniformly serious expressions.

'We leave our coats here?' Ben whispered.

'Back here in the cloakroom,' she said and led the way. The glances continued and she wondered about them.

The sailing master didn't appear to wonder. He hung up his cloak and hat and helped her, then leaned close to whisper, 'I think I know how the wind blows, Amanda.'

'What do you mean?' she whispered back, feeling surprisingly conspiratorial for St Luke's, where nothing ever happened except boring sermons.

'If I am not mistaken, those are the very people who ate in Mandy's Rose yesterday evening.'

She looked at him, a frown on her face, then felt herself grow too warm, not so much because he was standing close, which was giving her stomach a funny feeling, but because she understood. 'Oh, my,' she whispered. 'They are looking you over. Poor, poor Ben.' She leaned closer until her lips almost touched his ear. 'Should I just assure them that you'll be gone after Christmas?'

By the Almighty, she wanted to kiss that ear. An *ear*? Did people *do* that? It was probably bad enough that she was breathing in it, because he started to blush. A girl had to breathe, so she backed away.

He surprised her. 'Amanda, whether you know it or not, you have an entire village looking after your welfare. I'm not certain I would ever measure up. It's a good thing I'll be here only three weeks.'

'Nineteen days now,' she whispered and couldn't help tears that welled in her eyes. Thank the Lord the cloakroom was dark.

'Your coat?' he asked.

Silent, she handed it over, wishing she had never heard of choir practice, or Venable, or the Royal Navy. Why hadn't she been born the daughter of an Indian chief in Canada?

The humour of her situation saved her, because it surfaced and she started to breathe normally again. Three weeks, Royal Navy, her stupid half-brother, sailing masters and blue tattoos: beyond a smile or two over her silliness and a resolve to be smarter, she'd have forgotten the whole matter in a month or two.

'Choir practice awaits,' she told him, indicating the chapel. 'We're singing our choirmaster's own version of "O Come All Ye Faithful", and he does need another low tenor. But not necessarily in the worst way.'

There. That was the right touch. The sailing master chuckled and she knew he had no idea what she had wanted to do in that cloakroom.

Feeling brave, she introduced Benneit Muir to most of the people who had already met him yesterday at Mandy's Rose. She was casual, she was friendly. It only remained to introduce him to Mr Cooper, the solicitor, when the practice was over.

As it turned out, that wasn't even necessary. As men will, they had been chatting with each other while the choirmaster laboured with his sopranos on their descant, 'O come let us adore him', and the men had nothing to do. Out of the corner of her eye, she had watched Ben hand over that mysterious folded sheet of paper to the solicitor, who stood directly behind him in the bass section.

They walked home with other singers going in the

same direction. Again, Ben was quick to take her arm firmly. She knew better than to lean against his arm this time. Something told her that was a gesture best reserved for someone hanging around longer than nineteen more days.

Nineteen days! The thought made her turn solemn and then grumpy, but not until she was upstairs and in her room. She pressed her face into her pillow and resolved to be sensible and sober and mind her manners. After he left, the room across the hall would get dusty and that would be the end of lodgers. Mandy knew she would never suggest the matter again to her aunt.

Chapter Three

Good Lord, I wish you weren't just across the hall, Ben thought.

Sleep did not come, but the idea of counting sheep just struck him as silly. He had slept through hurricanes and humid tropical nights. Once a battle was over and he had done all he could, he had no difficulty in closing his eyes and not waking until he was needed. The way things were shaping up tonight in this charming room, he was going to still be awake at two bells into the morning watch.

He lay on his side, staring at the door, wishing Amanda would open it. He knew she wouldn't, not in a million years, but a man could hope. He lay there in utter misery, wondering how pleasant it would be to do nothing more than share a pillow with her. All the man-and-woman thing aside, how pleasant to chat with her in a dark room, talk over a day, plan for the next one. He felt his heart crack around the edges as he remembered the fun of bouncing into his parents' room and snuggling between them. He wondered now if he had ever disturbed them and that made him chuckle.

Thank the Lord she had no inkling how badly he wanted to kiss her in that cloakroom. But, no, he had reminded her that he was only there for three weeks. She had murmured something after he said that, so soft he couldn't be sure, into his bad ear. He pounded his pillow into shape and forced himself to consider the matter.

You just want a woman and any woman will do, he told himself. *Yes, Amanda is charming, but you know better. She is far too intelligent to care about a seafarer. Where are your manners, Benneit Muir?*

He thought of his near escape from the sister of the ship's carpenter several years ago. True, Polly hadn't possessed a fraction of Amanda's charm, which made bidding goodbye an easy matter, when he returned to Plymouth. He had paced the midnight deck off the coast of France a few times, scolding himself, until that was the end of it. This would be no different.

He put on his usual good show over breakfast, even though he couldn't overlook the smudges under Amanda's eyes, as though she hadn't slept much, either. *Ben, your imagination borders on the absurd*, he told himself as he ate eggs and sausage that might as well have been floor sweepings, for all he cared.

Amanda only made it worse by handing him his cloak and hat, and two sandwiches twisted in coated paper.

'I think you need more than one sandwich on a tray,' she said at the door. 'I put in biscuits, too. Have a good day, Ben.'

He took the sweet gift, bowed to her and left Mandy's Rose. By the time he reached Walthan Manor, he was in complete control of himself and feeling faintly foolish.

To his surprise, Thomas was ready for him, a frown on his face, but awake, none the less. Ben thought about a cutting remark, but discarded the notion. No sense in being petty and cruel to a weak creature, not when he himself had exhibited his own stupidity. Ben explained charting a course, and explained it again until a tiny light went on somewhere in the back of Thomas Walthan's brain.

Together, they worked through two course chartings. By the second attempt, Thomas nearly succeeded. A little praise was in order.

'Tom, I think you could understand this, with sufficient application,' he said.

The midshipman gave Ben a wary look, perhaps wondering if the sailing master was serious. Ben felt a pang at Tom's expression and an urge to examine his own motives in teaching. Was he trying to flog his own disappointments, show off, or was he trying to teach? The matter bore consideration; maybe now was the time.

Sitting there with Tom Walthan, inept midshipman, Ben took a good, inward look at himself in the library of Walthan Manor, of all places, and didn't like what he saw. He was proud and probably seemed insufferable to a confused lad. He had a question for the midshipman, a lad from a titled, wealthy family.

'Tell me something, Thomas, and I speak with total candour. Do you like the Royal Navy? Answer me with equal candour, please.'

Tom's expression wavered from disbelief to doubt, to a thoughtful demeanour that Ben suspected mirrored his own.

'I... I am not so certain that I do,' Tom said finally. He blushed, hesitated and had the temerity to ask the sailing master his own question. 'Do *you*, sir?'

Tom's unexpected courage impressed Ben. He thought a long moment and nodded. 'I do, lad. The navy was a stepping stone for me. My father was a fisherman and we lived in Kirkcudbright. He lives there still. I wanted more than a fishing smack. I discovered a real facility with mathematics, geometry in particular.'

'I hate geometry,' Tom said, with some heat.

'It shows. Do you like the ocean?'

With no hesitation this time, Tom shook his head. He stared at the ink-smudged paper in front of him. 'Not even a little.'

'I do. I love wind in sails and I feel I am greatly needed in this time of national alarm. For all that I am a Scot, I do care for England.'

Tom saw that for the gentle joke it was and relaxed.

'Then why, lad? Why? Could you find a better way to serve your country? You'll be an earl some day, I have no doubt. Why the sea?'

Tom said nothing for a long while. '*He* thinks it would make me a man,' Thomas said with considerable bitterness. 'I must do as he bids.'

'Must you?' Ben asked. He felt suddenly sorry for the miserable young man before him. 'Could you find the courage to tell your father that the navy will not do for you?'

'I don't know.'

'I hope you will.' Ben went to the window, turning deliberately to face Venable. He idly wondered what Mandy was doing, then shook his head, exasperated with himself. He turned back. 'I could pound this maths into your brain, Thomas, with a little help from you, but here is what I fear—some day you might be a lieutenant on a quarterdeck and you might make a fearsome mistake. Men's lives, lad, men's lives.'

Thomas nodded, his lips tight together. 'I don't think I can sit here any longer today,' he said. 'I need to...' He sighed. 'I don't know what I need, sir.'

'Do you have a good place to think?'

Tom gave Ben a half-smile. 'We can agree that I've never done much of that before. I'll find a place, sir.'

'I'll be back tomorrow and we'll continue,' Ben said. 'Give the matter your attention, because it does make a difference.'

I can give myself the same advice, Ben thought, as the midshipmen closed the door quietly behind him. They were inland here, but Ben had two sandwiches and biscuits. He could walk to higher ground and find a spot to see the ocean he was starting to miss.

He gathered up his charts and tools, then just sat there in the library. The sofa was soft and maybe he could lie down for a nap. No one ever came in the library and his eyes were starting to close. *Amanda Mathison, get thee behind me*, he thought, with some amusement at his own folly. 'You'll forget her in a week,' he muttered.

Mostly now, he wanted a nap.

Ben woke to the sound of angry voices. He sat up, startled, until the fog cleared and he realised the altercation wasn't going on there in the library. He tried to remember if there was side door to the manor where he could escape without notice.

He opened the door and peered down the hall. No servants lurked anywhere, which told him they had chosen discretion, too. The voices were so loud that he knew no one would hear him even if he stomped through. He should leave right now.

And he would have, if he hadn't recognised Mr Cooper's deep bass voice from the choir last night. The solicitor must have read the folded paper and gone directly to Walthan Manor. Still, the matter wasn't his business and Ben knew it. He started past the book room, then stopped, when Lord Kelso roared out Mandy Mathison's name like a curse.

Ben leaned towards the door. He had never eavesdropped in his life, but here he was, with no plans to move until he learned more.

'You cannot force me to honour this damned codicil!' Lord Kelso shouted.

'It is the law, my lord,' Mr Cooper said, his voice much softer, but distinct.

'Only you and that damned sailing master know!'

'The vicar witnessed it. I cannot just ignore a matter of the law, Lord Kelso.'

'Others do.'

'My lord, I am not amongst them.'

How will you feel if Lord Kelso flings open the door right now? was Ben's last thought before he sprinted to the side door. He stood on the lawn, furious at Lord Kelso, then suddenly worried for Amanda.

He wasn't much of a runner, considering his life spent on the confines of a frigate, but he ran to Venable, passing a surprised carter. He dashed into Mandy's Rose, then threw himself in one of the chairs, breathing hard and feeling every second of his thirty-one years.

Amanda came out of the kitchen. She took one look at him, snatched up a cloth napkin and pressed it to his sweating forehead. He gasped and took her hand, pulling her into the closest chair.

'Ben, my goodness. What in the world…?'

He said nothing until his breathing settled into an approximation of normality. Amanda had made no effort to let go of his hand, so he tightened his grip. 'We need to see the vicar right now,' he told her.

'What…why?'

'It's that paper I gave to Mr Cooper last night. Lord Kelso, damn his eyes, and Mr Cooper were in the middle of a mighty argument and your name came up. The vicar knows something. Will Aunt Sal mind if I drag you away?'

'I'll ask.'

She released his hand then and darted into the kitchen. When she returned, she had taken off her apron and the scarf was gone. She was trying to tie back her hair, with little success because her hands were shaking.

Oh, Lord, he thought, disgusted with himself. *Was I using my quarterdeck voice? I've frightened her.* 'Amanda, I didn't mean to shout. Here, let me do that.'

She handed him the tie and turned around promptly. He was almost less successful than she was, because her hair felt like Chinese silk in his hands and she smelled of soap, ordinary soap. He felt himself growing warm and then hot over soap. Good God, indeed. He tied up her hair, grateful he had not removed his cloak.

She threw on her coat and made no objection when he held her close as they hurried to St Luke's.

'He's in his study,' Vicar Winslow's wife said as she opened the door. Ben saw all the curiosity in her eyes, followed by the expression of someone who never pried into clerical matters.

If the vicar was surprised, he didn't show it. Ben knew they couldn't be the first couple who had ever burst into his study. The vicar showed them to two seats, then sat behind his desk.

Ben condensed the story as much as he could. 'I could hear Mr Cooper assuring Lord Kelso that he was not above the law,' Ben concluded. 'He said that since you had witnessed the codicil, it was valid.' He glanced at Amanda, whose eyes looked so troubled now. 'Would you tell us what is going on? I don't trust the earl.'

'Wise of you,' Winslow said finally. He focused his gaze on Amanda, who leaned forward. 'My dear, old Lord Kelso summoned me to his bedside the day before he died.

Said he wanted to make a little addition to his will.' He took a deep breath. 'He was determined to leave you one thousand pounds, to make amends of a sort. I suspect the family's treatment of you was preying on his soul.'

Amanda gasped and reached for Ben's hand. He happily obliged her, twining her fingers through his. 'I... I wouldn't take it!' she said.

Why the hell not? Ben wondered to himself. *Sounds like the least the old gent could do.*

'And so I told him,' Winslow said. 'I knew you would refuse such a sum.'

'I have to ask why,' Ben said.

Amanda gave him such a patient look. 'I neither need nor want money from that family. Aunt Sal and I have a good living without Walthan money.'

'I've been put in my place,' he said with a shake of his head.

'No, Ben,' she said. 'You're not the only proud person in the universe.'

And I thought I knew character, he told himself, humbled. Previously a man without a single impulsive bone in his body, Ben took her hand, turned it over and kissed her palm. She blushed, but made no effort to withdraw her hand.

'I stand corrected, Amanda Mathison,' he said. He thought about the vicar's words. 'What *did* you do, Vicar?'

'I convinced the old fellow to leave you one hundred pounds instead,' Reverend Winslow said to Amanda. His expression hardened. 'Apparently even *that* is too much for the new Lord Kelso.'

The three of them sat in silence. 'What should I do?' Amanda said finally. 'I don't even want one hundred pounds, especially if it comes from Lord Kelso.'

'Would you allow him to think he can trump the law?' Ben said.

'No!' She shook her head, then did what he had wanted her to do again, since their walk to church. She leaned her forehead against his arm. *In for a penny, in for a pound*, he thought, and put his arm around her.

When she spoke her voice was small and muffled in his cloak. 'It makes me sad to think that my mother once loved such a hateful man.'

Good Lord, he still had his hat on. Ben tossed it aside, and moved his chair closer so he could lean his head against hers. He could see Amanda was on the verge of tears and he still wasn't close enough. She would never be close enough. The thought filled up the bleak shell that war had turned him into and ran over.

'For all that he is wealthy and titled, I think the years have not been kind to your father,' the vicar said. 'Yes, his father annulled the marriage of your parents and pointed him towards the current Lady Kelso.'

'He's a weak man,' Ben said, feeling weak and helpless himself. 'A stronger man would have stood up to his father, defied him and stayed married to your mother.'

'You know Lady Kelso,' the vicar said to Mandy with a shake his head. 'I try not to speak ill of anyone, but...' Another shake. 'And his children seem not to be all that a doting father would want.'

'That's sadly true with Thomas,' Ben said. 'He's not promising. I hear he has a sister.'

'Violet,' Mandy said, which reminded Ben of the two failed London Seasons. 'You blame Lord Kelso's distemper on disappointed hopes?'

'I do,' Ben said, thinking of his own kind father in too-distant Scotland. 'I wish you could meet *my* father.'

Tears filled her eyes, and filled him with sudden understanding. *You want a father*, he thought, as wisdom bloomed in a vicar's parlour, of all places for a seafaring man to get smart. *I could hope you might want a husband some day—me, to be specific—but you need a father.*

Ben sat back, shocked at his own thoughts. *Me? A husband?* As the vicar stared at him, Ben considered the matter and realised that he had talked himself out of nothing. War didn't matter; neither did nonsense about not burdening a wife with fear as she waited for a husband who might never return. He thought of all the brave husbands and wives who took bold chances in a world at war and loved anyway. He was the worst kind of fool, a greater fool than any pathetic midshipman. He had tried to fool himself.

'So sorry, Amanda. I didn't mean to make you cry,' he said. Angry with his ineptitude, he disentangled himself from the weeping woman, picked up his hat and left the study.

'What do I do, Reverend Winslow?' Mandy asked.

'I suggest you go after him.'

'Indeed, I will,' she said calmly. 'I mean the one hundred pounds?'

'Accept it.' The vicar gave her his own handkerchief. 'It will drive Lord Kelso to distraction if you do. Sometimes that is half the fun.'

'Vicar!'

'My dear, I am human.'

She strolled along, grateful for the mist because she could keep her hood up and lessen anyone's view of her teary eyes. She watched the sailing master ahead, moving along at a substantial clip and probably castigating himself because he thought he had made her cry. Maybe he had, but she couldn't blame him for having a father who took an interest in his son.

'Sir, you have eighteen days and a visit to Scotland is not out of the question,' she said softly. Eighteen days. She stood still on the path, feeling hollow all of a sudden. What if he did go to Scotland? What if he gave up on Thomas Walthan and really *did* go to Scotland?

It hardly mattered. If he went to Scotland, he would not return here, but would go to Plymouth to spend the next three weeks dealing with rigging and ballast and what all. And then the *Albemarle* would return to the blockade and she would never see Benneit Muir again, end of story. 'This is most unsatisfactory,' she said, even as she knew that where he went and what he did must recede from her mind's eye, just as surely as he was becoming a small figure in the distance.

She sat on one of the benches placed here and there around Venable by some benefactor. She had much to do at Mandy's Rose and had promised a quick return to help prepare dinner, but suddenly it didn't matter. The enormity of her upcoming loss rendered her powerless to take one more step.

Sailors only come to go away, she tried to remind herself, but her heart wasn't having it. She thought he admired her; all signs pointed that way, at least. She was beginning to understand that he would never act on a man's impulse, because he plied a dangerous trade with no end in sight. Their generation had been born to war and like everyone else—there were no exceptions—it would influence their lives until death and destruction and one man's ambition ran its course. They were like chips of wood tossed into a stream and driven at random towards the ocean, powerless to change course.

She stared at the ground, then closed her eyes, wondering just when the pleasure of a good night's sleep had become a distant memory. She yawned and her own cheery nature

resurfaced. *You are facing a life crisis and you are yawn-*
ing, she thought as she yawned again.

She heard someone approach. She knew everyone in
the village and she didn't relish explaining her tears. But
these were familiar shoes. She had seen them under one
or other of the dining tables for the past three days. She
looked up at Ben Muir.

His face solemn, he sat beside her. It was only a small
bench and now they were crowded together. To accommodate matters, he draped one arm across the back of the
bench, which meant she had to lean towards him.

'There now,' he said. 'I looked back and saw you sitting so melancholy.' He peered closer and she saw that he
had freckles, too. 'One hundred pounds isn't a bad thing,
Amanda.'

'Certainly not,' she said, almost relieved that he had
nothing more serious to say. Relieved or disappointed?
This man could irritate me, she thought, then smiled. What
a ninny she was. He was only being kind.

'You can tuck the money away for a special occasion.
That's what I would do.'

He stretched his legs out and crossed them, which had
the effect of drawing her closer. Mandy knew she should
get up. The hour was late and Aunt Sal didn't like to prepare for the dinner rush by herself. She allowed herself to
incline her head against the sailing master, which proved to
be surprisingly comfortable, almost a refuge from worry
over a dratted inheritance.

'What is *your* special occasion?' she asked, curious.

'Don't have one yet.' His arm was around her now.
'After Trafalgar, when we towed one of the Spanish ships
into Portsmouth, the entire wardroom gathered together
and got stinking drunk.'

'I wouldn't spend any money on spirits,' she said.

'I didn't, either.' He took a deep breath. 'We drank dead men's liquor, Amanda. I was serving as second master on a ship of the line that was mauled during the battle. The sailing master and two lieutenants had died. I had assumed the master's duties during the battle, so the officers included me. We drank their stored supply— dead men's liquor.'

She turned her face into his chest, unable to help herself, which meant that both of his arms circled her now. 'How do you bear it?' she whispered into his gilt buttons.

'It becomes normal life, I suppose,' he told her, after much silence. 'Damn Napoleon, anyway.'

The unfairness of Ben Muir's life broke her heart. 'So… so you don't spend much time on land by choice? Is that it?'

'Partly. Granted, we have little opportunity, but you might be right.' He inclined his cheek towards hers. 'A sad reflection, but not your worry, Amanda.'

This would never do. A cold bench on a busy footpath was no place to discuss anything and Aunt Sal needed her. 'It is my worry,' she said softly. 'It should be of concern to each one of us on land who is kept safe by the Royal Navy. Let me thank you for them.'

She kissed his cheek. His arms tightened around her. She kissed his cheek again and, when he turned towards her, she kissed his lips. Right there on the footpath, she kissed a man she had known for three days, the first man she had ever kissed. She probably wasn't even doing it right.

His lips parted slightly and he kissed her back. He made a low sound in the back of his throat that Mandy found endearing and edgy at the same time. Warmth flooded her stomach and drifted lower, all from a kiss. Good God Almighty, Aunt Sal had never explained anything like this in her shy discourse on men and women. Of course, Aunt Sal was a spinster. Mandy could probably get better advice from the vicar's wife.

She ended the kiss, sitting back, wondering at herself, blushing hot, wanting him to leave, praying he would stay and stay. 'I… I don't think I know what I'm doing,' she said and stood up.

She thought he might apologise, but he did no such thing. He shrugged. 'I'm not certain what I am doing, either.'

They looked at each other and started to laugh. 'Have you ever met two more bona fide loobies?' he asked, when he could talk. He stood up and crooked out his arm. 'Take my arm, Amanda. This path is misty.'

She did as he said. 'That is a most feeble effort to get me to walk close to you,' she scolded, onto him and not minding it.

'I thought I was rather clever, for a man with no practice whatsoever,' he said, going along with her banter.

She stopped and faced him. 'You realise how…how odd this is. Neither of us is young, but listen to us!'

He nodded and set her in motion again. She looked at him, mature and capable, wearing that intimidating bicorn hat and sporting those curious blue dots on his neck. It was not her business, but he had to be a man with some experience with women, probably exotic, beautiful women in faraway ports. To say he had no practice whatsoever couldn't be true, but she thought she understood what he was saying. A man paid for those women for one night, a business transaction. He probably had no idea how to court a lady.

Not that she was a lady; she worked in Mandy's Rose. For all that, she *had* been raised gently by a careful aunt. He was no gentleman, either, just a hard-working Scot with ambition, who had risen perhaps as far as he could in the Royal Navy. They were really two of a kind, two ordinary people. With enough time, something might happen, but there was no time.

She also thought that he would never make another move towards her. After all, she had kissed him, not the other, more logical way round. He knew the clock ticked. Maybe he had forgotten that for a second when he kissed back, but he was a careful man, not likely to forget again.

'You're looking far too serious,' he said, as they came in sight of Mandy's Rose.

She took a deep breath, then let it out. What could she say? There would be no happy ending to this Christmas encounter because of Ben's vile mistresses—war and time. They were gruesome harpies she could not fight.

'I'll probably recover,' she told him. She gave his arm a squeeze, let go and hurried into the restaurant, late enough for Aunt Sal to scold.

He followed her inside, then walked up the stairs to his room. He didn't come down for dinner, but she heard him walking back and forth, back and forth. She worked quietly, distressed to her very core, uncertain, angry because until Ben Muir came into her life, she had known nothing would ever change. She and Sal would work and provide for themselves, and live a comfortable life, one better than so many could hope for.

Everything and nothing had changed. She would lie in bed a few more weeks, wondering what she would do if he tapped on her door long after Sal slept. When Master Muir left, all would return to normal, except down in that deepest recess of her heart. She would never be the same again, but how could that matter to anyone except her?

In growing discomfort, she listened to his footsteps

overhead. He walked slower now and paused often, perhaps looking out the window into darkness.

'What is the matter?'

Guilty for just standing still when there were tables to clear, Mandy turned around to face her aunt. She shook her head, tried to swallow down tears and failed miserably. She bowed her head, pressed her apron to her eyes and cried.

Tears in her own eyes, her aunt put her arm around Mandy's waist and walked her into the kitchen. She sat her down and poured tea.

I can't tell her how I feel about Ben, she thought, mortified. Thank God her father had given her an excuse that might brush past a careful aunt's suspicion. 'I told you about Ben finding that piece of paper in Lord Kelso's library.'

Sal nodded. 'I know he went with you to the vicar's, but you were gone so long.'

Careful here, Mandy told herself and sipped her tea. She told her aunt about the codicil that her grandfather had written the day before he died and which the vicar witnessed. 'He wanted to give me one thousand pounds, but Reverend Winslow said that would only frighten me. He settled on one hundred pounds and the vicar witnessed it. I am to receive one hundred pounds I don't want.'

Sal laughed and poured herself some tea. 'It's not the end of the world! You looked as though you'd lost your best friend and the world was passing you by!'

Exactly, Mandy thought.

'Into the counting house the legacy should go, until you need it,' Aunt Sal said. She started to clear the tables, then stopped. 'This will make you laugh, but I was afraid you...' she pointed over her head '...were starting to fall in love.'

'Heavens, Auntie! How can you imagine such a thing?' Mandy asked, as her insides writhed. Head down, she stacked the dinner plates.

'Silly of me,' her aunt confessed. 'I can't imagine a less likely match.' She set down her dishes and rubbed her arms. 'They seem like marked men, almost, working in wooden ships and facing enemy fire. What does that do to some-one?'

What does that do to someone? Mandy asked herself as she washed dishes later. *It's killing me.*

To her relief, Sal had taken a bowl of soup and basket of bread upstairs. Mandy stopped washing when she heard laughter overhead, then washed harder, grateful that the sailing master wasn't mourning over something that wasn't there. It remained for Mandy to chalk this up to experience, a wonderful experience, yes, but only that.

Sal came downstairs a few minutes later, a smile on her face. 'Such a droll fellow,' she said. 'He told me how your eyes widened at the idea of one hundred pounds and how you protested.'

'I suppose I did,' she said and made herself give an elaborate shiver that made her aunt's smile grow. 'I reckon I will have to make an appearance at Walthan Manor, un-less Mr Cooper can arrange this in his office.'

'We can hope, my dear.' Sal kissed her cheek, while Mandy prayed she wouldn't pick up the scent of lemon soap from someone else's cheek.

Nothing. Obviously the fragrance had worn off, if it was ever there in the first place.

Sal started drying the dishes. 'It's odd, though,' she mused. 'Remember how he said he wanted peace and quiet to read that dread book of mathematics? Well, there it was still on his bedside table, still un-slit. And after I left the food and we chatted, he went to the window when I left the room. I wonder what he is thinking?'

'Maybe that he really should be in Scotland for Christmas to see his father,' Mandy said. She nudged her aunt. 'Not everyone has a father like mine!'

Chapter Four

Life resumed its normal course in the next few days, as normal as anything was before Christmas. Aunt Sal spent more time sitting with clients in the dining room when the meals were done, planning Christmas catering, and one party at Mandy's Rose itself.

Mandy continued fixing extra sandwiches for the sailing master to take to Walthan Manor and let him tease her about her legacy, still not forthcoming. Perhaps her father had changed his mind. Ben didn't linger over dinner any more and spent time on solitary walks. She was usually in bed before he returned, but never asleep. Her heart sad, she heard him pace back and forth in his room. She wondered if he was trying to wear himself out so sleep would come. She convinced herself that he was wishing for Scotland and his father. 'I would want to be with my father, if I had a good one,' she whispered into her pillow, trying to drown the sound of pacing on boards that squeaked.

In the next week, a solemn-faced fellow in livery delivered a note to Amanda Mathison, requesting her presence at Walthan Manor at eleven of the clock. She nodded her acceptance to the servant, then hurried into the kitchen.

'Here it is,' her aunt said, after she read the note.

'I would rather go to Mr Cooper's office,' Mandy said, then tried to make a joke of it. 'I doubt my father will invite me to luncheon with him.' She sat down, struck by a sudden thought. 'I have never seen him up close. Aunt, did he ever lay eyes on me?'

'I can't recall a time,' Aunt Sal replied. She fixed a critical eye on Mandy. 'I wouldn't wear Sunday best, but perhaps your deep-green wool and my lace collar will do.'

Mandy changed clothes, her eye on the clock. The simple riband she usually wore to pull back her hair would have to do. She looked down at her shoes that peeped from under her ankle-length dress, grateful she had blacked them two days ago, when she was desperate to keep busy so she would not think about kissing the sailing master. It hadn't worked, but at least her two pairs of shoes shone.

Her aunt attached the knitted lace collar with a simple gold bar pin. She indicated that Mandy should turn around so she did, revolving slowly.

'I believe you will do, my love,' her aunt said. 'Hold your head up. Use my woollen shawl. Heaven knows it only goes to church on Sundays. This will be an outing.' She settled Mandy's winter hat square on her head.

'I don't even remember when you grew up,' Aunt Sal said. 'Could it be only yesterday?'

'I grew up quite a few years ago, Aunt,' Mandy teased. 'You know very well that I will be twenty-seven soon.' She fingered the fringe on her aunt's shawl. 'With the money— let's think about a little holiday at Brighton this summer. We can close the Rose for a week and visit the seashore.' She recognised Aunt Sal's worry frown. 'We'll be frugal. We have never had a holiday. We are long overdue.'

Mandy took a deep breath and started for Waltham Manor. The morning mist had broken up enough for weak sunshine to lighten the normally gloomy December. Soon she would have to hunt the wild holly and ask the butcher prettily for some of the ivy on his house. She had finished the stockings she had knitted for Aunt Sal, useful stockings. She had wrapped them in silvery paper the vicar's wife had found in the back of a drawer.

Mandy wished she had something for the sailing master. If she hurried, she could knit him stockings, too, because stockings weren't a brazen gift. Maybe he would think of her upon occasion. She knew she would never forget him.

Her courage nearly failed her at the long row of trees, with Walthan Manor at the far end. The leaves were gone now and no one had raked them into piles for burning yet, which suited her. She left the drive and walked through the leaves, enjoying the rustle and remembering leafy piles in the vicar's yard. He had never minded when she stomped through the church leaves, because Mandy's Rose had only three windows and two storeys in a row of buildings. There were no leaves to run through, so he had shared all of God's leaves at St Luke's with one of his young parishioners.

I could never leave Venable, she told herself, her heart full. There would never be a reason to, which suited her. Why she sighed just then puzzled her. Maybe Brighton this summer would be the perfect antidote for the sudden melancholy that flapped around her like vultures around the knacker's yard.

The dry crackle kept her company all the way to the gravel half-moon driveway that fronted the manor. She had never been so close before and she sighed with the loveliness of the grey stone and white-framed windows. Certainly there must be grander estates in Devonshire, but this was so elegant, despite the small-minded people that lived within. She looked at the ground-floor windows and saw the sailing master looking back at her, his hands behind his back. On a whim she regretted immediately, she blew him a kiss. He was far too dignified to do anything of the sort in return, but his head went back in what she knew was silent laughter. Obviously her half-brother was in the room, probably sweating over charting a course.

She knocked and the door was opened immediately by a grand personage that might even be the butler, although something told Mandy that the butler himself wouldn't open a door for her. At least the man bowed her in and didn't tell her to find the servants' entrance. Whether the supercilious look on his face was worth one hundred pounds, she couldn't have said. *Think of Brighton in summer*, she reminded herself. *Aunt Sal deserves a holiday.*

With a motion of his hand, he indicated she was to follow him down the hall. He didn't slow his pace, so she hurried to keep up.

Mandy stopped for a moment at the grand staircase, because a young woman had started down from the floor above. She hadn't seen her half-sister Violet in several years, not since the time Violet and Lady Kelso stopped in Mandy's Rose for tea. She wanted to say hello, but there was nothing in the look Violet gave her that suggested she would respond. *Two London Seasons*, Mandy thought, feeling suddenly sorry for the young lady who glared at her down a nose too long, in a face designed by a committee.

The servant Mandy decided was a footman opened the door and she entered a small room lined with ledgers and a desk so cluttered that it lacked any evidence of a wooden surface. There sat her father.

She had seen him a time or two from the dining room window of Mandy's Rose, once on horseback, but generally in a barouche in warm weather and a chaise in winter. The years had not been gentle to his features. His red complexion suggested he drank too much, as did the myriad of broken blood vessels on his nose.

The nose was familiar; she looked at it when she gazed in the mirror: a little long for general purposes, but thankfully not as long as his other daughter's nose. Beyond that, she saw little resemblance.

Elbow on the desk, his chin in his hand, Lord Kelso appeared to be studying her, too, perhaps looking for a resemblance to the young woman he had loved so many years ago. Mandy knew she bore a pleasing likeness to the miniature that Aunt Sal kept on her bedside.

'My lord?' she asked, when the silence continued too long.

Mr Cooper was on his feet. He took her hand and led her to the chair beside him, squeezing her fingers to either calm her or warn her. She could not overlook his serious expression and vowed to make this interview brief. The air seemed charged with unease.

The silence continued. Mandy leaned forward, ready to rise if no one said anything. Glancing at the solicitor's deep frown line between his eyes did nothing to reassure her.

After a put-upon sigh from the earl, Mr Copper cleared his throat. 'Miss Mathison, you are no doubt aware of the codicil to your…grandfather's will that the sailing master found.'

'Yes, sir. Master Muir told me about it and took me to see the vicar, who had witnessed the codicil. Reverend Winslow explained the ma—'

'A damned nuisance,' the earl said, glaring at her.

'It is the law,' Mr Cooper said with firmness. He looked at Mandy. 'Lord Kelso has agreed to the hundred pounds.'

She nodded, afraid to speak because she saw the warning in the kindly man's eyes. In her mind, *I should leave,* warred with, *I'm no coward.*

With a great show of ostentation, Lord Kelso rummaged on the desk and finally picked up the document right on top. 'Pay close attention. "Lord Kelso, James Thomas Edwards Walthan, earl, agrees to pay Amanda Mathison, his daughter, one hundred pounds, at the rate of five pounds annually for the next twenty years, if she will come to Walthan Manor and petition for it." Sign here.'

Mandy's mouth went dry. She swallowed and blinked back tears at the humiliation.

'My lord, what did I ever do to you to deserve this?' Her own words startled her, even as she started to rise, eager to leave the presence of a man who was no father at all.

'Sit down!' he shouted and slammed his hand on the desk, which only caused the inkwell to tip over. He stared at the spreading stain, his face as pale as milk, then changing to an unhealthy brick red.

'I will not sign anything so humiliating. Good day to you.'

Her eyes cloudy with tears, she turned towards the door, only to see Ben Muir standing there, Thomas Walthan looking over his shoulder, his mouth open. 'Please move aside, Ben,' she said.

'No.'

The sailing master's eyes were mere slits and his cheeks alive with colour. 'Lord Kelso, you are going to make this kind lady crawl to you each year for five pounds?'

'The codicil does not say how I have to deliver her… inheritance.' The earl spat out the word.

'What…? Father, what is going on?' the midshipman asked.

'Oh, don't…please don't,' she whispered to Ben, when the realisation dawned that her half-brother probably had no idea of their relationship, if he even knew who she was.

Ben took her arm, even as she tried to pull away and

get to that door that looked miles away. 'Thomas, let me introduce your half-sister, Amanda Mathison.'

'Please, no, Ben!'

'You're bamming me,' Tom said and started to laugh. When no one else laughed, he stopped.

'Your father married my mother over the anvil in Gretna Green,' Mandy said, since there was no retreat now. She shook off Ben's hand and moved closer to the door. 'Your grandfather annulled it.' She looked at her father, terrified at what she saw. His choler had been replaced by something worse—a cold stare that turned his eyes into specks of granite. 'Believe me, Lord Kelso, I had nothing to do with any of this.'

She couldn't help herself in the face of her sudden anger, anger building over the years without her even aware of its breadth and depth. She pointed a finger at her chest. '*I* was the baby! None of this was my fault!' She took quick strides to the desk and slammed her hands down, too, in perfect imitation of her father. 'I wouldn't take even a ha'pence from you now, you vile man. I hope you choke on your wealth.'

She ran from the room, snatching up her cloak from the astonished footman and taking the front steps in one leap. She pounded along the lane. The wind had picked up, banishing the few leaves still clinging to the elms. The unfairness of the situation washed over her, drenching her with shame at actions not of her own making and sorrow for Thomas, of all people. He had no skill for mathematics and no interest in the career his father must have chosen for him. And now he had learned that he was brother to a woman who served people at Mandy's Rose.

With any luck, she could get all the way home before Ben came after her, as she knew he would. She ran across the field, taking a roundabout route that he didn't know. *You have made my life immeasurably more difficult*, she thought. What told her that, she couldn't have said, but she knew it.

Mandy stopped, breathing hard, dreading what she would have to tell Aunt Sal. There wouldn't be any little holiday to Brighton, as modest as it would have been. There would be no momentary easing of her dear aunt's life of constant work. Maybe that was the lesson, she decided. Depend on no one, and for God's sake, never count chickens before they are hatched.

The sailing master had paid six shillings for three weeks. As little as she knew her father, Mandy knew he would not keep the sailing master near his son, even if it improved Tom's chance of passing his lieutenancy exam. Ben would want some of his shillings back, before he returned to Plymouth, or wherever he had a mind to go. She couldn't help the tears that filled her eyes.

Mandy started walking, her chin up, the same way she had walked towards Walthan Manor. She slowed down even more, not eager to face her aunt. Her plans for a pleasant Christmas had evaporated. Whatever his motives—and she was not inclined to extend her surprising charity from Thomas to their father—Lord Kelso had reminded her of her own insignificance in cruel fashion.

'What will happen now?' she asked the geese high overhead, the last stragglers from the north of Scotland, bound for Spain or North Africa. 'Take me with you, please.'

'Can this nonsense possibly be true?' Thomas asked, his eyes unpleasantly pop-eyed. 'Really, Father.'

'Yes, it's true,' Lord Kelso snapped. He looked at Mr Cooper, who returned his levelling gaze. 'I made my offer and she has refused.'

You really are a bastard, Ben thought, disgusted. 'I am done here,' he said quietly, appalled at the scene he had witnessed and full of sudden dread for Amanda, a woman he admired. Oh, hang it—the woman he loved. He doubted supremely that she would ever speak to him again. By blurting out Amanda's relationship to Thomas, he had muddied the waters beyond repair. Only a foolish woman would take him now and he knew Amanda Mathison was not foolish.

'I won't pay you a pence,' Lord Kelso said. 'For all I know, it's your fault that he cannot pass the stupid mathematics test! Why should this be a requirement, anyway? My son is Quality and you are less than nothing.'

Ben heard Mr Cooper's sudden intake of breath. There was far more at stake than his pride, however much the earl might wound it. The last thing Ben's beloved navy needed was one more nincompoop with gold lace and epaulettes. He took a deep breath, trying to frame his thoughts carefully, because he knew every word out of his mouth would make Amanda's life more difficult.

'My lord, every midshipman must pass a test detailing his knowledge of navigation. He must also sit before a board of four captains or ranks above, who ask a series of questions, all for the good of the service.' Ben spoke softly, even as he edged towards the door. Lord Kelso seemed a simple sort of spoiled man. Maybe out of sight, out of mind would ease Amanda's way.

But he couldn't stop yet, not for the good of the service. He turned his attention to his unwilling pupil, who still needed to think about his own future. 'Thomas, think this through.' Ben hoped his words didn't come across as bare pleading and then he didn't care. 'I have seen too many good men dead because of foolishness on the quarterdeck.'

'How dare you?' Lord Kelso stormed. 'I will talk to the Lords Admiral about you! We'll see how long you remain in the Royal Navy!'

Ben shrugged, in no mood for another moment in such

a poisonous place. No wonder Thomas was a weak excuse for a midshipman. He turned on his heel and left. He took his time gathering up his charts and navigation tools, certain that Amanda would be long gone.

He was right. She was nowhere in sight. Ben walked down the lane, head bowed against the wind. On the way through the village, he stopped at the posting house and enquired about the fare to Kirkcudbright. He couldn't face Plymouth right now—Plymouth and more duty, endless duty—and a return to the blockade. His plans for Christmas had settled around his ankles like trousers with no braces to hold them up. For the first time in years, probably since he had received a year-old letter telling him of the death of his mother, Ben Muir, senior warrant officer on one of His Majesty's frigates, was desperate to go home.

He sat a long while in the kitchen of Mandy's Rose, sipping tea with Sally Mathison. With sad eyes, she listened to his version of the events in Lord Kelso's book room and the shame on her niece's face.

'Mandy told me as much,' she said when he finished his recitation, and poured more tea for them both.

'I would like to speak to her,' he asked. 'Apologise, at the very least. Lord knows I made a muddle of the whole business.'

It was Sal's turn to look uncomfortable. 'She told me she would rather be alone. Let's give her the evening off and all should be better tomorrow.' She passed him a plate of biscuits. 'Besides, what can Lord Kelso do, except fume and froth?' She gave him a worried glance. 'Do you fear for your own career?'

'Oh, no,' he assured her. He looked down at his cup, wishing absurdly that he could read tea leaves and have a medium tell him his own future. 'It's just… Miss Mathison, would you be surprised if I thought I was in love with your niece?'

She gave him a genuine smile. 'I'd be astounded if you weren't.'

'It's out of the question, I know, but...'

'Why do you say that?'

She caught him by surprise. 'I am thirty-one,' he said, casting about for a good reason.

'Mandy is twenty-six.'

'I'll be gone all the time, until Napoleon decides to end this war, and he shows no such inclination.' Even to his own ears, it sounded like a weak argument.

'She has ever been a resourceful child,' said the lady who had raised the woman he adored. 'Mandy would be lonely, but she would manage. You would get amazingly wonderful letters.'

Why that made him blush, Ben couldn't have told a roomful of Mr Coopers, or even a chief magistrate. He stood up. 'Some things are not meant to be,' he told her.

'Why?' she asked so quietly.

'What man in his right mind would marry, when the prospect of death in battle is so high aboard each Royal Navy vessel that plies the waters?' There. That should do it.

'Oh, I expect that a man who loves a lady would do precisely that,' Sal replied, as calmly as you please. 'P'raps it's better this way, since you have no respect for the bravery of women in general and my niece in particular. Good day to you, Master Muir.'

She had him, even as he cringed inside at the complete truth of her words. 'I'll be leaving in the morning.'

Ben ate dinner in silence, wishing with all his heart that Amanda would come down the stairs. She did nothing of

the sort and his forebodings grew. He knew how poorly
he had shown himself to Sally Mathison, probably the
one person that Amanda would believe. He had a greater
worry. He had met vindictive men before and he feared
what Lord Kelso might do.

By the time he went to bed, he had convinced himself
that his fears were unfounded. After all, what else could
Lord Kelso do? Ben packed his clothes, took a long look
at *The Science of Nautical Mathematics*, still untouched,
then lay down to compose himself for sleep that he knew
would not come.

He stared at the ceiling all night. In the morning, he
got up, washed and shaved in cold water and dressed. He
had already told Sal that he was leaving on the northbound
mail coach before dawn and just to leave a pasty for him.

His timepiece told him that he had better hurry. He
opened the door to his room to let himself out quietly and
there stood Amanda in her nightgown and shawl.

He exclaimed something because she had startled him,
but she didn't step back. Without a word, she put her hands
up on his shoulders, which made him stoop a little.

She kissed one cheek and then the other. 'God keep you,
Ben Muir,' she whispered, her eyes on Aunt Sal's closed
door. 'I was a ninny yesterday and I apologise.'

'I am the fool,' he contradicted.

'Bother it,' she whispered and kissed him again.

He picked her up and kissed her back, then set her
down. Her body pressed against his had given him a bigger jolt, but he had to hurry to the mail coach. He touched
her nose, which made her sob, then put her hand to her
mouth to stifle it. Unsure of himself, he who was self-assured in every aspect of naval operations, he went down
the stairs quietly.

He turned back to look up at her, wanting to declare himself, wanting to propose to her, wanting to tell her the deepest feelings of his heart. A realist, he knew he could do none of those and still catch the mail coach, so he remained silent. No, not a realist; a coward.

'Wait a moment.'

Miserable, Ben stood still in the darkness of the hall that led into the dining room.

'Catch.'

He held out his hand as the love of his heart, the mother of children he would never have, tossed something soft to him.

'I only had time to knit you one stocking,' she whispered, 'so it's a poor kind of Christmas. Perhaps one is better than none.'

With that, she blew him a kiss and disappeared back into the upper-floor gloom. He heard another stifled sob and then a door close on every one of the expectations he hadn't known he possessed, until he went to Venable to tutor a miserable excuse for a midshipman.

He tucked the stocking into his uniform front and let himself out Mandy's Rose for the last time.

He had forgotten the pasty, so he bought pasteboard and lint at the posting house and ate that instead. As he chewed and swallowed doggedly, he wondered if there was a more cowardly man in all of England. Someone else would make her a good offer some day. Besides, he didn't even know how to propose marriage.

He would have managed quite well, if the mail coach hadn't passed Mandy's Rose on its journey to take him briefly to Plymouth, and a change of coach onto the Great North Road. He should have known better than to look out the window.

There Amanda stood in the rain, that shawl still clutched tight around her nightgown, her feet bare. She locked her eyes on to his and he could have died with the pain in his heart.

'Shameful, forward piece,' said the woman seated next to him. 'She'll come to no good end.'

Ben closed his eyes in perfect agony.

Aunt Sal scolded her for standing in the rain, but Mandy could tell her heart wasn't in it. She let her aunt lead her upstairs, strip off her wet nightgown and towel her dry, then wrap her tight in that towel and hold her close.

Neither of them spoke. Sal finally turned to the door. 'Get dressed, missy,' she said. 'We have a lot of work to do today and we have Christmas plans.'

Mandy stared at the closed door for a long time, then did as her aunt had dictated. She had wasted a whole day yesterday. Breakfast seemed like a burden, so she shook her head over pasties when she came downstairs.

'Amanda Mathison.'

Mandy looked up, startled, as her dearest aunt took her chin firmly in her hand and gave her a shake. Wounded at ill treatment, she let Aunt Sal slap that pasty in her hand and obeyed her command to eat. She had the hardest time swallowing around the lump in her throat, but she managed because Aunt Sal expected her to manage.

'Aunt Sal, why didn't he declare himself?' she asked finally, when she knew she wasn't going to cry. 'I believe he cared for me.'

'He more than cared for you,' Sal said finally. She hadn't eaten, but there seemed to be an impediment in her throat, too.

'Doesn't he understand that the man has to do the asking?'

Aunt Sal seemed to consider the question. 'Perhaps he didn't know how to declare himself,' she said. 'I doubt anyone teaches that in the Royal Navy, and didn't he say a ship has been his home since he was thirteen? And there's a war to consider. He probably convinced himself he was sparing you.'

'That is utter nonsense,' Mandy said, and her aunt nodded.

They sat close together in silence, just breathing in and out, probably what women had done since for ever, when matters went contrary to desires.

'Will I recover?' Mandy asked finally. 'We didn't do anything to regret.'

'I almost wish you had,' her aunt whispered.

'Aunt!' Mandy put her hands to her face. 'I wanted to, oh, I did.' Miserable beyond words, she looked up as the morning light changed. The rain had changed into snow. She sat there and watched the snow fall, covering ugly woodpiles and ash heaps. If only there were such a remedy to disguise a broken heart.

Mandy folded her hands in her lap. *You can survive Ben Muir*, she told herself. *Look at Aunt Sal. She never married. Look how well she has done.*

She looked at Aunt Sal, shocked to see tears on her cheeks. She wondered if, years ago, there had been a Ben Muir for her aunt. She put out her hand and clutched her aunt's balled fist. *We'll just sit here and breathe*, she thought.

Just breathing never paid a single bill, so Mandy turned the horrible day into a usual day, with work and diners who expected her good cheer and happy commentary. By the time the last dish of the evening was dried and the dough set for tomorrow's bread, Mandy knew she could manage.

She wasn't so certain next morning, when everything fell apart with an official-looking document delivered by Mr Cooper, more solemn than she had ever seen him. She wanted to offer him some refreshment, but she accepted the blue-sheathed document instead, with *Sal Mathison, Mandy's Rose, Venable, Devon*, written in plain script.

Sal had come into the dining room, wiping her hands and ready to chat with Mr Cooper. She stared at the paper in Mandy's hand, then took it. Her face went white and she dropped the document. Mandy picked it up and read without permission. She read it again, then looked at Mr Cooper's equally stricken face.

'He can do this?' she asked.

'He can and did.' The solicitor took the pages from her slack grip. 'He has entered into verbal agreement with your landlord to purchase this row of buildings for the sum of three hundred pounds.' His voice shook with emotion. 'You will be gone by December the twenty-fourth, 1810.'

Sal burst into tears and buried her face in her apron. Mandy watched her in horror, beyond tears because she had already shed all the tears in the entire universe last night in her bedroom. There weren't any more, so she did not cry.

'Do you have any money at all?' Mr Cooper asked.

Mandy knew the books as well as her weeping aunt. She shook her head. 'Nothing beyond fifty pounds,' she said. 'How…?'

Mr Cooper paced the room, his rage evident with each step he took. 'Lord Kelso paid a visit to Mr Pickering. You know how foggy the dear old man is! I doubt Mr Pickering has any idea what he has done.'

'Has any money changed hands yet?' Mandy asked.

'No, but Mr Pickering gave his word and I have been charged to draw up the papers, to be signed as quickly as possible. Mandy, I cannot tell you how sorry I am.'

He let himself out of the tea room and Mandy held her aunt close. A wave of anger passed over her as she remembered the scene in the book room—from her father's indignation, to her half-brother's stupefaction, to Ben Muir's fury and his ill-timed revelation to Thomas Walthan. She thought forgetting Ben Muir might suddenly become much easier. She could blame this mess on him, except that she couldn't. After all, who had refused the terms of the codicil and stormed out of the room?

So much blame: if Lord Kelso had been a stronger man, he could have resisted old Lord Kelso's decision to annul that Scottish wedding so many years ago. If the old earl hadn't experienced some change of heart through the years, he would never have altered his will and raised even miniscule hopes. If Ben Muir hadn't been looking in Euclid's *Elements* he never would have found that scrap of paper and given the damned thing to Mr Cooper. If she had accepted her father's humiliating terms, the matter would have rested, with her half-brother none the wiser.

Without a word, she helped her sobbing aunt upstairs and set to work by herself. When the first diners arrived, Aunt Sal had joined her in the kitchen, her eyes red-rimmed and her lips pinched, but her fingers as sure as ever as she chopped and diced. Her love for her aunt nearly took Mandy's breath away. They were in this mess together.

Mandy was almost on time to choir practice, even though she had to run. She slipped and slid along the snow-covered path, yearning for Ben Muir's steady hand. She knew she would be late, but Aunt Sal lost all strength after the last dinner guest left. She helped her aunt upstairs to bed again, told the dishes just to rest for a while in the dishwater and hurried to church.

She paused inside the chapel door to catch her breath. 'Angels We Have Heard on High' calmed her heart, even though she missed Ben Muir's commanding second tenor, that voice he had assured her was only half the size of his voice in battle when his crew manoeuvred the *Albemarle* close to enemy guns and he kept his ship trim through turmoil she couldn't imagine.

When the rehearsal ended, Mandy remained. The wind blew cold as the other choir members opened and closed the door. She likened the cold wind to the disaster soon to envelop Mandy's Rose and knocked on the vicar's study door.

Reverend Winslow didn't seem surprised to see her. She saw the worry on his face and knew that Mr Cooper must have whispered something to him during the rehearsal. She told him everything.

The vicar paced the room much like Mr Cooper that morning. 'Christmas Eve?' he asked. She knew he had heard her, but she also understood his disbelief. Her disbelief had faded more quickly, but Mandy was only beginning to appreciate her own courage.

'I fear so,' she told him. 'Sir, do you know of anyone in Venable who could use a cook and an assistant?'

His tear-filled eyes dismayed her, but she kept her gaze clear. She had already cried every tear, but she wanted advice. 'I need you to think of something,' she said. 'Please help us.'

Her quiet words seemed to brace him. 'Mrs Winslow and I need a cook and an assistant,' he said, after long thought. 'Her joint ache is growing worse by the day and you know how busy I am.'

She nodded. 'You needn't pay us.'

'We can't afford to,' he said with real apology in his voice and not a little shame. His expression hardened and, for just a moment, he was an angry man and not a servant of the Church of England.

Mandy shook her head. 'We'll cook for you this winter, and maybe by spring we'll think of something else.' What, she couldn't imagine, but her own grief hadn't driven away all her optimism.

He gave her a searching look then. 'Would you consider writing a letter to Master Muir? He might take an interest.'

She had mulled over the matter for a long time that afternoon, then tucked it away. 'I'm not the brazen sort,' she said. 'I have no leave to write him a letter.'

Reverend Winslow nodded. 'Just a thought.' His slight smile died on his lips. 'I doubt the Royal Navy pays sailing masters much, if he took a tutoring job with Thomas Walthan.'

He stood up as the clock chimed nine. It was time for Mandy to hurry home and lie in bed wide awake for another night.

'Perhaps you and your aunt could come here *before* Christmas Eve.' Anger gleamed in the vicar's eyes again, plus something else, a stubbornness she had never noticed before. Evidently vicars were not perfect, either. 'Let's not give Lord Kelso the satisfaction of ordering the magistrate to evict you. There's room here for you to store whatever you wish. I'll send round a note to some of my able-bodied parishioners and we'll move the matter along.'

She gave her vicar the bob of a curtsy, feeling a weight leave her shoulders. Perhaps they could avoid the poorhouse, after all. Her heart full, she left the vicarage, relieved to have good news for Aunt Sal. *It is good news*, she thought, as she walked with her eyes down, since snow was falling again. *Perhaps not as good as we would like, but better than destitution.*

She stopped by the bench where she and Ben had sat so

close together. She brushed aside the snow and sat there again. She closed her eyes, thinking of what Christmas catering they could complete before Mandy's Rose closed forever.

Her heart nearly failed her at the thought of all the cooking equipment and furniture to pack and store in the shed behind the vicarage. If they could hold an auction, they might be able to eke out a few weeks or months of independence. Someone else would have to represent her and Aunt Sal, if there was an auction. The idea of watching her life and livelihood selling to the highest bidder was harsh and wrong. Her father would get what he wished— they would have to leave Venable and try their fortunes somewhere else, never to embarrass him again.

Maybe Christmas truly was the season of forgiveness. As she sat there, Mandy began to feel sorry for Ben Muir, instead of distressed at him. If happiness with a tired and wrung-out but immensely capable sailing master had come to nothing, well, no one ever died of a broken heart.

'I will keep Christmas,' she whispered to the falling snow. She decided to knit that other sock and mail it care of the *Albemarle* in Plymouth. 'I am better off than many.'

Chapter Five

As much as he would have preferred to avoid Plymouth, Ben Muir accepted the fact that the Royal Mail had its routes. He walked to the Drake, surprising Mrs Fillion, who knew he wasn't due until after Christmas. She made no comment, but he hadn't expected any, since he was wearing his sailing-master expression. His quick visit to Brustein and Carter should have sent him out smiling, because his prize money was doing nicely, but it didn't.

He walked to the dry dock in Devonport and looked up at the *Albemarle* as workers swarmed about. The masts were bare of yardarms and rigging, which made the frigate appear as vulnerable as an enemy hulk after Trafalgar. He would bide his time in Scotland for a week or so, then return to supervise what made him so valuable to the fleet. This time, no matter how hard he stared at his ship, all he saw was a barefoot woman standing in sleet.

He shook his head over the continuous game of whist at the Drake that had been going on since at least the Peace of Amiens. He slept only because a man can't stay awake more than three days in a row. He woke up tired, and began his mail-coach journey from one end of England to Kirkcudbright on the River Dee, hating himself with every mile.

He arrived three days later, bleary-eyed and unshaven, at Selkirk Arms, the posting inn with such a view of the river. He wasn't sure if the landlord recognised him, even though they had gone to grammar school together. Ben was not in the mood for conversation, so he shouldered his duffel like the common seaman he really was and walked home, past MacLellan's Castle, by St Cuthbert's and up Church Row to Number Nine.

His Aunt Claudie opened the door. She stood a moment in shocked silence, then held out her arms to him. 'Benny, Benny,' she crooned, apparently not minding his travel smell. 'I didn't know you were coming.'

He knew he had been away too long because he had trouble understanding what she had just said. With some regret, he knew he had tidied up his own brogue so he could be understood aboard ship. The gentle burr of his aunt's welcome eased his Scotsman's heart.

'I hadn't planned to come home,' he explained, as he let her drag him inside. 'Where's t'auld man?'

'Ye'd better sit down, lad,' she said and pushed him into a chair in the parlour.

He gave Aunt Claudie a long look, but saw no sorrow there. 'What has he done?' he asked.

'He went on a trip to *that* country,' she said as she relieved him of his cloak and hat.

'Good God, did he go to *Canada* and my brothers?' He couldn't help shouting.

'Nay, lad, nay, England!' she exclaimed, her hands over her ears.

He took a deep breath and lowered his voice. 'Why, in God's name?'

'It was something you wrote in your letter. He wouldn't tell—such a stubborn man is my brother—but don't you know he left immediately.'

Ben sat back in the chair, aware of his deep-down exhaustion. What had he ever written in his two letters from Venable of such urgency that would make a seventy-year-old fisherman, retired and comfortable before his own fire, scarper off?

Aunt Claudie returned his stare with one of her own. 'Are ye ill, Ben Muir? Is that why?'

'No. Good God, he has never even left the district!'

'Don't I know? As I remember, he got your last letter, muttered something like, "He's never done this before and he's messing up." He was aboard the mail coach in the morning.' She gazed at him with a twinkle in her eye. 'Laddie, ye probably passed each other on the road!'

In the morning Ben secured a seat on the outgoing mail coach to Plymouth. He had a few minutes, so he re-acquainted himself with the innkeeper and sat down to sweetened porridge and tea, vexed and troubled that his sole remaining parent had a peculiar bee in his bonnet.

He had just finished his tea when the innkeeper brought a letter to his table.

'Ben, last night's Royal Mail dropped off the mail sack. There's one addressed to you.' He chuckled. 'Likely you rode all the way here with this letter in the mail coach.'

Mystified, Ben took the letter. As he read, he felt his whole body go numb. Reverend Winslow had begun by apologising for his presumption, then spent a close-written page telling what had happened to the proprietor of Mandy's Rose and her niece. *I thought you should know*, the vicar concluded. *If I am mistaken in your affections, I do apologise. Yours sincerely...*

Horrified, Ben realised he had badly underestimated Lord Kelso. The mail coach stopping at every town would never be fast enough. He put both hands on the innkeeper's shoulders. 'What's the fastest way I can get to Devon?'

The innkeeper didn't flinch. 'This is a matter of grave national emergency, isn't it?'

'Without question,' Ben lied. 'I'll trust you not to mention that you even saw me here. Suppose Napoleon's agents find out? What can I do?'

'Post-chaise,' the keep replied. 'Barring snow, you'll be there in two days.'

He arrived in three days. No amount of willing the horses to go faster could defeat snow around Carlisle, and then at York. The worst moment came as they rolled into Venable, past a darkened Mandy's Rose. Bright lights burned everywhere else, making the closed and shuttered tea room appear long-abandoned, as though the last proprietors had left during the War of the Roses. Funny how quickly old buildings—and old ships, for that matter—could appear almost haunted.

He knew his postmen had tried to do what he demanded, so he paid them liberally and wished them merry Christmas. He stowed his duffel at the posting house and walked to St Luke's. The vicar would know where Amanda and Sal Mathison had taken themselves. He cursed his stupidity again, resolving to do what he could for the woman he loved, who by now probably wouldn't speak to him until the twentieth century, if either of them lived that long. And then he had to find his father. For the first time, the blockade of France and Spain sounded almost like going on holiday.

He heard the choir singing as he opened the church door. All of Venable must have chosen to forget work and worry and petty strife to celebrate the birth of Our Lord, the Prince of Peace in a world sorely in need of peace. Well, why not? It was Christmas Eve. He had forgotten.

Tired, discouraged, Ben shucked his cloak and hat and stood there watching the choir. The choirmaster was waving his arms about with his usual fervour, as if his exertions would get more tune and music from his amateurs.

There she was. He saw her when the choirmaster swayed to one side, carried away by his efforts. 'Amanda,' he said, so softly that no one looked around. 'Please don't hate me.'

He stood there in the aisle, unable to move forward or leave, or do anything except stare at her like a drowning man desperate for a life preserver.

The choir had begun a series of crescendoing 'Hallelujahs' when Amanda noticed him. The love of his life threw down her choir book and wormed her way past a row of astonished sopranos. She ran down the aisle as the choir kept singing and threw herself into his arms.

She nearly bowled him over, but he grabbed her and steadied them both, he who knew something about ballast and balance on a pitching deck. 'Hallelujah!' sang the choir as he kissed her.

'Ben, we are idiots,' she whispered in his ear.

'I know. Do you love me?' he whispered back, acutely mindful that the anthem had ended and no one was paying attention to the vicar. He glanced at Reverend Winslow, cheered to see that the vicar didn't appear overly concerned.

'Yes, I love you, you ninny,' his dear one said. 'You should be kept on a short chain.'

Someone else caught his eye. Grinning as broadly as the others, his father sat next to Aunt Sal. Ben took Amanda by the hand as they walked down the aisle. Aunt Sal obliged by moving over and he squeezed in next to his father. There was nowhere for Amanda to go except on his lap, which appeared to bother no one.

'I need an explanation, Da,' he whispered.

'In good time,' Maxwell Muir whispered back.

Reverend Winslow beamed at them. 'Are we all settled?' he asked and the congregation laughed.

The service continued. The choir sang again, after a reading of Luke 2, but nothing could induce Amanda to leave his lap and rejoin the singers. With a sigh that went right to his heart, she rested her head on his chest and closed her eyes. Her even breathing told him that she slept. That was just before his eyes closed, too.

At least the congregation didn't tiptoe out and leave them slumbering. Ben's father prodded him in the ribs before the recessional and they both stood, holding tight to each other, as the vicar and his acolytes walked down the aisle and into a snowy night.

Ordinarily, the gathering that followed the midnight service would have been a small one, as parents carried sleepy children home and elderly parishioners followed. No one left early this time. There was wassail for the adults and punch for the children, and Mrs Winslow's exquisite desserts, made more special because Sal Mathison and Mandy had added their talents. Mandy's Rose might be shuttered and dark, but it was plain to see that the real heart of the tea room carried on in the vicarage.

As much as he wanted to cuddle Amanda and work up the nerve to declare himself, Ben had another matter to discuss. 'Da, what was it in my letters that sent you barrelling down the pike to Venable?'

His father traded glances with the suddenly shy lady who was probably going to become Ben's wife. 'Laddie, your letters were full of Amanda this and Amanda that.

I wanted to see her for myself,' he said simply. 'At each change, the coachmen made certain I got on the right coach.'

Did I speak only of Amanda? he asked himself, his arm around her again. 'And you wanted to make sure I stepped up to the mark,' he said to his father.

'For all that you sail in a dangerous occupation, you are the most cautious of my sons,' his father informed him. He leaned forward to look at Amanda. 'My dear, I thought he might try to talk himself out of a very good idea. Besides, I wanted to meet you. Ben said you needed a father. Here I am.'

Ben couldn't help his tears when Amanda gave her father a deep curtsy. 'And here I am, Father,' she whispered.

Touched beyond words, Ben raised her to her feet. 'Ben, we have had a pleasant visit, these past few days,' she told him. 'I have heard some diverting stories about your childhood.'

Ben rolled his eyes. He saw Aunt Sal's smile and knew nothing had been settled. 'Sal, I owe both of you an apology. This whole bad business with the loss of Mandy's Rose wouldn't have happened if I had kept my mouth shut. Can you forgive me?'

'I can and will,' she said in her forthright way. 'Mandy and I are working for the Winslows now, and I—'

'Pardon me, dear, but perhaps the curtain has not quite closed on this whole mess,' Reverend Winslow said. The vicar ushered a little man forward, someone Ben had seen in Mandy's Rose for a few meals, but unknown to him.

'May I introduce Andrew Pickering?'

Ben made his bow.

'Mr Pickering owns that row of buildings that our esteemed Lord Kelso has decided to purchase.'

'A good row, sir, a good row,' the little fellow said. He frowned. 'The vicar tells me I have done a hasty thing, but perhaps we can make all right again.'

'I believe you gave your word, Mr Pickering,' Ben reminded him.

Mr Pickering shook his head. 'I was duped.' He gave a snort of indignation. 'Promised me, he did, that there would be a signed contract by half-six on Christmas Eve.' He shrugged until his high collar rode up past his ears. 'It is midnight.'

Mr Cooper continued the narrative. 'Lord Kelso had me prepare the contract, but he sent word this afternoon that he was too ill to do business until the first of the year.'

Serious nods all around. Ben felt his spirits begin to rise.

'I reminded him that the deal was to be closed today and he just laughed. Said no one wanted it,' Mr Cooper said.

'Insulted me, he did!' Mr Pickering declared.

'I propose this, Master Muir,' Mr Cooper said. 'If you will make Andrew Pickering a better offer, the row will be yours to do with as you see fit.'

Amanda returned to Ben's side, her face rosy with embarrassment for him, because she knew nothing about his finances. 'Mr Cooper, you needn't put Ben on the spot. I don't think…' She stopped.

Ben looked at the woman who might actually share his pillow soon. He gave his attention to Mr Pickering. 'Three hundred pounds, did you say?'

'Aye. You offer will have to be higher, to flummox Lord Kelso.'

'You're a shrewd gentleman,' Ben said, which appeared to delight Mr Pickering. 'How about four hundred pounds?'

Amanda gasped and grabbed his hand, towing him to

a corner of the room. 'Ben! Is that your life savings? You can't!'

He pulled her close, amused to look over his shoulder and see everyone leaning towards them. Amanda moved even closer to him, which brought some heat to one of his appendages.

'I guess that means you're not marrying me for my money,' he teased, stepping back a bit because they were the attention of mixed company.

'Do be serious, Ben.'

He whispered in her ear about Brustein and Carter, and prize money. 'We all get a percentage, not just the captain and admiral of the fleet,' he concluded. With unholy glee, he saw that her eyes had begun to glaze over when his lips tickled her ear. 'I can afford any number of Mandy's Roses.'

Amanda took a deep breath and another, looking around as if aware for the first time that they were the centre of attention. 'You would to that for Aunt Sal and me?'

'That and more.' He whispered in her ear again, since results were so positive. 'I love you.' He turned to Aunt Sal. 'Everything I ever said about not inflicting myself on a good woman in time of war was poppycock and base cowardice. Do excuse it, Miss Mathison.'

'I am inclined to,' Aunt Sal told him, 'particularly since Mandy seems to want to hang about your neck.'

Ben returned his attention to the pretty girl whose eyes were little chips of blue, because she was smiling so big. 'Please marry me as soon as possible.'

She nodded and gave him a fierce hug, which caused a curious phenomenon: the room suddenly seemed empty of observers. No one was there except the two of them and a fierce hug deserved an equally fierce kiss.

They stood together, locked in a tight embrace, as their audience applauded, then returned to their own Christmas food and cheer. The vicar shook his hand, tears in his eyes, and his father just looked on in amusement and what looked like pride. Aunt Sal's lips trembled and her smile made Ben shaky. He was marrying Sal's treasure. The responsibility settled on his shoulders, right next to duty to his king and country. It was more of a caress than a heavy weight.

'I'll buy the building block and you won't lose Mandy's Rose,' he told Aunt Sal.

He thought she would agree, so her headshake surprised him. 'I can afford it, dear lady. Please let me.'

'I think not,' she said, with a smile at the vicar, who had just been joined by his wife. 'I rather like cooking in the vicarage and I know Mandy would rather be in Plymouth, for those times when the *Albemarle* comes to port.'

'Would you?' he asked his dear woman.

'Venable would be too far away,' she said, her voice so shy.

'It's only ten miles,' he reminded her.

'Too far.'

Ben nodded; she was right. He could already see her standing dockside in Devonport, waiting for him. In a few years, if the war ground on, she would probably wait for him there with a child, maybe two, if this wedding happened soon and he came into port occasionally.

'Very well,' he agreed. 'But there will be this condition, Reverend Winslow: I will pay Sal Mathison's salary. Consider it my contribution to the health and well-being of the Winslows and my tithe to the Church of England. No argument.'

No one argued. He saw the relief in Mrs Winslow's

eyes. He glanced at her hands, knotted with arthritis, and understood. He turned to Mr Pickering. 'Alas, I think you must wait for Lord Kelso to recover from his choler and accept his offer, after all.'

'I don't mind. It's still a good offer and I'm getting old,' Mr Pickering said. 'Eighty-five next week. I need a holiday.'

Everyone laughed, including Amanda, then she gave Ben a searching look. 'His choler? How would you know what is really wrong with Lord Kelso?'

'It's only a suspicion,' Ben said. 'When I stopped in Devonport and talked to the harbour master, he told me about a visit to my captain from Thomas Walthan.'

'Thomas?'

'Aye. He surrendered his midshipman's berth. I cannot begin to express my relief, but I doubt his father sees it that way.' He chuckled. 'Let's draw a curtain over life at Walthan Manor right now.'

He turned to the vicar. 'I need a special licence. My ship is my parish, but I'd rather not wait three weeks to have my captain cry the banns there.' Ben laughed. 'Besides, after all my declarations on never marrying, he would find this vastly amusing. Do you suppose the bishop is in Plymouth?'

'Alas, he is not,' Reverend Winslow said.

'We will elope,' Ben said, biting off each word, as his darling Mandy blushed.

'No need,' the vicar said. 'I saw the bishop only yesterday at Lord Baleigh's seat just a little south of here, celebrating with wassail.' He leaned forward. 'He is a patriotic man, Mr Muir. Go in all your finery and describe a lonely night on the blockade. Get Mandy to squeeze out a tear or two and he will grant a special licence, even if he is on holiday. Shall we say December the twenty-sixth?'

'What say ye, Amanda?' Ben asked, his eyes on his love, who struggled to keep back tears. She nodded.

'Lad, it might be hard to find a nice place to stay, inns being what they are at Christmas,' Maxwell Muir said.

'Hardly.' Mr Cooper reached into his pocket and pulled out a key. 'Mandy's Rose is available. No one is taking possession until Lord Kelso gets around to signing the contract.' He bowed to Mr Pickering. 'No objections, sir?'

'None whatsoever.'

'I don't have a dress,' Amanda said, but it sounded to Ben like a feeble protest.

'Good God, woman, then what are you wearing?' he teased. *It'll come off soon enough*, he thought.

The dress lasted through a wedding, a quick reception in the vicarage on leftover Christmas refreshments, and a walk to Mandy's Rose. They sat for a moment on the bench by the road, where he promised to find her a wedding ring as soon as they got to Plymouth and the Drake.

She took off the dress—that nice green wool—as he watched, her face a deep blush. He did duty on the buttons to her camisole, which afforded him a most pleasant view of what he had already imagined was a lovely bosom. There was even a wonderful mole between her breasts, which he kissed. That led to her hands on his trouser buttons. She was good with buttons.

When his trousers and shirt were off, and his small clothes halfway gone, she made him turn around so she could see the blue gunpowder dots on his back. He would have laughed at her cheerful scrutiny, except that she started kissing each dot, which moved matters along handsomely.

She didn't even fumble with the cord holding up her petticoat and she hadn't bothered with drawers. She was a sailor's dream come true.

* * * * *

The Viscount's Christmas Kiss

Georgie Lee

To my family.
Thanks for making every Christmas memorable.

Dear Reader,

I think it was Shakespeare who once said, "the course of Christmas never did run smooth," or something like that. As with anything, life can step in to mess with the best-laid plans for the holidays. Sometimes it happens in sad and poignant ways, like the year my family carried our good cheer, along with our presents, to the hospital to celebrate what would be my grandfather's last Christmas. Sometimes the interruption is exciting and happy, like the year we journeyed to the same hospital on Christmas morning to welcome a new baby into the family. All our plans for that joyous Christmas Day changed as we moved back dinner and asked guests to arrive later so we could visit the little bundle of joy who'd arrived early. I even braved the mall the day before to buy a Baby's First Christmas ornament.

No matter what surprises or sorrows Christmas brings me, family will always be at the heart of my celebrations. *The Viscount's Christmas Kiss* is my attempt to capture the craziness and the love that fills a family and a house at Christmas. It's also about the unexpected surprises life sometimes throws into the celebration mix, and how they can change us and our lives and strengthen our bonds with those we love. I hope you enjoy sharing Christmas with Lily and her family, and the unexpected surprise that changes all of Lily's expectations and plans.

Georgie Lee

Chapter One

Yorkshire, England—1818

'What do you mean, he's coming here?' Lily paused over her canvas and a large drop of red paint dripped from the tip of her paintbrush.

'Laurus is bringing him,' her younger sister Daisy announced as she strolled across the wide sitting room, waving the letter with the shocking news. 'He's to stay with us for Christmas.'

'Here?' Lily squeaked as she wiped the red spot off her easel with the corner of her old smock. 'To Helkirk Place?'

'Of course. What other here might I be referring to?' Daisy flounced to a nearby chair and dropped into it, tossing their older brother's letter on the table beside her to pick through the other envelopes she carried. At ten, Daisy enjoyed a more vigorous correspondence than Lily did at twenty.

Lily shoved the paintbrush in its holder and rushed across the room, disturbing the pack of small terriers sleeping on the hearthrug before the fireplace. They jumped to their stubby feet and began loudly protesting.

Aunt Alice continued to snore in her chair by the fire, immune to the indignity of her precious darlings.

Lily snatched up her brother's letter and read through it, the words nearly lost in the jumble of yapping canines.

'Quiet down, all of you,' she commanded, but it did nothing to silence the tiny pack or calm the panic racing through her. 'He's coming tonight, on Christmas Eve?'

'I imagine so if he's to be here for Christmas.' Daisy shrugged, the red ribbon in her brown hair as askew as those around the terriers' necks.

Lily crushed the letter to her chest as she took in the sorry state of the sitting room. With the exception of her corner where the easel sat neatly over the oil cloth protecting the floor, nothing else was as it should be. The house was already filled to near bursting with family. Besides Aunt Alice, their eldest sister Rose had descended on them yesterday with her husband, Edgar, and their five-year-old twins, James and John. The boys' shoes littered the stone hearth where they'd been discarded when they'd torn by after coming in from playing in the snow. Their mittens fared no better, one having been tossed over the back of a wooden chair, the other flung across the seat to wet the sturdy fabric. The rest were strewn about the room, except for the one being chewed on by Pygmalion, the smallest terrier with the longest name. Her other sister Petunia had arrived this morning with her husband and daughter, increasing the chaos. This wasn't the festive atmosphere in which to bring someone unaccustomed to the confusion of the Rutherford family, especially one as arrogant as Lord Marbrook.

'Did you tell Mother about Laurus's plan?' With any luck she'd object, what with the staff already overwhelmed and, if the butler was any judge of things this afternoon, sampling the wassail brewing in the kitchen.

Lily also hoped, for once, the family might side with her against a man such as Lord Marbrook, though she wasn't sure why, since they never had before. Because he was Laurus's oldest school friend, they'd been all too willing to overlook his slight of her. The indignity of it still stung.

'Mother thinks him being here is a wonderful idea. You know her, the more the merrier.' Daisy kicked her legs over the arm of the chair to recline across them and read.

Lily grabbed Daisy's ankle and tossed it off the embroidered arm. 'Why? Did she feel we didn't expose our family to enough ridicule the last time Gregor St James was in our midst?'

They hadn't seen Gregor St James, Viscount Marbrook, since Petunia's wedding to Charles Winford, fifth Baron Winford, four years ago. St James had only been a second son then. Now, with a title hanging in front of his name, he was sure to be even more arrogant than before and all too eager to sneer down his sharp nose at her and her family again.

'You were the only one who made a fool of herself, tripping while dancing with him during the Scotch reel,' Daisy pointed out.

Aunt Alice snorted in her sleep as if agreeing with Daisy, the slurp of the dog chewing the mitten punctuating it.

'Thank you very much for reminding me.' Though she'd never forgotten it, or the callous way Lord Marbrook and his family had treated her afterwards. Their very public disdain had encouraged the most vicious in society to follow their lead, making her the focus of wicked ridicule and turning every subsequent ball and soirée into a drudge. She'd left London less than a month later and hadn't returned since.

'I have no desire to attend our Christmas ball and face the entire countryside, most of whom were at Petunia's wedding. It's bad enough I have to endure Sir Walter's cracks about my graceful dancing every year, but to have Lord Marbrook there when he does is more than anyone should have to bear.'

'I don't know why you care about what wrinkled old Sir Walter says. No one else does.' Daisy turned over a page of her letter. 'Beside, Lord Marbrook is sure to have forgotten your tumble by now. Mother said he was with Wellington at Waterloo, before his elder brother died and he inherited.'

Lily didn't share her sister's confidence in Lord Marbrook having been changed by his time in France. Nor could she imagine a Marbrook sullying his hands on a battlefield or taking orders from anyone of lesser rank, not with the way the whole family revelled in their lineage more than the Prince Regent.

'He probably wasn't anywhere near the fighting but the aide-de-camp to some fat general with a higher title than his father's,' Lily retorted as she stomped back to the canvas and snatched up her palette. She mashed together yellow and blue with her knife, the memory of Lord Marbrook standing arrogantly over her while the other dancers had laughed, not bothering to acknowledge her or even help her rise from where she'd fallen, still made her cheeks burn. Yet it wasn't so much the haughty man's condescension which enraged her as how little she'd deserved it, especially after all she'd done for him in the hallway outside the ballroom before the dance.

She set down the knife and took up her brush, but fumbled the smooth wood. It dropped to the canvas covering the floor. She reached for it, but it disappeared in a flash of brown fur as Pygmalion snatched it up.

'No, Pygmalion, bad dog.' Lily chased after the animal, wincing as it scurried beneath a table with its prize, painting the bottom of one oak leg as he moved backwards. Lily knelt down in front of the table and reached for the brush. 'Give that back.'

The toll of the front bell echoed through the house, sending the dogs scurrying from the hearthrug in a hail of yapping and toenails scraping across the wood floor. Pygmalion, still gripping his treasure, darted past Lily to join the pack, leaving a streak of red on the white door moulding as he passed.

'It must be Laurus and his guest.' Daisy tossed aside her letter and, like one of the dogs, hurried off down the hall. Aunt Alice continued to snore in her chair, oblivious to the excitement of her darlings.

Lily sat back on her heels, ready to run in the opposite direction, but she could hardly hide from the family at Christmas. Nor could she leave Pygmalion to mark up the house, not with such an *esteemed* visitor about to grace it with his presence.

She hurried after the pack, jumping over the twins' discarded lead soldiers and tin horns, wrinkling her nose at the red bits of paint blobbed on the floor and streaked along the low bottoms of the walls. She hurried down the hall, eager to catch the dog before it did more damage and made the house, which was already in sixes and sevens, even worse. Her family wasn't slovenly, but there was a messiness to Helkirk Place, as if it wasn't just lived in, but well-worn. Her mother was too lenient with the staff, allowing them to shirk their cleaning duties, as Lily often reminded her. However, attending to such matters would involve her parents looking up from their precious plants long enough to give more care to what the servants were doing.

Passing the long tapestries and dark panelling of the Tudor-era house, Lily inhaled the woodsy scent of the pine boughs covering the sideboards and mixing with the savoury spices from the roasting pig's head wafting up from the kitchen. In the smell was every Christmas they'd ever spent here, except for the year they'd ventured to London for Petunia's wedding, the one Yuletide Lily did her best not to recall.

'Laurus, you made it.' Lily's elder sister Petunia embraced their brother. Behind her stood Mrs Smith, the nurse, with Petunia's toddler daughter Adelaide perched on one hip. Charles, Petunia's husband, stepped forwards to shake Laurus's hand. Beneath them, James and John ran in circles like the dogs around the adults.

'Uncle Laurus, what did you bring us?' the boys demanded, stopping to dig in Laurus's pockets.

'Boys, don't pester your uncle,' Rose chided as she and Edgar entered the foyer.

'They aren't bothering me. Besides, I need to get rid of this twist of sweets.' Laurus withdrew a small paper cone from inside his coat pocket and dangled it over their heads before depositing it in James's hand. He and John tore at it, extracting their treats while the dogs waited at their feet for the crumbs.

In the midst of all the wagging and whimpering, Lily spied Pygmalion, who bolted towards the stairs, determined to hang on to his treasure. She cornered the terrier between a high clock and the wall, stopping him before he could ascend and decorate the already bough-laden banister with more Christmas colour. The little dog growled as he shifted this way and that, trying to get past her, each turn of his head adding a new dollop of paint to the already marred wall.

'Lily, stop playing with Pygmalion and come greet

your brother.' Lily's father, Sir Timothy's, deep voice carried over the noise as he and Lily's mother descended to greet their only son. As always, his dark jacket was dusted with yellow pollen. Woe to those who were made to sneeze by flowers—the Rutherfords had lost more than one maid to the affliction.

'I will as soon as I get my paintbrush back,' Lily insisted.

'Lily, let the dog be, he isn't doing any harm,' Lily's mother added before turning her attention to Laurus.

Lily grabbed the end of the paintbrush and began to tug. Her mother might not care about marking the plaster, but Lily did.

'Perhaps I can be of some assistance?' a male voice offered as Lily continued her tug of war with Pygmalion.

'No, I have him.' The dog's little jaws were no match for Lily's determination and she tugged the paintbrush from Pygmalion's mouth. It came free so fast, it sent her stumbling back. She whirled, trying to reclaim her balance, only to hit the hard chest of a man with the soft end of the brush. It left a wide, red streak across the camel-coloured coat.

'Oh, Laurus, I'm so sorry.' She reached out to wipe off the spot, then froze. This was not Laurus, or Edgar, or Charles, but none other than Gregor St James, Viscount Marbrook.

She snatched back her hand, waiting for his green eyes, a shade more like grass in a meadow than the dark holly leaves decorating the family portraits, to turn as cold as they had in the ballroom four years ago. In the expanding silence, every humiliation she'd experienced as she'd sat on the dance floor rubbing her sore ankle with everyone staring at her except Lord Marbrook, who'd refused to even acknowledge her, filled her again.

'I'm sorry,' she squeaked, horrified at the stain and appearing in front of him in her old smock and dress. This wasn't how she wanted to meet this man again. Curse Laurus for bringing him here.

She pulled the smock from her shoulders and draped it over one arm, squaring herself to face Lord Marbrook and daring him to cast whatever insults he wanted at her. She wasn't the same Lily he'd so publicly disdained in London and she'd make him see it.

He slipped a white handkerchief from his pocket and wiped at the stain, regarding her with more humour than horror. 'It's all right. I've never much cared for this coat anyway.'

Lily's chin dropped in shock. If she didn't know better, she'd think Lord Marbrook was making a joke. Apparently, so did everyone else for the entrance hall grew quiet. Even the twins ceased their chatter, sensing the adults' astonishment, even if they didn't comprehend the reason for it.

Lord Marbrook folded the linen square and tucked it back in his pocket, drawing Lily's attention to the increased width of his chest and shoulders. The candles in the chandelier overhead brought out the strands of red in his dark hair which was cut short in the Roman style. A slight curl made it wave instead of fall over his forehead, captivating her as much as the height and muscle he'd gained since she'd last seen him. His face was more angular than before and graced with a seriousness which seemed to deepen the faint lines at the corners of his mouth and harden the set of his chin. She didn't want to stare, but she couldn't help herself. It'd been the same at the wedding ball when she'd glanced past her cousins to watch him with his brother, mother and father. While his family had sneered at the guests, he'd watched the celebration with the longing of a child pressing his nose against a bakery window.

Then, when he'd slipped away from his family, she'd followed him. Having heard so much of him from Laurus, she'd felt bold enough to approach him, her heart fluttering when he'd asked her to join him on the bench in the alcove. While they'd sat there, he'd told her how his father had purchased a commission for him and was sending him off to France because he wasn't the heir, only the disappointing second son who'd failed to comprehend the importance of the Marbrook name. His revelation had increased the darkness which had tightened his angular jaw and hardened his green eyes, revealing the depth of his pain. She'd comforted him in his distress, thinking such intimacy made them friends. She'd been horribly mistaken.

'I see Lily has painted you.' Laurus laughed, breaking the silence. 'It's only fitting since she's painted everyone else in the family.'

Laurus's joke brought the merriment back to the greeting and soon the twins were talking in their loud voices, imploring Daisy to try one of their sweets. She ignored them, staring up at Lord Marbrook in near adoration as he spoke to Rose, then pestering him with questions about his journey. She wasn't the only one troubling him with unchecked excitement. Pygmalion stood on his hind legs and scratched at Lord Marbrook's riding boots, fighting for the Viscount's attention as much as Daisy.

'Pygmalion, get down,' Lily demanded, wishing someone would show some sense of decorum, but like her family, the dog ignored her entreaty to behave.

Lord Marbrook picked up the dog and tucked him under his arm as though he were a riding crop and not a usually nippy terrier. 'Is he yours?'

Lily gaped at him, as did the entire room. 'No, he's my aunt's.'

'Am I not allowed to touch him?' Lord Marbrook ran his hand over the dog's head and down its back. The dog closed its eyes in delight, his tongue hanging out of his red-stained muzzle.

'No one is,' Laurus explained with some of the same wonder as Lily. 'Even Aunt Alice can't pick him up without risking losing a finger.'

'It's a season of miracles with even the most ferocious beast living in love and peace with its fellow creature,' Sir Timothy announced in a voice better suited to the family chapel than the hall, though he had to nearly yell to be heard over the noise of the twins, and Edgar and Charles debating the merits of their own pointers.

Lord Marbrook's opinion of the chaos surrounding him was difficult to gauge. He didn't sneer as Squire Pettigrew did whenever he visited, but stood with Pygmalion tucked under his arm, a reserve worthy of a king masking his thoughts. Whatever his opinion, and Lily was sure it wasn't good, when he left here he'd probably tell everyone in London of the coarseness of the Rutherfords, and Lily in particular. It would set the tongues wagging against her and her family all over again. Everyone else might not care what society said about them, but Lily did.

'I'm so glad you could join us for Christmas,' Lily's mother offered in a calm voice, as though nothing, not a houseful of guests or a viscount with a stained coat holding a vicious little terrier, could ruffle her. Lily wished she possessed her mother's poise. It would make living in the bedlam of Helkirk Place much easier.

'It's I who am grateful for your warm invitation, Lady Rutherford,' Lord Marbrook responded with all the manners expected of a viscount.

'I'm sure such feelings won't last long,' Lily murmured much louder than intended, hazarding a frown from her father.

'What do you mean, girl?' he demanded.

If she hadn't wanted to slip away unnoticed before, she did now.

Laurus dropped a hand on his friend's shoulder. 'What she means is, Lord Marbrook will regret it when I insist he join in our celebration of the Lord of Misrule. You will help us, won't you, Marbrook?'

Lily imagined the old viscount, if he were here to see this, would clutch his cap in horror at a mere baronet's son addressing a peer in such a manner. If Lord Marbrook minded, it was impossible to tell for very little in his expression changed as he answered.

'I'll gladly help you.'

Lily imagined he didn't share Laurus's excitement for the coming festivities and she wondered how her good-natured brother could have ever become friends with such an aloof man.

'You'll find our way of celebrating Christmas a little different here, as opposed to London,' Sir Timothy announced. 'We enjoy our Christmas feast tonight and to-morrow hold a ball for all the country families.'

'I assure you, any customs you keep will be heartily enjoyed. My last few Christmases have not been happy ones.' Gregor stroked the dog, the green of his eyes darkening with his disquiet and, to her surprise, making her own heart constrict. She hated to imagine anyone, even Lord Marbrook, so unhappy at such a pleasant time of year.

'Yes, we were very sorry to hear of your brother and father,' Lady Rutherford offered.

Lord Marbrook had lost a father and an older brother

in the space of a year, all after enduring who knew what horrors in France. It softened Lily's attitude towards him, but not her desire to escape and avoid any more silent judgement or unintended missteps. With the red paint stain on his jacket mocking her, she backed slowly away from the group. They were so busy chatting, they didn't notice her as she made for the sitting room and the peace of her painting.

Over Lady Rutherford's shoulder, Gregor caught Miss Rutherford stealing off down the hallway. She didn't run, but moved with the same timid grace he remembered from outside the ballroom four years ago, only tonight she was sneaking away from him, not to him. He couldn't blame her. She'd been kind to him once and he'd treated her with the disdain all Marbrooks showed anyone they thought beneath them. So many times his father had railed against Gregor's friendship with Laurus, but he'd defied the man to maintain it. If only he'd possessed the courage to defy his father the night of the ball, but at seventeen, he'd still hungered after his father's approval and in an effort to secure it, he'd hurt a young woman who didn't deserve it.

Miss Rutherford paused near the centre of the hall and looked back at the group. Catching his eye, she stood up a little straighter and Gregor silently applauded her spirit. Regardless of the incident with the paintbrush, she'd faced him with sufficient resolve to impress a man used to commanding men and he admired her for it. While she studied him, the candles on a nearby sideboard brightened the whites of her eyes and caught the faint amber strands in her brown hair. Despite the simple style of her grey dress, it couldn't hide the roundness of her high breasts or the faint curve of hips just beneath the paint streaks. In the four years since he'd last seen her, she'd lost the plumpness of girlhood and gained the more sinewy curves and lines of a woman. The supple changes made Gregor's breath catch in his throat and for a moment he thought he saw her own sweet chest pause in its rising and falling. Then it was gone and with it the faint connection holding her here. With her lips pressed tight together in disapproval, she turned and fled into the room at the far end of the hall.

Gregor ran his hand over the dog's wiry fur, trying to draw comfort from the creature, but there was little to be found. He'd hesitated to come to Helkirk Place, unsure how the family might accept him after the *débâcle* at the wedding. Their kind welcome only increased his guilt, yet still he was glad to be here, for he had sins to atone for with Miss Rutherford.

'I'll have my maid see to your coat,' Lady Rutherford offered, taking his arm and leading him upstairs to show him to his room. The rest of the family followed, especially the youngest girl who lingered by his side, watching him like the dog did. Behind them, everyone else talked and laughed loudly, the sound echoing off the walls.

The noise drove Gregor into silence. He wasn't accustomed to such an animated family. Despite his many years of friendship with Laurus, his father had never allowed him to come here during the holidays, insisting Gregor spend a lonely six weeks in the mausoleum which was Marbrook Manor. It was easier for his parents to berate him for not meeting their high expectations with him under their roof than through the few letters either of them bothered to write to their least favourite son.

It was a pleasure to be in the midst of so much happiness.

'You needn't trouble yourself or the staff about the coat.' He owned twenty others like it and not one of them warmed him as much as this house and family did.

Chapter Two

'He's quite a good person, once you get to know him,' Laurus pressed, standing beside Lily's canvas, his brown eyes, identical in colour to hers, focused on the painting.

'Which I have no intention of doing.' Lily brushed a stripe of orange along the horizon line, working carefully so as not to get paint on her blue-velvet dress. She'd crept upstairs some time ago to change, determined to appear more refined and ladylike the next time she encountered their grand visitor.

'I'd like to be his friend,' Daisy gushed from her place by the fire, her hands folded in the lap of her long brown-wool gown. It seemed Lily wasn't the only who'd changed in honour of their guest.

'I think you've already captured his attention.' Laurus winked at their sister and Lily swiped at her brother with her hand, trying to warn him off encouraging Daisy.

The Rutherford trait of making a fool of one's self in front of others was the strongest in Daisy, for she didn't possess the maturity to mind her manners or her tongue, and their mother had long given up trying to instil such a trait in her youngest child.

'Enchant him enough and perhaps he'll wait for you to

reach your majority,' Laurus teased, stepping out of Lily's reach as she took another swing at him. 'You might even become a viscountess and outrank Petunia.'

'Do you really think so?' Daisy clapped her hands in front of her in hope.

'No,' Lily answered. 'No Marbrook is going to sully the family name with the daughter of a baronet.'

'Or perhaps you're afraid Daisy might take him from you?' Laurus prodded.

'Don't tease her or she might ruin your jacket like she did Lord Marbrook's.' Daisy laughed with the smugness of a ten-year-old.

'What are you all jabbering on about?' Aunt Alice demanded, shuffling into the room on her cane.

Lily set down her brush and hurried to help her aunt into her favourite chair by the fire. 'Nothing, we're only discussing our guest.'

'A fine young man that one.' Aunt Alice sighed as Lily fetched a blanket to lay over her aunt's knees. 'Mind you don't let him get away from you like you did last time.'

Lily struggled to not groan as she propped her aunt's feet up on a low stool.

'Oh, he isn't interested in Lily,' Daisy protested.

'Mind your tongue,' Lily demanded as movement near the sitting room door silenced her.

Lord Marbrook entered, the dark green coat which had replaced his ruined tan one sharpening the colour of his eyes. The sternness of his father didn't harden his piercing look or make rigid his stance. Instead, he stood with the discipline of an army officer and the humble hesitancy of a guest, one respectful of his place as an outsider instead of the worshipped scion of a titled family.

Lily rose and hurried back to her canvas. Daisy wasn't so timid, rushing up to him and dragging him into the room to speak with Aunt Alice. The older woman raised her lorgnette to inspect him as Pygmalion, roused from his nap in front of the fire, trotted over to sit beside him.

'What are you doing in this godforsaken part of the country?' Aunt Alice demanded in a tone brusque enough to make Lily wince.

'It's far more festive here than anywhere else I might spend Christmas.' Lord Marbrook's smile dropped a little about the corners, so subtle it might have been missed, but Lily noticed the change. Knowing something of his family, she wasn't surprised by his pain or his willingness to come to Helkirk Place. She stepped back behind her canvas, hiding from Lord Marbrook and the dangerous notion of caring about him. He hadn't appreciated her concern for him before, and he wasn't likely to now, not after she'd ruined his jacket.

While Lily worked, Aunt Alice and Daisy chattered away to Lord Marbrook. Lily listened with half an ear, trying to ignore the deep roll of his voice whenever he answered one of their many questions about London. More than once the heady melody of it drew her out from behind the canvas to admire the way his crisp white collar framed his face. Then his eyes would snap to hers and she'd duck back behind the painting, willing her heart not to race and feeling like a foolish girl for peeking around corners at a man.

'Don't let Daisy command his attention,' Laurus whispered as he came to stand beside her.

She nearly wiped the knowing look from his face with her orange-tipped paintbrush as her brother sauntered off to sit near his guest. Whatever he imagined might transpire between her and his friend, it most certainly wasn't what Lily had mind. While Lord Marbrook was here, she intended to avoid him. It would be difficult, what with supper and festivities tonight and the ball to-morrow, but she'd find a way to manage it. Hopefully, he wouldn't be here for the entire twelve days of Christmas. At least the weather offered no reason for him to linger. Although there was snow on the ground, it wasn't overly thick and the sky was blue and clear, adding to the frost decorating the trees.

It didn't take long for Aunt Alice to change from asking questions to telling Lord Marbrook one of her many stories of Christmas past, including the one about the Christmas goose who nearly escaped. Lily listened with a smile. She was one of the few people in the family who never tired of her aunt's stories. Daisy wasn't so patient, coming to stand beside Lily, arms crossed over her chest in a huff.

'I can't believe she's boring him with that old tale.'

'I can't believe he's listening.' As her aunt paused to take a breath, Lily waited to hear Lord Marbrook make some excuse for rising and escaping the way Charles and Edgar often did. He didn't, but instead listened to Aunt Alice as though she were in the House of Lords delivering some great speech. It seemed an odd amount of politeness from a Marbrook. The dowager viscountess hadn't been subtle in her eagerness to escape from Aunt Alice and her tales at Petunia's wedding.

'I think she's starting in on the time Grandfather spilled the wassail bowl on Lord Creighton,' Daisy whispered. 'I'd better rescue poor Lord Marbrook.'

'Leave him be.' Lily grabbed her sister before she could walk away. It was bad enough Aunt Alice had cornered Lord Marbrook, Lily didn't need Daisy fluttering around him like some lovesick butterfly and shocking his already sure-to-be stunned sensibilities. 'He's a man and capable of looking after himself.'

'And a very handsome one, too. Now, let go of me before you get paint on me like you did on him.'

Mortified of being reminded of her blunder, Lily let go and her sister practically floated across the room to stand beside Aunt Alice and stare at the object of her admiration.

Then the French doors flew open and the twins rushed in with a whirl of cold air, mud and snow. The dogs jumped to their feet to bark at the intrusion, the noise making Lily's brush slip, leaving an orange streak across the white. She scraped at the mark with her palette knife, wishing her family would better control themselves.

'Uncle Laurus, come sledding with us. There's just enough on the rise beyond the portico to really make the sled fly,' John demanded, his brown hair scattered wildly over his head.

'Yes, come at once,' James added, identical to his brother except for the increased number of freckles covering his snub nose. The boys didn't wait for an answer, but hurried back outside, leaving the door open behind them and a trail of wet footprints across the wooden floor. The dogs followed them into the crisp afternoon, their barks fading off over the lawn.

'What do you say, Marbrook? Are you up for the snow?' Laurus asked, shrugging on his heavy coat.

'Oh, yes, let's go outside and sled,' Daisy pleaded, plucking her coat from the fender where it'd been left to dry beside Lily's after their walk outside this morning.

'Only if Miss Rutherford will join us,' Lord Marbrook added.

Lily peered around the edge of her canvas, stunned by the invitation.

'I, well, you see—' Lily's mind turned to mud as she

tried to think of a suitable excuse for staying indoors and failed.

'Don't stand there like one of your father's oak trees, go on outside,' Aunt Alice commanded. 'The air will do you good.'

The matter decided, and not to Lily's liking, she laid down her brush and palette, arranging them on the small table so they wouldn't be dislodged by anyone passing by.

'Stop dawdling, girl,' Aunt Alice snapped.

'I'm coming.'

'So is Christmas.'

Lily slid her coat off of the fender and pulled on the heavy wool, then followed Daisy, Laurus and Lord Marbrook outside.

Her breath rose in a cloud around her head as she walked across the stone portico to the railing on the far side. Just below it, her nephews threw themselves down the short hill on their wooden sleds, leaving wide troughs in the thick snow. At the bottom, they stood and waved at the adults.

'Uncle Laurus, pull us up the hill,' James begged.

'Please,' John pleaded.

'Will you help me, Marbrook?' Laurus asked.

'I'm afraid I can't,' he answered plainly, offering no further explanation.

'Then it's up to you and me, Daisy,' Laurus informed her.

'But... I...' she protested, looking back and forth between him and Lord Marbrook.

'Come on or we'll have no peace.' Laurus took her arm and pulled her down the hill to where the twins were waiting on their sleds for their obliging uncle and pouting aunt.

'I suppose it's below a Marbrook to frolic in the snow with boys,' Lily remarked with more edge than intended.

'If only I could.' He let out a long breath and it rose like a wraith around his head before fading away. 'I took a musket ball in the thigh in France and have a difficult time managing hills, even small ones, when they're slippery with snow.'

'Oh, I see.' Lily wrapped her arms around herself, shivering more in embarrassment than cold. It seemed nothing she did around Lord Marbrook was ever correct.

They stood together in silence for some time as she struggled for a topic to fill the awkward quiet. 'Would you like to see Father's hothouse? A friend in Mexico sent him a beautiful new plant, though I don't suppose such things interest you.'

They rarely interested anyone outside her parents and their botanist friends.

'I'd like to see it. Please, lead the way.'

She gaped at him before she recovered herself and led him across the portico and down the steps. They followed the curving stone path past the square beds of bare rose bushes, accompanied by the boys' laughter and Daisy's complaints. Pygmalion trotted beside Lord Marbrook, as loyal as any hunting dog. They made for the end of the garden where a brick-and-glass building with four faux chimneys and an arched door meant to mimic the front of Helkirk Place stood. Numerous windows made up the walls, each covered with a fog marred by large beads of water which streaked the grey surface. Lord Marbrook moved forwards to pull open the door and Lily sighed as the moist heat swept over her. Inside, the air was heavy with the heady aroma of the lilies and the large rosemary bushes along the sides. She revelled in the smell of warm earth and herbs as she moved down one side of the long table covered with green-leafed plants with long stems topped with brilliant red flowers. Lord Marbrook strolled down the other side, admiring the plants.

'They're called poinsettias. The priests in Mexico decorate their churches with these as a reminder of the star of Bethlehem,' she explained as they stopped near the centre, facing each other across the flowers. 'Here they don't thrive outside the hothouse.'

'Very few things bloom in the absence of warmth.' He shifted on his feet, grimacing as he moved.

'There's a bench there if you need to sit.' She motioned to the nook behind him, not wanting him to stand in pain on her account.

'I'm not quite so fragile, Miss Rutherford. My time in the army taught me to deal with deprivation.' He fingered one red petal, pulling it down a touch before letting it go to bob back into place. 'Cold, hunger and musket balls don't care whether a man is a viscount's son or butcher's brother.'

'Was it very painful being shot?' She near groaned at her stupid question as his mouth turned down at the corners. She should have limited the conversation to the plants instead of alighting on such a dreadful topic, one which demanded a certain intimacy she was reluctant to engage in. This kind of leading question had been her downfall with him before.

He stared past her out the far window at the garden covered in snow and she knew he saw more desolation than the bare trees encased in ice and the small winter birds hopping among the few bushes poking up through the snow. 'Not as bad as laying in a barn for three days until another officer found me.'

Lily's hands flew to her mouth in horror. 'How awful.'

'Yes, but at least it kept the surgeons from taking the

leg and allowed the wound to heal without corruption.' He brushed his thigh with his fingers and she knew at once where he'd been struck. 'I was one of the lucky ones. Most of my men died in the mud or on the surgeon's table.'

He pressed his fingers against the table top and leaned hard on his shoulders. His jaw moved as if he wanted to say more but couldn't. She waited patiently for him to continue, as ready to listen now as she'd been four years ago, her grievances paling in comparison to his. As many times as she'd cursed him, she wasn't cruel enough to wish something so terrible on him, or to think it just deserts for what he'd done to her.

At last he straightened, tossing her the kind of small smile meant to convince her his experience didn't still haunt him, but it was plain it did. 'Please excuse my melancholy turn.'

'I'm very sorry you had to suffer so,' she offered with genuine concern.

'It wasn't all hardship.' He tapped the table in thought. 'Before my wound, my men and I used to play like those boys in the snow at our winter quarters.'

'It's difficult to imagine grown men frolicking.'

'But we did,' he added, the sadness of mourning tainting the happy memory. It was clear he'd lost friends in France, people he cared deeply about and now missed. 'I enjoyed the camaraderie of army life. It wasn't something I'd ever experienced before my father purchased my commission, not even at school. It was almost as if we were a kind of family, albeit a strange one.'

'Yes, I know something about strange families.' She motioned to the window through which they could see Laurus and Daisy hauling the laughing twins back up the rise.

'I enjoy your family. Mine isn't quite as—'

'Eccentric?'

'Welcoming,' he finished. 'It's impossible to cultivate many acquaintances when your father believes himself higher than everyone but the greatest dukes and marquesses. The fact our family is descended from a king's mistress troubled him less than when people didn't pay him the respect he believed his birthright.'

She was just about to agree with his assessment of the Marbrook family, but for once managed to catch her tongue before it made a fool of her. 'Laurus told me your father didn't approve of your friendship with him.'

'He didn't approve of any friendship, not even between me and my brother, who was too much like him to care for me. We never played together like those two boys.' He picked a brown leaf off one of the stems and flung it away, the loneliness she remembered draping him in the ballroom hallway haunting his words. Then he raised his eyes to hers, the green filled with a regret Lily could almost touch. 'I tried to emulate my father once, in order to garner his approval. It didn't work and all I did was treat poorly someone who deserved kindness.'

Lily sucked in the humid air, his expression as bracing as the cold outside. Surely he wasn't referring to his behaviour at the ball? It must be another situation with a fellow officer or soldier, some comrade-in-arms he'd disappointed, not her. He'd been so mean and aloof after she'd tripped it was difficult to imagine he might regret his behaviour, and yet...

'About what happened at your sister's celebration—' He glanced down to where Pygmalion stood beside him, flecks of snow dotting his black nose.

'You needn't bring it up. I've quite forgotten it.' Heaven help her for lying on Christmas Eve, but she didn't want him to suspect how much that night had affected her or changed her life. 'It was a long time ago.'

'It was, but, well, you see...' His voice faded like the wind through the open glass vent at the top of the hothouse.

'Yes?' she urged. If an apology was coming, she wanted to hear it, simply because she couldn't believe it. Everyone knew the Marbrooks were not people to make apologies, but to demand them, even from those they'd wronged.

'I—well—'

'We have you cornered.' The twins burst into the hothouse and Lily and Lord Marbrook raised their arms to protect themselves from a hail of snowballs.

'Not in here. Father will kill you if you hurt his plants.' She rushed after them into the biting cold, stopping outside the hothouse door to snatch up a handful of snow and fling it at the mischievous imps. They easily ducked her projectile and she was about to reach for more snow when cold hit the back of her neck and slid inside the collar of her coat.

'I got you,' Daisy proclaimed while Lily packed another snowball.

'You won't stay dry for long.' Lily hurled the snow at her sister, but it flew past her curls to hit Laurus's jacket.

Soon, he, too, was throwing snow or ducking behind trees and statues to avoid being hit. Only Lord Marbrook didn't join the fight. He stood outside the greenhouse, arms crossed over his chest as he leaned against the glass and watched, a grin decorating his lips.

She glanced at him as she hid behind an urn to pack another ball, irked to see him standing outside the fun after claiming he'd enjoyed such frivolity in France. He was probably horrified to see two adults acting like children and laughing at the expense of those around him, not in solidarity with them. Let him judge, she wouldn't allow him to dampen her mood, even if it meant another story for him to share with those in London who continued to sneer at her lack of grace.

With snowballs flying this way and that, fresh snow began to grow scarce. Lily spied some piled against the low stone wall surrounding the rosebushes. She had rushed to gather it up before the others reached it when her boot hit a patch of ice. She pitched forwards, tightening as she fell towards the thorny branches when a firm hand about her waist caught her.

She whirled in Lord Marbrook's embrace to face him. His hot breath warmed the cold tip of her nose as his tall body arched over hers. She clasped his shoulders to steady herself, her heart pounding in her chest more from his nearness than her near miss of the sharp bush. His lips parted and for the briefest of moments she thought he might lean down to kiss her. Their faces were so near, all it would take was one small movement to close the distance, and to her shame, she wanted him to.

Instead, he straightened and turned to set her on the centre of the path. He didn't part from her, but remained close with his hand on the small of her back. The weight of it made her entire body tingle and she locked her knees to stop from sinking against his chest and stomach. For a moment it was just the two of them together, as it'd been in the alcove in London when she'd been naïve enough to comfort him. She removed her hands from his arms and stepped out of his embrace, his former slight dampening her appreciation of today's courtesy.

'Oh, you were so chivalrous.' Daisy rushed forwards, beaming at Lord Marbrook like some besotted heroine in a novel. 'Too bad Lily is so clumsy.'

'I'd do the same for you, Miss Daisy, should you need it.' He bowed to Daisy, but as he rose he caught Lily's eye.

She looked away, embarrassed by both her sister and herself. Despite the poise she'd shown with him on the portico, it seemed as if falling in front of Lord Marbrook was a predetermined reality, not a mere happenstance.

'Boys, it's time to come in and dress for Christmas Eve supper.' Rose's voice carried over the clear air from where she stood at the open doorway, her willowy frame, so much like their mother's, draped by a puce dress. Like their mother, Rose was refined and serene, a definite contrast to Lily's clumsiness. 'You, too, Daisy.'

'But I'm not ready to come in,' she whined.

'It doesn't matter. It's time to dress. Bring her along, will you, Lily?'

Lily reached for Daisy's hand, but her sister tugged it away. With a warning arch of her eyebrow, Lily forced Daisy to comply and pulled her out of the garden and up to the house before she could say anything else to Lord Marbrook which might embarrass her, the family or Lily.

At the French doors, Daisy trudged past Rose, in as dark a mood as her twin nephews. It wasn't the children Rose watched, but Lily.

'I saw what happened,' she said as Lily tried to slip past her into the warmth of the house. 'Lord Marbrook was quite gallant.'

'If only he'd been so courteous in front of all London. What a difference it would've made.' To both her future and her past.

Rose laid a comforting hand on Lily's shoulder, the diamonds in her wedding band catching the low winter sun and sparkling. 'If you'd face those who laughed at you, you'd defeat them. Join me and Edgar for the Season and we'll have a grand time and show everyone we don't care a fig for what they think.'

'No. I'd rather stay here than be ridiculed in London again.' She stormed inside and towards her room, eager for some solitude. After the dance, with society's cruel taunts and whispers making her ears burn, she'd retreated to Yorkshire, determined never to set foot in town again. It was a quiet life and despite her ever-present family, at times a very lonely one. Her sisters might have wed, gained houses of their own, husbands and children, but it was difficult to see such a future for herself. Lord Marbrook had played no small part in her current state. An account of his snub had been printed by the newspapers, along with their usual society gossip, so all London could snigger over the incident. Despite his catching her today, and the hint of an apology, there was little he could do short of writing a letter to *The Times* praising her to undo the damage he'd already wrought on her reputation and her present circumstances.

Gregor didn't follow the others inside, but retreated back into the warmth of the hothouse, Pygmalion close on his heels. He wandered the length of the room, the heat easing the slight pain in his thigh from his old wound aggravated by the long carriage ride today. He approached the centre of the table and the bright red plants, reaching out to touch the pointed leaves. He rubbed one between his fingers, the softness of it reminding him of Miss Rutherford's dress against his palm and her supple curves pressed to him.

When he'd seen her slip, he'd rushed to her, despite the stiffness in his leg, eager to keep her from tumbling into the thorny bushes. He hadn't expected the weight of her in his arms to singe him as if he'd grasped a hot iron. It'd taken every ounce of gentlemanly control not to claim her parted red lips as she'd stared up at him, her deep brown eyes wide with surprise. If he'd given in and tasted her, it would have confirmed her low opinion of him, the one he'd caught in her comments and the wary looks she'd flung at him from across this very table.

It'd hurt to let go of her on the path, just as it'd burned to turn away from her on the dance floor four years ago, but both times he'd had little choice. Decorum demanded he let go of her today. His father had commanded him to disregard her at the ball. Determined to show his father he was a Marbrook and deserving of paternal respect, he'd done the old man's bidding. In the end, it'd gained him nothing but regret and wounded the person who'd shown him the most kindness that day.

'I should have ignored my father and helped her up. I should have apologised today.' He banged his fist on the rough table, making the plants shiver, unable to comprehend what had tied his tongue when he'd faced her. 'I can direct estate workers, command men into battle, yet I can't spit out one much-needed and long-overdue apology. What's wrong with me?'

He looked down at the dog sitting beside him. The dog licked its lips but did nothing more, as silent on the matter as Gregor had been with Miss Rutherford.

'Yes, I know, the army taught me a number of things, but not how to seek a woman's forgiveness.' He picked the animal up and plopped it down on the table where it sat, its wagging tail brushing the terracotta pot holding the plant. 'Neither did my father, nor my mother for that matter.'

He rubbed the dog behind its ear, making it cock its head to one side in dreamy satisfaction. 'I might have had difficulty today, but there's still tonight and tomorrow. Correct?'

The dog yawned and Gregor picked him up, tucked him under his arm and made for the house.

There would be other opportunities to speak with Miss Rutherford and correct at least one of the wrongs he'd committed in his life. He'd apologise to her and be worthy at last of the warm friendship extended to him by the Rutherford family.

Chapter Three

Noise filled the dining room as the entire family—children, the aged aunt, parents—and Gregor sat around the long mahogany table. It'd been quite a feast and the half-devoured pudding still decorated the centre, with two tall, silver candlesticks festooned with evergreens standing guard on either side. To Gregor's surprise, the children had been included in the supper and were still seated at the far end of the table and attended by their nurse. The twins chattered together, joined by their three-year-old cousin and Miss Daisy, who didn't look happy at being seated with them. Once in a while she would flash Gregor a bright smile which he gladly returned, more amused than annoyed by her fascination with him, though it was Miss Rutherford's attention he longed to capture tonight.

She sat beside him, appearing as unhappy about her place at the table as Daisy. It was as if the laughing woman hurling snowballs at her sister and brother had never existed and he very much wanted her to return. Whenever he tried to draw her into conversation, she offered him little more than simple answers to his questions before turning away to speak with her brother-in-law, leaving him to the aged aunt who sat on his other side and had no end of stories to tell.

When at last the aunt fixed her attention on Laurus, and the brother-in-law turned to speak to his wife, Gregor leaned close to Miss Rutherford, catching the notes of her lily-of-the-valley perfume over the rich nutmeg spice of the pudding. He took a deep breath, allowing himself the brief indulgence of her scent before he spoke.

'I may have to adopt him.' He nodded to where Pygmalion sat beside his chair. 'He won't leave my side.'

She studied the dog. 'Aunt Alice is very attached to her dogs, all of them. She isn't likely to part with even this little terror. Pygmalion may make you stay here.'

'Won't your parents mind?'

She tossed him a sly little smile and even without the glow of sheer joy on her face, she was gorgeous. Her hair was drawn up in ringlets at the back of her head, the faint gold in the brown made darker by the red ribbon wound through her locks. She wore a dark-green velvet dress dotted with leaves embroidered in a lighter green thread which shone with the candlelight whenever she moved. 'As long as you don't disturb them while they're with their plants, or trample the seedlings, you could be a herd of elephants residing in the house and they wouldn't notice.'

He fingered the small spoon next to his plate. 'Then I think I'll stay.'

This struck the smile off her face and she reached for her wine glass, taking a long sip before seeming to regain her courage. 'Won't your mother miss you?'

'No.' Gregor let go of the silver before his tight grip bent it. 'I wasn't her favourite son, as she insists on reminding me every time she tells me it should have been me and not Stanton who died of smallpox.'

'How can she be so cruel?'

'She didn't want me. She barely wanted my brother, but Stanton was her duty. I was the spare my grandfather, who controlled the money at the time, demanded. My mother is none too happy about Stanton's death proving my grandfather right.'

'I'm sorry she's so severe.' She touched his arm, the sweet care which had first drawn him to her years ago filling her round eyes. He stared at the creamy hand resting on the dark blue of his coat, the pressure of each fingertip as vivid as if she'd touched him naked. As if feeling the spark, and remembering their place among so many people, Miss Rutherford withdrew her hand and folded it with the other in her lap.

'They were as severe as yours are amiable...' Gregor breathed.

She settled her shoulders and glanced around the table, pursing her lips in disapproval. 'My parents are too amiable. As you can see, they allow everyone and everything to run wild.'

'Don't wish for too much discipline. My father was a man of stern self-control who expected obedience from his wife and children. He demanded we always behave in ways which would instil awe, if not fear, in those around us. It's why we didn't get along. I didn't hold with his notions of our importance because I knew it was a lie. My parents put on a façade of unity and strength in public. In private, they were bitter, miserable people with no love or real purpose in life except to make everyone around them wretched. We never celebrated anything like your family does, or enjoyed a house filled with such laughter. Your parents love each other and you, as do your siblings. Learn to embrace it, Miss Rutherford.'

If only it was so easily done. All her life, she'd stood in the midst of her family's chaos, attempting to carve from it some tranquillity, yet they kept intruding, laughing and calling her dour when she asked them to understand. They didn't, they couldn't and they never would. Even when it came to Lord Marbrook, they didn't see things the way she did. Once when Lily had asked her mother why she continued to encourage Laurus's friendship with Lord Marbrook, her mother said if he was Laurus's friend, then he must be good and it was only Lily taking things much too seriously which left her tainted by the ball. Lily had tried to make her mother see how Lord Marbrook's actions had influenced others against her, but it was no use. Her mother agreed he'd behaved poorly, but thought there must have been a good reason for it, though Lily could never guess what beyond Marbrook arrogance it might have been. Her mother failed, like the rest of the family, to realise the damage the viscount had done, though recognising reality was never a Rutherford strength.

She looked around the table at her sisters and their husbands. Rose's hand rested lovingly on Edgar's forearm as she smiled at her sons where they sat at the end of the table. James smiled back, but John was too busy stroking Toddy, the second-smallest dog and the most docile, the one he liked to carry around whenever he was here. The dog would muddy up the boy's bed later and track in more dirt than was already soiling the carpets. Yet Lily seemed the only one to ever notice or care. Even Lord Marbrook was taken in by the charm of it, but he couldn't see the extra work it meant for the servants or how yet another set of sheets would be stained beyond repair, money paid to replace them.

Nor could he see how far outside the circle of love and contentment she sat. While her sisters enjoyed the comforts of husbands, homes and children, she was left to grow old with nothing but her paintings. She was fast becoming a spinster aunt.

'Miss Rutherford, our conversation in the greenhouse—I wish to discuss what happened between us at your sister's wedding,' Lord Marbrook cautiously began in a low voice, drawing Lily from her gloomy musing.

'Now you're threatening the merriment of the evening by bringing up such a distasteful subject.' She tried to laugh, but her throat was so dry it hurt. She reached for her wine, the indignity of her current situation, the one he had no small hand in, burning like the brandy-soaked raisins in the pudding.

'I don't wish to upset you, but I feel I must apologise for what happened.'

Lily jerked around in her chair so fast, she thought she might split the silk seat covering. 'Why? What can your apology achieve except an easing of your own conscience? It can't undo the opinion your behaviour created of me, or force the gossips to take back every nasty thing they said about me.'

Her voice rose, briefly attracting Aunt Alice's attention before Laurus drew it away.

Gregor stared at his plate and the half-eaten slice of pudding covering the fine rose pattern of the china. His jaw worked, but he said nothing and regret began to creep up Lily's spine. He'd been humble enough to apologise and she'd thrown it back in his face, but there was truth in her accusation, one they both couldn't ignore.

At last he let out a long breath to make the candles in front of his place dance. 'You're right, but I don't know where else to start. I've regretted what I did from the moment my father escorted me from the ball. It was he who ordered me to cut you, who insisted I act like a Marbrook. I wanted to please him because I thought it would make a difference in how he regarded me and convince him not to send me to France. It didn't. I should have ignored him and helped you, the way you'd helped me in the alcove.'

So Mother was right, there had been a reason beyond arrogance to explain what he'd done and it was a good one. It eased a portion of her anger, but didn't banish it. In the end, no matter what his motives, he'd attempted to relieve his problems at her expense.

'Lily, what is Sir Winston's daughter's name?' Petunia asked from across the table, watching her with a strange little frown, as though something about Lily's conversation with Lord Marbrook didn't sit well with her.

'Catherine Fordham,' Lily replied and Petunia resumed her conversation with Rose and Mama, though not without casting more curious scrutiny in Lily's direction.

Lily picked up her napkin and raised it to her mouth, whispering to Lord Marbrook from behind it, eager not to attract any additional attention from anyone else in the family. They weren't known for their discretion. 'Why apologise now when it no longer matters?'

As if sensing Petunia's scrutiny, he turned slightly in his chair to face Lily, looking at her from beneath his brows with an intensity to make her shiver. 'Because it does matter, I see it in your eyes when you look at me, I hear the pain in the few barbs you've allowed yourself, every one of which I deserve.'

'Lord Marbrook, do you have any experience with water dogs?' Charles asked, leaning around Lily to address him.

'I'm afraid not,' he politely answered, as if he and Lily were only discussing the weather and not her disgrace.

An answer received, Charles returned to his discussion with Edgar.

Lord Marbrook leaned closer to Lily, his voice heavy like distant thunder. 'I'd intended to visit your home the day after the ball and apologise, but I couldn't. The next morning my father packed me off to France. With little more than an hour's warning, he sent me away to a hell I wasn't prepared for. Now it's over and I wish to make right the wrongs my family has done to its tenants, to other families and you.'

Lily took another sip of wine, struggling through the confusion of her feelings to think and breathe. She didn't doubt his sincerity, or his need for absolution, yet she withheld it like Pygmalion had gripped her paintbrush, unable to let go of the pain and embarrassment she'd endured in exchange for something as wispy as words. It was wrong and she knew it, but she couldn't help herself. 'What do you possibly hope such a belated apology can achieve?'

He was about to answer when Daisy called out from across the table in a voice loud enough to silence all but Aunt Alice, 'Lord Marbrook, what are you and Lily discussing in such a serious manner?'

'Daisy, mind your manners and stop making a fool of yourself,' Lily responded, the interruption disturbing her as much as Lord Marbrook's sincere revelations. Never before had she wanted her family to leave her alone as much as she did at this moment and all of them seemed intent on intruding, as usual.

Silence swept up one side of the table and down the other. Even the boys paused in eating their pudding to stare at her with big eyes.

'Lily, apologise to your sister at once,' her father demanded. 'The remark was uncalled for.'

'It wasn't.' Lily kept her back straight despite the scrutiny being given to her. 'Can't you see how she's behaving?'

He levelled a forkful of pudding at her. 'That's for me and your mother to worry about, not you.'

'You should worry about it. It might be fine here with the family, but what if she does it somewhere else, in front of someone who might mind.' She looked pointedly at Lord Marbrook. 'She'll embarrass herself and all of us.'

'You're the only one embarrassing yourself tonight,' her father snorted and stuffed the pudding in his mouth.

She looked down at her hands in her lap and the orange paint still staining the corner of one thumbnail. She scratched at it but it wouldn't budge, the skin around it turning red with her effort. She'd wanted so much to appear confident in front of Lord Marbrook. Instead, she'd once again been made to look ridiculous, this time by the people who were supposed to love her the most. A loneliness she hadn't experienced since she'd sat on the ballroom floor while the other young ladies had laughed at her filled her again.

'Enough scolding for one night.' Lily's mother rose from the table, bringing the men to their feet. 'It's Christmas Eve and we must enjoy ourselves. If the men don't mind forgoing their port, we'll play charades, then Aunt Alice will play the pianoforte so we may all sing carols.'

'I think we can sacrifice our port for tonight of all nights,' Sir Timothy offered, his usual joviality returning as he held out his arm to his wife. 'Come along, everyone.'

The adults filed out of the room, ushering the children along in front of them. The young ones resumed their lively banter, all except Daisy, who stomped away on Rose's arm complaining bitterly about Lily.

Lily didn't rise, but stared at the uneaten pudding in the silver dish in the centre of the table until only she and Lord Marbrook remained.

'You should go with the others, or you'll miss charades.' She wished he'd leave, she very much wanted to be alone, but he didn't.

'I'm sorry about what happened, I didn't mean to cause you distress.'

'This time it's not your fault, it's mine, always mine.' She snatched the napkin off her lap and tossed it on the table. 'My family can act as ridiculous as they please, but if I dare point it out, or suggest they show some restraint so they don't become laughing stocks, I'm the wicked one, not my sisters, my brother or even my nephews. Only me.'

He laid his hands on the back of the chair beside hers, his fingers long and graceful beneath the crisp white of his shirt cuff. 'I know what it's like to sit outside the circle of your family and feel they don't understand you and how lonely it can make you, even in the midst of so many. Unlike my family, yours is happy and they love you. It's something to cherish far more than the opinions of others.'

He was right and she didn't want him to be right, she didn't want anything except to be alone with her paints and the patience of the canvas. Instead she was here, being reminded again of her awkwardness and loneliness. If only someone would cherish her. Rose and Petunia had Charles and Edgar, but there was no one to stand beside her and support her when people scolded her for trying to be sensible and there likely never would be.

Swallowing hard against the pain in her chest, she rose and at last faced Lord Marbrook. The tender sympathy in his eyes tore into her as much as her father's rebuke. She didn't want Lord Marbrook's sympathy, or to appear so pathetic in front of him.

'If you'll excuse me, I don't want to miss charades.'

She fled the room, afraid if she stayed he would see her tears.

* * *

It was some time before Gregor slipped into the sitting room to join the Rutherfords in their game of charades. Laurus stood in front of the fireplace, entertaining everyone with what could only be described as a feeble attempt to depict an elephant. It amused the children who sat in a half circle on the carpet in front of him guessing all manner of large animals and roaring with laughter. Gregor allowed himself a small smile at the sight. He'd never sat at his parents' feet to watch some relative make a spectacle of themselves. He'd never sat on the sitting room carpet in his entire life, even the carpet on the nursery floor had been for walking on, never sitting, or playing or, heaven forbid, laughing.

Miss Rutherford sat in the back of the room near the French doors, the glow of excitement surrounding the others failing to reach her. The moonlight from outside spilled over her sadly rounded shoulders while the fire from the Yule log warmed her high cheeks and flickered in her eyes, though the light wasn't enough to reignite the sparkle which had filled them this afternoon.

Pygmalion trotted away from Gregor to join Miss Rutherford, rising up on his back feet and placing his front paws on her knees. She frowned at the small dog and raised her hand. Gregor thought she meant to shoo him away. Instead, she drew the dog up into her lap, clutching her to him and stroking his fur as though he were her last friend in the world. The sight of it tore at Gregor and he moved around the back of the room, behind the family, to join her.

'I think the rumours of the beast's ferociousness are unfounded,' Gregor offered as he settled himself in the lyre-backed chair beside hers.

'I'm stunned.' She shook her head at the animal. 'He's never sat with me before.'

'Perhaps he recognises someone in need of a friend.'

Her hand paused between the dog's ears before she resumed her steady scratching, making the dog's eyes narrow with delight. If it could sigh, Gregor felt sure it would. Miss Rutherford did, a small one which whispered across Gregor's hand where it rested on his thigh, making him want to slide his arm around her and draw her head down on to his shoulder, the same way her eldest sister now sat with her husband.

Damned fool, his father would have said if he'd seen such a display, always disapproving of the regard Gregor had shown to others, but he wasn't here to stand over him with censure at best and indifference at worst.

'You asked me in the dining room what I hoped to achieve with my apology,' Gregor hazarded, determined to finish what he'd come here to do. 'I'd very much like to be your friend and for you to be mine.'

Lily stroked the dog, staring straight ahead as her brother finished his turn and relinquished the floor to Lord Winford. 'Why?'

Gregor took a deep breath, then began in a voice just above a whisper. 'Many times in France I thought of you and the way you'd sat beside me in the alcove listening to my complaints. We were strangers and yet you treated me with the tenderness of an old friend. It would have been nice while I was in France to have received letters from you and known there was someone, besides Laurus, who cared if I came home safe.'

Lily drew the dog a little closer to her chest. 'Surely your parents cared, even a little.'

'They didn't. I wasn't my brother, only an unwanted disappointment best got out of the way.' He rubbed his thumb in a circle over the scar on his thigh hidden by his breeches. 'I'm sorry, Miss Rutherford, to burden you with such things. I know it isn't proper, but for some reason I feel you more than anyone else will understand.'

She shifted in the chair, holding tight to the dog as she moved, and he thought she might rise and flee from him as she'd done in the dining room, but she didn't.

'I do understand and please call me Lily. Only not in front of the others. If they heard us on such intimate terms, there'd be no end to the teasing.' The smile she blessed him with dipped all the way down to his toes, bringing one of equal joy to his lips.

'I'll call you Lily in private, and you'll call me Gregor. Will that suit?'

'Yes, very well.'

They sat together watching Lord Winford take his turn at charades, listening as the children and adults called out animals only for Lord Winford to shake his head in reply.

'He's a goose,' Lily said, but only loud enough for Gregor to hear.

'You think so? I thought he might be a carriage.'

'No, Charles does some kind of fowl every year. Once it was a duck, another time a swan. He's quite taken with fowling.'

At last Lady Winford guessed her husband's character and he sat down, relinquishing the floor to Sir Timothy, who squatted down, then rose, throwing out his limbs in a display Gregor could only imagine was meant to imitate a flower blooming.

While the family called out guesses, Gregor leaned in close to Lily, noting the slight separation between her full breasts above the fitted bodice of her gown. He swallowed hard, very much wanting to press his lips against the soft skin and revel in the heat of her. His body began to stiffen at the thought, but he forced it back, determined to behave like a gentleman.

'What did Laurus mean earlier when he said you'd painted the entire family?' he asked, his breath disturbing the small curl at the nape of her long neck.

Lily turned to face him, so close to him he could see the single small freckle just beneath her right eye. He expected her to lean away, but she remained near him, her voice sliding like satin across his cheek. 'The portraits in the entrance hall are mine. I did them.'

An unmistakable pride filled her voice.

'Will you show them to me?'

She looked back and forth between him and her family, the small curl dangling near her ear brushing her cheek as she moved. 'Now?'

'Unless you wish to be chosen as the next person to do a charade, then yes.'

She grimaced at the thought. 'Then we'd better hurry before someone guesses Father is a rose.'

She set the dog on the floor. It didn't bark, but trotted behind them as they slipped out of the room and down the hallway. Candles twinkled in their holders, catching the red of the berries pressed among the shiny holly leaves decorating each table and painting. Down the opposite hall, in the far wing of the house, the high strings of a fiddle drifted in like snow through the open ballroom door. The music was joined by the laughter of the maids and footmen and the sounds of their shoes banging over the wooden boards in time to the lively song as they enjoyed the servants' Christmas Eve celebration.

The candles glittered as much in the entrance hall as they did in the hallway, but without the heat and fire of the Yule log, the air took on something of the crispness of the cold night outside.

'I painted these.' She waved her hand at the numerous portraits of her family lining the walls and following the rise of the stairs. On either side of the door hung the ones she'd done of her parents. They looked back into their house and up at the line of children arranged on the wall above the stairs, each with hair the same shade of brown as their mother's. 'I'm to do little Adelaide's soon, and John and James once they learn to sit still.'

'Then they may be adults by the time you manage it,' he observed, making her eyes dance with delight.

'And perhaps not even then for I don't think they'll ever settle down.'

'I'd like to sit for you while I'm here, if you don't mind.'

The suggestion seemed to catch her off guard and she chewed the bottom of one full lip before an impish smile to mimic the ones her nephews often wore split the tender bud. 'If you'd like, though I'd have thought you'd been painted enough today.'

She was teasing him and he wanted more of it. His father would never have allowed such humour at his expense, but Gregor wasn't his father, or his brother, and he never would be.

'I assume Pygmalion shares your talent for oils?' He pointed to the slashes of paint on the wall at the bottom of the stairs, the faint stain of blue and yellow sitting just beneath the bright red.

Instead of the frustration she'd exhibited with her family at dinner, she rolled her eyes with some humour at the marks. 'That brush wasn't the first one the little beast has snatched from me. He's quite well behaved now, but usually he's stealing all manner of things. If the holly and mistletoe weren't so high, he'd have them, too.'

She pointed to the sprig of mistletoe with one last

berry clinging to the leaves hanging from the brass chandelier. Only then did either of them realise they were standing beneath it, in the centre of the stone circle inlaid in the floor. Lily slowly lowered her hand, as aware as Gregor of what their present position implied. He studied her face, noting the eager nervousness in her eyes, as if, like him, she wanted a kiss, but feared it at the same time.

Gregor remained where he stood, allowing the tinkling of 'Here We Come A-Wassailing' on the pianoforte and the voices of the family singing the carol at one end of the hall and the servants' laughter at the other to cover the stretching silence between them. He could drop a quick peck on her cheek, pluck the last berry from the hapless branch and they could smile and laugh and return to the sitting room, but he didn't move. He couldn't manage something so innocent because he wanted to enjoy the feathery caress of her fingers against his neck while he took her in his arms, pressed her body to his and felt her breasts flatten against his chest as he tasted her full lips. He'd asked for her friendship and she'd granted it, but in this moment, he wanted a great deal more.

He took a hesitant step forwards and she didn't move, looking up at him with anticipation. She wouldn't flee if he dared to claim her lips, nor would she push him away or chastise him. It was as frightening a prospect as it was exhilarating and her silent entreaties drew him closer. He raised his hand to her face, his fingers so close to her skin he could feel the heat of it. The embroidered leaves on her dress shimmered as she took in one deep breath after another, waiting, as eager as him to steal the last berry off the mischievous plant.

Gregor leaned closer, his lips aching to know hers, all

desire to be a gentleman forgotten. He'd won her forgiveness and friendship, now he wanted her heart.

'There you both are. I wondered where you'd gone to.' Laurus's voice cut through the moment, dampening the waver of the candles across her face and making them jump apart.

With some frustration Gregor glanced to the plant, the lone berry mocking him as much as Laurus's knowing look as he hustled into the entrance hall.

Gregor exchanged a worried glance with Lily, wondering if she blamed him for this near compromise of her in front of her family. He'd made such small gains with her, he hated to think his weakness might lose them. Whatever irritation she experienced, it didn't reveal itself in her eyes, which crinkled at the corners with the same frustration at the interruption Gregor felt as he flexed his cold fingers behind his back.

Lily watched her brother's approach, not sure what to expect. She'd nearly kissed Gregor and in front of Laurus no less, but instead of wanting to creep away in shame she was mad at her brother for interrupting them. Thankfully it was Laurus who'd stumbled on them and not someone else. He was far more discreet than either Rose or Daisy, but even he wasn't above commenting on such a discovery. Standing beneath the mistletoe, St Nicholas himself might forgive her for extending a viscount a kiss. However, for all her desire to claim the near indiscretion was simply a result of the season, she knew it was something more and the idea was as terrifying as it was exhilarating.

'Come on, we must prepare.' Laurus grabbed Lily by the hand and linked his arm with Gregor's to lead them down the opposite hall towards the ballroom.

'Prepare for what?' Lily demanded, her slippers rustling over the stone as she worked to keep pace with the men.

'The arrival of the Lord of Misrule. We must be ready to appear before the carols end.'

'You need us to help you get dressed?' Lily asked as Laurus stopped outside a door set in the panelling of the hallway walls.

'I'm not going to be him this year, Gregor is. And you're to be his Queen of Folly.'

Oh dear. 'But you love being Lord of Misrule, why won't you do it again?'

'Because the twins are expecting it and I want to surprise them. No one will suspect Lord Marbrook, especially if you're with him. Everyone knows you don't like him.'

Lily's cheeks burned as she glanced back and forth between her brother and Lord Marbrook who seemed to be taking his friend's ribbing in his stride. 'That's not true. How can you say such a thing?'

'I'm glad to discover I've been mistaken in my assumptions.' He pulled open the door, revealing the large cupboard behind it. It'd been a priest hole in the days of King Henry, but was presently used to store linens, candlesticks and other odds and ends. 'Now inside, both of you, and get changed before Aunt Alice reaches the end of her repertoire.'

He hustled Lily and Gregor inside where the clothes he'd pulled out for the masque were strewn over the old trunk where they were usually stored. A single candle burned in a brass holder on one of the shelves, its dancing shadow casting a strange eeriness over the room already believed to be haunted by the children and a few of the older servants.

'As soon as you're ready, we'll go back. I can't wait to see John's and James's faces when they realise it isn't me who's the Lord of Misrule this year.' Laurus closed the door on them, leaving them alone.

'I suppose we'd better prepare,' Gregor suggested, picking up a velvet doublet in a shade of red to make a cardinal jealous.

'Yes. Aunt Alice only knows about five of the old carols and I believe she's already through two of them.'

Lily picked up a robin-egg-blue damask gown with a wide neckline and full hips, both cut more in the style of Old Queen Anne than the current Queen Charlotte. She wrinkled her nose at the mustiness of it as she slipped it over her head, catching the wide sides before it fell past her shoulders to puddle on the floor. Whatever great-grandmother had worn this had been much wider than Lily, who'd have to find a way to make do for there were no other dresses in the trunk.

Across from her, Gregor cast aside his coat and dark grey waistcoat and stood only in his breeches and shirt. A touch of chest was just visible through the openings between his shirt strings. As Lily stared at the contrast between his skin and the linen, the chilly priest hole grew a great deal warmer. The idea that this was wrong, very wrong, whispered through Lily's mind as did the music from the fiddler down the hall. With Gregor standing so close in a state of simple undress, it was too intimate and, were it not Christmas Eve, too scandalous. Whatever new faith she'd developed in Gregor, she hoped he deserved it. Otherwise he'd return to London and tell who knew what tales of his time alone with her in the priest hole and she'd never be able to set foot in society here or in London again.

'Can you do up the doublet?' Gregor slid on the velvet, then turned his back to her.

Beneath the short-waisted garment, his dark breeches sat tight against his buttocks and the sight of the round, solid firmness made her blush. Thankfully he couldn't see her red cheeks or her curiosity as she stood behind him, fingers trembling as she did up the laces. She tried to breathe evenly, to give no hint of her nervousness but it was difficult with the hue of the skin of his back just visible through the shirt. She wanted to trace the curving arch, feel the sinew and muscle of it, but she didn't dare let one finger accidentally slide along the line of it. She was as much afraid of how he might react to such an intimate touch as how she would.

'I'm done,' she said at last, both regretting and relieved by the end of her task.

He turned, regarding her as he had under the mistletoe, as though there was more to this than simply the merriment of the moment, or his desire for friendship. It was the same sense of belonging and need she'd experienced with him in the alcove four years ago, the one which had been as badly interrupted now as then.

'Hurry up in there,' Laurus called through the door. 'Aunt Alice is already halfway through "The Twelve Days of Christmas".'

'I'll do up your gown now,' Gregor instructed, taking her by the shoulders and turning her around, his finger sweeping the open neck of her dress before he let go. 'We don't want to keep the little ones waiting.'

The bodice only grew a touch tighter as he tied the laces, but it could have been strangling her for all the trouble she had breathing with him so close.

'Turn around and let me see,' he instructed.

Gripping the skirt of the dress, she turned with stiff

steps to face him. If he didn't look so strange in the doublet, she'd feel silly standing here in a dress which was
much too big. Already the heavy damask was sliding from
her arms. With no shoulders to help keep the dress in
place, she'd barely make it down the hall before it would
sink around her feet. 'It's still too large.'

He snatched a red bodice from the pile of clothes. 'I
have an idea.'

His sandalwood scent teased her as much as the closeness of his cheek to hers when he dipped down to slide
the satin under her arms and around her waist. She stared
straight ahead at the faded outline of a saint on the far
wall, determined not to meet his eyes as he paused beside
her, so close she could hear him breathe, feel the heat of
his skin against hers. All she need do was turn and their
lips would meet. She forced herself to remain still, but
she wanted to turn, very badly.

At last he straightened, slowly as if he regretted moving away.

She let out a long breath, then looked down at the red
satin around her waist, holding the wrinkled thing closed.
'It's backwards.'

'It doesn't matter.' His fingers worked the laces through
the eyelets, brushing hers as he tightened the strings. She
tried not to breathe too deeply, afraid of bringing his
hands closer to her breasts than they already were. Her
nipples grew taut against her stays as his hands moved
lower towards her waist, making her head swim as if she'd
had too much wassail.

When at last he tied off the laces, he stepped back to
admire her, not with a critical eye, but with the heady interest he'd shown beneath the mistletoe. She was thank-
ful the little branch was still on the chandelier and not

in here, for if it was, she'd surely throw herself against him and claim the last berry, and his lips, for her own.

She laced her hands in front of her, determined to put an end to such ridiculous notions. This morning she'd detested him, now she wanted to forget herself with him? Even during a magical season like this it was beyond comprehension and belief. He'd asked for friendship, not passion. 'How do I look?'

'It only needs one more thing.' He plucked a wreath of dusty fake flowers from the top of the pile of clothes. 'A crown for the queen.'

He lowered it over her hair, his hands lingering by her temples as though he meant to gently take hold of her before he lowered them to his sides. His eyes remained fixed on hers as she adjusted the crown, frowning when a few silk petals fell off to decorate the skirt of her dress.

When she was done, she slid a domino off the old clothespress where Laurus had draped it. 'And you must have a mask and a cape.'

His fingers brushed hers as he took the cape from her. In a swirl of musty black velvet, he flung it around his broad shoulders, then tied the ribbons at his neck. Lily picked up the matching black mask and held it out to him. Instead of taking it, he bent down, inviting her to slide it on. He held it to his face as she tied the laces at the back of his head, the thickness of his hair like sable brushing against her palms as she worked.

When she was done and he straightened, there was something more rogue than misrule about him, an air of confidence not diminished by the red doublet, but enhanced by the mysterious darkness of the domino. Taking him in, Lily wondered what it would be like to stand beside him at a London masque in a dress better suited to her than the old blue damask. In masks, no one would know who they were and she'd be free to whirl and turn about with him, enjoying his smiles in a crowd as easily as she did in this closet. For the first time in years, she contemplated accepting Rose's invitation to join her in London for the Season. With Gregor by her side, even in a mask, she felt sure she would not fear society as much as she did.

'What do you think?' he asked, turning as well as he could in the cramped confines of the priest hole.

'No one will guess it's you and not Laurus. You're matched in height and the domino and mask hides your hair and most of your face.'

'Then let's be off to make our mischief.' He held out his arm to her, throwing back the side of the short cape with the flourish of a musketeer.

She clung to the hardness of his arm beneath the shirt, the heat of him spreading through her and settling low inside her stomach. It'd been like this before when he'd escorted her onto the dance floor at Petunia's wedding, the eyes of all the guests on them as they'd taken their place in the line. For the first time the thrill of dancing with him, not the moment it had all turned sour, dominated her memory of that night.

'You two make quite a Christmas pair.' Laurus whistled as they stepped into the hall. 'Now come on. I can't wait to surprise everyone.'

He led them back to the sitting room, waving them to a stop outside the door. He leaned forwards just enough to peer inside without being seen, watching as everyone drew out the last line of the long song. 'And a partridge in a pear tree.'

The family clapped and Laurus waved Lily and Gregor forwards.

If Lily expected their entrance to be one of the measured Marbrook ilk, she was pleasantly disappointed. With a mischievous wink, Gregor clasped her hand and pulled her into the room. Just over the threshold he let go and flung out his hands to announce his appearance in a booming voice to startle the children and amaze the adults.

'The Lord of Misrule has arrived!'

'It's Laurus,' James and John cried at once and, along with Daisy, jumped to their feet to rush at the Lord of Misrule. Poor little Adelaide, too young to understand, buried her face in her mother's chest and let out a wail.

'It isn't Laurus.' Lily's brother stepped in behind the Lord of Misrule and John and James's eyes grew as wide as pewter plates, along with half the adults.

'Then who can it be?' Daisy cried.

'You must follow me to find out.' Gregor led the children in a merry dance around the room, snatching one of the tin horns off of the floor and blowing a very off-key but lively tune. The children followed, jumping and skipping around the furniture in imitation of the Lord of Misrule while the adults clapped and laughed at the sight. Lily followed in amazement, stunned to see Gregor so carefree. Though he was nothing like the rest of his family, even he possessed a distinguished reserve which he happily cast aside tonight.

As he rounded the sofa, he caught her hand and pulled her to the door. 'Come, my fair queen, we must lead the way to the servants' ball.'

His hand was tight in hers as they marched together in time to the boys' loud singing and tooting of horns. Lily's sides hurt as she laughed and spun with Gregor, turning with him to enjoy the beaming faces of the children and the adults who followed behind them as they led the way to the servants' celebration.

The ballroom, at one time the great hall, was a long room with a high timber ceiling and a wide stone fireplace at one end. The parade of merrymakers broke into the centre of a country dance, taking up places in the line to join the servants who clapped and twirled to the lively tune of the fiddle. Rose partnered with the butler and joined him in the dance, while Petunia, holding a now-mesmerised Adelaide, stood along the sides as Charles swept the old housekeeper nearly off her feet. Daisy promenaded with a footman while the two young scullery maids danced with John and James. Lily's parents joined in the line, taking their place just beneath Lily and Gregor, who led the reel as the top couple.

Lily held on tight to Gregor's hand as he led her through the steps, his laughter rising with the music. Past the darkness of the mask, his green eyes were alight with his excitement and, when the dance made her and Gregor face one another to sashay down the line, something more.

When all the couples had passed, James and John began to chant, 'Unmask! Unmask!'

The servants and adults soon joined in until Gregor led Lily back into the centre of the line. Holding up her hand, he had the two of them bow to one side and then the other before he let go of her to pull back the hood and sweep the mask from his face.

A gasp of surprise rushed through the room, nearly snuffing out the candles before the servants' murmurs of astonishment silenced even the fiddler. If Gregor was aware of the stir he created, he didn't show it as he smiled at Lily, his hair ruffled over his forehead and damp with perspiration.

'Well done, well done.' Laurus appeared now and

clapped, snapping all out of their astonishment to join him in their thanks.

Soon the fiddler struck up the next dance and the servants, bidding goodbye to Sir Timothy and Lady Rutherford, resumed their celebration while the family wandered back towards the other wing.

Gregor and Lily were the last to leave, lingering far behind the family which said their goodnights at the bottom of the stairs. Rose and Edgar led their tired boys up to their rooms, the twins protesting going to sleep even while they yawned and rubbed their eyes. Even Daisy moved with heavy feet as mother and father ushered her up to bed, followed by Petunia and Charles and little Adelaide, who snored on her father's shoulder.

Lily was sad to see them go and for the evening to come to an end. The troubles in the dining room seemed so long ago and she didn't want to lose the lightness and excitement surrounding her now. It stretched out to encompass Gregor, the smile on his face not dimming as they stood together at the bottom of the stairs. The flush of excitement illuminating his face made him seem younger, as though the troubles with his family and his time in France no longer haunted him.

'Well done, Marbrook, well done.' Laurus clapped his friend on the back.

'A very exhilarating reign.' Gregor took off the cape, then shrugged out of the doublet.

'I expect the same level of enthusiasm tomorrow night at the ball.'

'We'll make it one you won't forget.' Gregor laughed as he exchanged with Laurus the doublet for his waistcoat and coat.

'I hope so.' Laurus winked at Lily as he took from her the crown of flowers before she slipped the bodice and dress down over her hips and stepped out of the old garment. Then Laurus pointed over their heads. 'With only one berry left, it seems a shame to leave the poor thing hanging.'

'Goodnight, Laurus,' Lily cried, half-serious, half in jest as she tossed the old gown over her brother's shoulder.

'Goodnight.' He skipped up the stairs, disappearing into the darkness at the top with a whistle.

Lily should have been angry at Laurus for his implication, but it was difficult to think of anything with Gregor standing so close. Here before her wasn't the arrogant lord who'd refused to acknowledge her after her fall, but the young man who'd told her of his troubles in the alcove. What might have happened between them if the secret heartaches they'd shared hadn't been interrupted by his family's arrogance? There was no one to interrupt them now.

While he did up the buttons on his coat, Gregor examined the sprig of mistletoe and the lone berry still clinging to it. 'It does seem a shame to leave it.'

'You must excuse my brother, he has quite the teasing sense of humour,' Lily remarked, trying to change the subject and draw Gregor's attention away from the sprig hanging over them like some sword of Damocles. The intimacy was already too much without the encouragement of the small plant. 'Even when he isn't the Lord of Misrule he can't completely relinquish his duties.'

'I know. He was like that at school, always moving Parson Verrell's books. It's why I liked him. He was everything my brother and father weren't.'

Some of the merriment faded from his eyes and he ran his fingers through his hair.

She didn't want him to be sad, but as happy as he'd

been in the ballroom. 'Laurus may regret appointing you Lord of Misrule. Everyone is sure to insist you come back next year and he'll find himself dethroned.'

He straightened the collar of his coat. 'I'd gladly come back, if your family will have me.'

'I'm sure they will.'

He raised his eyes to meet hers, a fire burning in their depths which nearly stole her breath away. 'Would you?'

'I'd welcome you much sooner, if you'd like.' Her boldness surprised her, but she didn't regret it.

Gregor reached up and plucked the last berry off the sprig, then stepped closer to tower over her. He raised one hand to her face, cupping her cheek with his palm, the pulse in his fingertips fluttering against her temple.

Her toes curled in her slippers as he leaned in, his breath sweeping her face. She closed her eyes, expecting the brush of his lips over her cheek, so she wasn't prepared for the meeting of their mouths. As his firm lips enveloped hers, she fell against his chest with a sigh, raising her arms to encircle his neck. He met her embrace, deepening the strength of his kiss as he wrapped his arms about her waist, his hands wide on her back as he drew her closer to him. He bent over her ever so slightly as though wanting to draw her inside of him. She would gladly disappear into him if she could, remove the thin obstacles of her dress and his shirt to meld completely with him. In the openness of the entryway, she could only part her lips and allow his pressing tongue to caress hers.

She'd studied so many classical paintings of nymphs possessed like this by gods, but until this moment, she hadn't understood the sheer power of a man holding a woman, his breath drawing out hers.

Lily clutched Gregor even tighter as her knees went weak from the pressure of his tongue against the line of her lips, curling and drawing her tongue out to meet his. Low down against her stomach, she felt the hardness of more than his hips, the heat of it increasing the fire already licking up inside her. If he were to ask her for more, she'd gladly give it, surrendering to him and the desire threatening to consume them both.

'I'll see if Adelaide left her doll downstairs, Miss Smith, while you look in the nursery.' Petunia's voice from the hall upstairs broke through the haze of Lily's passion, snuffing it out like a drop of water from an icicle on a candle. 'She must have it or she won't sleep.'

Lily broke from Gregor's embrace and took a few steps back. With shaking fingers, she straightened her dress, smoothing out the wrinkles. Petunia's light step filled the entrance hall before she reached the bottom, pausing on the last stair to look back and forth in curiosity at them.

'Lily, what are you still doing up?'

'I was showing Lord Marbrook my portraits.'

'In almost complete darkness?'

'It isn't that dark,' Lily challenged, though even she could see the candles had burned down far enough in the chandelier to make the hall far darker than propriety allowed.

Before Petunia could challenge Lily, Miss Smith appeared at the banister above them.

'I've found Adelaide's doll, ma'am. I'll see to it she gets it at once.'

Petunia nodded, then fixed her attention back on Lily. 'You should get bed. Tomorrow will be a late night.'

'Of course. Goodnight, Lord Marbrook.' Lily dropped a delicate curtsy, glad for the low light for it hid the blush she was sure covered her chest and neck.

'Goodnight, Miss Rutherford.' He pierced her with a singeing glance from beneath his brow as he bowed.

Petunia turned and with a flick of her head instructed Lily to follow her. Far from being irritated at her sister's command, she followed, nearly floating up the stairs and ignoring her sister's searching looks. Let her wonder, she didn't care. Gregor had kissed her, not the playful peck of the Lord of Misrule, but the passionate embrace of a powerful man. It made Lily shiver in the darkness and anticipate the rising of the Christmas sun more than any child in the house. It would mean seeing Gregor again.

Chapter Four

Little voices warbling 'Hark the Herald Angels Sing' drew Gregor from his dressing table to tug open the bedroom door. On the threshold stood the twins, their youngest cousin standing behind them gripping Miss Daisy's hand. Their voices faded away as Gregor smiled down at them. The excitement of last night had taken hours to leave him and he'd spent the better part of his time in the dark trying to forget the memory of Lily in his arms and the heaviness it created low in his body. Sleep had at last come to him early in the morning, but it hadn't lasted much past dawn. Too restless to remain in bed, he'd risen and dressed, eager to see the woman who'd filled his thoughts through most of the night.

'Aw, this one's already up and dressed. There's no fun in that,' one of the twins complained.

'Then let's try someone else,' his brother suggested and the two of them shot off down the hall, leaving Miss Daisy and her tiny cousin behind.

'Merry Christmas, Lord Marbrook,' Miss Daisy offered, her cheeks as red as if she'd been out in the snow.

'Merry Christmas, Miss Daisy, and Miss Adelaide.'

He bowed to the toddler who watched him with wide eyes, one fat hand in her mouth.

'Come on, Daisy, stop dawdling,' one of the twins called as they stood at the door of their next victim.

Daisy looked back and forth between Gregor and her cousins as if debating whether to stay or go. Her youthful exuberance won out over her girlish infatuation and she rushed off, dragging little Adelaide behind her.

Once they were all together at the next door, the children sang their carol at the tops of their lungs. The door to the room opened and out stepped Sir Timothy, still clad in his nightshirt, his cap askew over his grey hair.

'A merry Christmas to you all,' he boomed, scooping Adelaide into his arms and whirling her around to the delight of the other imps.

Gregor watched, enjoying their laughter and high voices. There'd never been such Christmas morning joy at Marbrook Manor. He'd tried it once a very long time ago, knocking on his parents' door in excitement, only to receive a stern whipping which had made sitting through the dull sermon in church difficult.

The butler appeared at the top of the stairs, chuckling as he passed the scene before approaching Gregor. He held out a silver salver with a letter on top. 'My lord, this arrived for you.'

Gregor recognised his mother's handwriting at once. He was tempted to refuse the missive, sure it was not full of cheerful Christmas wishes, but he picked it up, eager to be done with the unpleasant task. As Gregor broke the seal, the butler made for downstairs, trailed by the singing children.

Gregor leaned against the doorjamb as he unfolded the letter, the merriment of the morning draining from him as he read the elegantly written lines.

I can't tell you how disappointed I am that you've chosen to spend Christmas in the north and with the Rutherfords of all people. They're so below us in rank and station. I don't know why you favoured them with a visit.

Your brother never would have shown such poor judgement, nor left me to oversee your duties at Marbrook Manor, but since he is gone I suppose I must deal with you. I've distributed the beer as you instructed, but saw no need to waste an entire cow on such coarse people as the tenants.

What with your raising of their wages and forgiving their debts last year, something your father never would have approved of or done, surely they now have more than enough to purchase their own beef with which to celebrate.

Please do not linger too long in the north. Your presence there has already been remarked upon by your uncle and heaven knows who else.

There was no loving postscript to close the chiding missive and Gregor folded it in half, running his fingers over the crease, wanting to rip the thing to shreds. Instead, he must answer it at once and send separate instructions to his steward about distributing the beef as originally intended. The order would not reach Marbrook Manor before the day was out and he could well imagine the disappointment of many tenant families when their tables were much lighter for their feasts this year, but he would see to it they had something for Boxing Day. He'd even instruct the housekeeper to put together gifts for them in order to make amends for his mother's meanness at such a generous time of year.

'A hearty greeting to you on this merriest of mornings.' Lily's beautiful voice broke through the cloud of Gregor's ire.

A deep red dress of velvet trimmed with blue ribbon wavered around her legs as she approached from the other end of the hallway. The bright fabric set off the whiteness of her neck and the delicate *décolletage* just visible beneath her snow-white fichu. For a brief moment Gregor forgot the letter and everything but the memory of her lips against his last night.

'Good morning, my queen.' He dropped into a bow, noting the slight furrow of her brow as he rose.

'What's wrong?'

'I've received tidings from my mother and they aren't of great joy. I'm afraid I must remain behind from church to see to it my tenants receive the good wishes intended for them, the ones my mother is thoughtlessly denying them.' He didn't mention the rest of the missive, or the aspersions his mother threw on Lily's family. The reminder of every cold and lonely holiday he'd ever known at home was already dimming the warmth of last night and the cheerfulness of the day.

'But you'll be here when we return and you'll attend the ball?'

Her eagerness to be with him brought back a measure of the happiness with which he'd first greeted the morning. 'Most definitely.'

'Then I'll leave you to your work and see you very soon.'

He peered up one side of the hall and down the other to make sure no one was about. Then he took her hand and raised it to his mouth. He pressed his lips against her soft flesh, rubbing one finger against her palm and enjoying the shiver it sent racing through her to make her skin pebble against his. What he wouldn't give to draw her into his room, close the door and forget his problems with her in the deepest of embraces. He couldn't, and with his mother's letter acting like a ballast stone on his mood he let go of Lily and straightened.

Lily rubbed her hand in disappointment as Gregor quickly retreated into his room and closed the door, leaving her in the hall, confused. Despite the heady press of his lips and his teasing caress, it was as if the Lord of Misrule had abandoned him completely and he couldn't be free of her fast enough. Was it just the letter troubling him or was it something more, something to do with seeing Lily? Maybe he regretted being so open and intimate with her last night and this morning was an attempt to make clear to her there could be no more between them than a Christmas Eve kiss.

Lily's stomach tightened with worry, and the shame she'd experienced when he'd turned from her on the dance floor swept in to blot out the excitement from last night until she forced it back. Surely whatever was distracting him this morning had nothing to do with her. He'd told her so and she'd seen it in his face when he'd mentioned his mother and the troubles at home.

Lily raised her hand, tempted to knock and offer him some of the comfort she felt he needed, but didn't. Her parents might be lenient with many things, but even they would look askance at a single young lady alone in the bedroom of an unmarried gentleman.

She wandered off down the hall towards the stairs, knowing she must wait until later for Gregor to look to her for support, assuming he decided to do such a thing. Despite the kiss last night, there was no promise of more between them and no reason why she should expect further confidence and intimacy than what they'd already shared.

Ahead of her, Rose's bedroom door was cracked open and she could hear her and Petunia talking inside. She headed for Rose's room, eager to join them and forget her worries, when Petunia's voice made her freeze.

'You shouldn't encourage her with Lord Marbrook.'

Lily leaned towards the opening to listen, careful not to call attention to her presence.

'Why not? I think it'd be an excellent match. They're very much alike in temperament,' Rose countered. 'And imagine Lily as a viscountess.'

'It isn't likely to happen.' Petunia sniffed.

'Afraid our little sister will outrank you?' Rose teased.

'I'm afraid she'll be humiliated again. It's troubling enough Mother allowed him to come here at all, but for him to show Lily special attention is beyond the pale, especially since everyone knows a Marbrook, no matter how amiable he is to our family, is never going to disgrace his own grand name by marrying so far beneath him.'

'I think you've misjudged Lord Marbrook. His brother might have been arrogant, but I've seen no such tendency in him, at least not now.'

'But what about four years ago?'

'He was a boy then, and Lily just a girl. They've both matured a great deal since.'

'Perhaps, but I've heard rumours his mother is pushing him to marry Viscount Daunton's daughter. Most people expected an announcement last Season.'

'If he didn't ask her last Season, he probably won't. Beside, Lord Marbrook doesn't strike me as a man to be pushed into a marriage he doesn't want, especially not by his mother.'

'Nor is he the kind to rush into anything. He might play the fool at the servants' ball, but he won't do so in London, especially not with Lily,' Petunia insisted.

Lily's chest constricted and panic surged through her. Last night, in the dark of her room, when the moon was high and reflecting off the small arches of snow snug in the corners of the window panes, she'd allowed herself to believe there might be something more between her and Gregor. Hearing Petunia state the truth so plainly, she realised there wasn't. Petunia was right, it was one thing to make merry in the country and quite another in the stately homes of London.

Lily balled her hands and pressed them against her forehead. She'd been weak and foolish with Gregor, granting him favours no young lady should give a man of such slight acquaintance. Then to further lower herself, she'd told him about her troubles with her family, pouring out her heart like the lonely drunk in the public house she'd once read about in a novel. For all she knew, she'd been dallying with a man on the verge of a betrothal and the letter from his mother had something to do with Viscount Daunton's daughter and not Marbrook Manor. It would certainly explain his quick retreat from her at his door, the memory of which made the shame sting even more.

'What are you doing skulking around doorways?' Laurus's voice rang out from behind her.

Lily pushed away from the wall and, catching her brother by the arm, pulled him to the stairs.

'Do you ever speak softly?' she hissed.

'No more than anyone else in this family.' He stopped at the top of the stairs to study her, concern furrowing his brow. 'Is something wrong?'

She twisted her hands in front of her, wanting to confide in the one sibling who understood her, but she hardly knew where to begin, or if she wanted to reveal her humiliation and confusion. Everything Petunia had said was right, she knew it, yet it contradicted everything she'd come to feel about Gregor last night. Surely he wasn't the man Petunia described, though the one who'd greeted her this morning was so different from the one she'd kissed, confusing her more than her father's Latin names for his plants.

'Lily?' Laurus prodded as she struggled to bring her thoughts under control like she always did at her easel, when everything around her was a whirlwind of noise and motion.

'Nothing's wrong, only we must go down for breakfast. If we don't eat soon we'll be late for church and you know how Father is about Christmas service.'

As Lily began to descend, she glanced back at her sister's room to catch Rose standing in the doorway. Petunia watched anxiously over her shoulder, the pity in her expression as irksome as the worry drawing Rose's lips thin.

Lily hurried down the stairs, refusing to give them any hint she'd heard their conversation, though it was plain to all she had. She gripped the banister tight as she descended, trying to fight back the panic and not let it trip her on the stairs. She'd made yet another mistake trusting Gregor, one which would heap more derision on her if it was ever made known. She might not mention it, not even to Laurus, but what might Gregor say to his friends or at his club in London? He might laugh and talk about Lily's morals being as clumsy as her dance steps. Such a story would ruin her reputation for good. She'd worried last night about Daisy's behaviour reflecting badly

on the Rutherfords. Her father had been right to scold
her for it, especially since it was Lily's behaviour which
risked tainting them now.

Overhead, grey clouds began to blot out the blue sky
which had greeted them this morning. There would be
snowfall by this evening, nature's decoration for the
Rutherford ball. For now, ice clung to the bare branches
of the trees and the top of the portico balustrade. Gregor
paced back and forth across the cold stone, his boots
crushing the ice as he moved, his leg a touch stiff this
morning because of the cold and his exuberant dancing
last night. Pygmalion sat inside at the window watching
him, willing to remain his constant companion, but not
loyal enough to wander too far from the hearth. Gregor
didn't blame the little creature. If he possessed any sense,
he'd be inside too with a cup of tea instead of torturing
himself out here in the frost.

The distant bells of the church began to toll, bringing
Gregor to a halt. Church was over and soon the family
would return to the house and their Christmas celebration. Their happiness would help lift the dreariness which
had descended over him while he'd composed a letter to
his estate manager, instructing the man to distribute the
beef as Gregor had promised his tenants. Then, it'd taken
time for the Rutherford's butler to find a man willing to
travel so far to deliver the missive on this festive day. A
few pounds from Gregor's pocket had at last persuaded
a local farmer with no family to ride south to Marbrook
Manor and undo the damage of Gregor's absence.

Turning to make his way back across the portico, he
vowed some day to see the kind of joy he experienced
at Helkirk Place light up the halls of Marbrook Manor.
There would be children to laugh and run through the

halls like the ones did here, sons and daughters he would raise up to care for one another without fear of expressing it. They'd be kind to those around them and as full of life and love as a woman like Lily. He stopped at the far end, the image of Lily as a mother as startling as the scratch of Pygmalion's paws against the glass urging him to come back inside. Gregor hadn't come to Yorkshire with the intention of finding a wife, only forgiveness, yet the thought of pursuing the young lady with the eyes like coal and an open, welcoming nature warmed him more than his thick redingote. In the eagerness of her kisses he'd tasted her passion not for the Viscount Marbrook, but for Gregor, the soldier and the second son, and he didn't want to let it go.

The image of her troubled face as he'd closed the bedroom door on her this morning rose up to disturb him. He wanted to enjoy again the lively woman from last night, the one who'd danced and laughed with him as he'd shrugged off the shadows of the last few years. He'd never experienced such freedom and mirth with anyone. He paused to take in the white-and-grey garden, wondering how different the last few years might have been if he'd defied his father, helped Lily to her feet, then stood beside her in her embarrassment and furthered the friendship they'd started.

As beautiful a fantasy as it was, he knew it would never have come to pass. His father would have seen to its end, one way or another, and at the time there was no way of knowing if he would survive France. Nor could he have imagined inheriting the title and the freedom it offered. With both in his possession, he was determined to not let the next few years slip away without Lily in his life.

The crunch of carriage wheels on gravel and the jangle of equipage carried through the chill air, announcing the return of the Rutherfords. Gregor stepped inside, pausing before the fire to warm his hands as he considered what to do next. Pygmalion watched him from his place on the hearthrug, the small bells on his collar tinkling each time he moved. Gregor could hardly rush down the hallway to greet Lily, not with her whole family watching. Perhaps she could be tempted out to the greenhouse and he might taste again her sweet lips. Or they could walk down the snow-covered lawn and engage in the lively sport which had sent her laughing over the garden path yesterday. Her bright smile and glittering eyes would drive back the blackness brought on by his mother's callousness.

The twins' voices filled the hall, joined by the noise of the adults and the patter of the dogs' feet as they hurried down the stairs to meet their mistress. Gregor wanted to rush with them, but with measured steps made his way to the entrance hall, Pygmalion jingling at his side.

He spied Lily before she noticed him, watching in amazement as she pushed the red-velvet hood of her cloak off her hair. She adjusted a couple of pins holding the luscious mahogany curls against the back of her head, then turned, catching his eye from across the room. She didn't smile as she had this morning, but appeared troubled, as if something had happened between their parting and this meeting. He thought of last night at dinner and wondered if someone had said something to her to dull the excitement of the morning.

Gregor exchanged Merry Christmas greetings with the other ladies and gentlemen as he pressed through the Rutherfords to reach her. She watched him with more anxiety than anticipation, and the gut feeling it was he and not her family which had brought about the change in her mood began to creep in beneath his desire to be near her. Then she flicked a glance at her second-eldest sister, the one Gregor knew the least. He dared to follow the line of her gaze, noting the wariness in Lady Winford's eyes before the demands of her small daughter drew her attention away. When Gregor looked back, Lily was gone. He hurried to the front door to see her walking quickly down the drive and he dashed out into the chill to follow her.

'Lily,' he called when they were some way from the house.

She stopped, but didn't turn around. He came to stand in front of her, the cloud of their breaths mingling in the crisp air between them. 'What's wrong?'

She drew the hood back over her hair, settling it just above her forehead so it framed her face. 'Nothing is wrong, only the carriage was so crowded, I needed some fresh air.'

'Then allow me to escort you in your walk.'

'No.' She looked back at the house, twisting her gloved hands in front of her before fixing him with a wan smile. 'I'll only be out here a moment. Father always likes me to help him oversee the last arrangements for the ball. He says I have a mind for organising things.'

Gregor laid one hand over hers, squeezing it gently. It was a bold move, especially here in the open where anyone upstairs might see them, but he couldn't let her get away, not with such worry shadowing her. 'Lily, please tell me what's troubling you.'

She pressed her lips tight together, studying his face as though debating whether to trust him with her concerns. Then the hesitation fled, replaced by irritation, and she pulled away her hand. 'Don't be so intimate with me. Have you no care for my reputation?'

'I care very much for it and you.'

'If you did, then you wouldn't have taken such liberties, not last night and not this morning.' She stomped off down the drive and Gregor rushed to fall into step beside her, not caring for the cold or the way it cut through his coat.

'Did someone see us? Did someone say something to you?' he pressed, trying to get to the heart of what was vexing her.

'No, but I overheard my sisters talking.'

At once he understood the change in her attitude. 'They don't approve.'

'Rose does, but not Petunia.'

'And you agree with her?'

They walked in silence, the gravel crunching beneath their feet. Around them a few birds twittered, making the bare tree limbs rub together as they took off from their perches. At last Lily took a deep breath and spoke with measured words. 'I think our freedom with one another last night was a mistake. I was foolish to forget myself with you when I know I'm nothing more to you than a mere country dalliance.'

Her words stung as much as the cold air in his lungs. 'You're very mistaken.'

She whirled to face him. 'Am I? You already cut me once and everyone who hungered after your family's approval or based their behaviour on their opinion followed suit. Why do you think I haven't returned to London? I couldn't face the whispers, the derisive looks.'

Gregor toed the snow at his feet, uncovering a clump of brown weeds. 'I didn't realise.'

'Of course not. Like all Marbrooks, you only think of yourself.'

His head jerked up to meet hers. 'Don't lump me in with my family. I'm nothing like them. I never will be.'

'You have been once already. I won't let you make a fool of me again.'

The remark hurt like a slap. There'd been so little time for him to show her his true self, but he thought she'd recognised it and understood—he was beginning to suspect he was wrong. 'Have you heard nothing of what I've said to you about my past, my life or these last four years?'

'I have, if I hadn't I never would have accepted your apology.'

'Yet you haven't, not really, or you wouldn't doubt my sincerity, integrity and my concern for you.'

'I trusted you once and you let me down.'

'And you'll always hold it against me, no matter what I say or do.'

'How can I forget it when I can't escape it?'

'You could if you truly wanted to, but instead you've hidden yourself away here, imagining your troubles to be much greater than they really are.'

'How dare you.' She marched off around the corner of the house and out of view of the upper windows.

Gregor followed, quickly closing the distance between them before he grabbed her arm and spun her around to face him. She landed against his chest, clutching his upper arms to steady herself. Her breath caressing his neck above his cravat nearly startled the words from him, but they didn't abandon him completely. They were driven out of him by the anger welling up from deep inside him, fuelled by France, his parents and his own failings. 'You think you know suffering, but you don't. It isn't rumours or people staring, it a field full of shattered men bleeding and dying, your friends alive one moment, then ripped from your side by a cannonball the next. It's lying in an abandoned barn for three days with your leg bleeding, passing in and out of consciousness, your tongue swollen with thirst while you watch the sun set, wondering if it will be the last time you see daylight.'

He shifted closer, his chest brushing against her as she listened. The care he'd craved from her only half an hour before filled her eyes and tore at him the way the musket ball had torn through his leg.

'I'm sorry, Gregor, I didn't know,' she whispered, reaching up to brush the hair off his forehead.

Tears for him glittered in the corners of her eyes, but with the cries of his men and the cannon fire echoing in his ears, he couldn't accept her sympathy. 'How could you? You talk of my faults, but what of yours? You hide here, afraid to be embarrassed by me, your family, yourself, looking for the worst in others because of how it might reflect on you.'

This time she didn't object to his words, but lowered her head and sagged a touch in his arms. He'd humbled her as much as France and his father had once humbled him, and he hated himself for it.

Sliding a finger beneath her chin, he raised her face to his. 'You were brave once, approaching me when you thought I needed a friend, despite my family name and rank. Be that brave woman again, Lily, and you'll stun yourself and everyone.'

Lily stared into Gregor's green eyes. He was right. She'd lived for so long in fear of being embarrassed she hadn't really lived at all. Yes, the ball four years ago was unfortunate and he'd made a mistake, but the time afterwards was her mistake, not his. He'd learned to battle on in spite of the heartlessness of his family and in the face of his horrors in France. Instead of picking herself up and carrying on with the fortitude of a Rutherford, she'd hidden herself away, more ashamed than proud of her family and herself. While she'd imagined herself wronged, Gregor had suffered real tragedies, ones she couldn't fathom. Then, when he'd come to her for understanding, she'd scorned him, too blinded by her own slight troubles to see his.

She wasn't worthy of his friendship. She deserved to be alone.

She let go of his arms and stepped back. He didn't cling to her, but opened his fingers and let her go. Whatever had passed between them last night was gone now. She'd killed it with her fears and accusations. It was as terrible a misstep as the one she'd made with him at the wedding ball.

Snow crunched beneath her boots as she fled off towards the garden, rounding the house to make for the greenhouse standing alone at the end of the flower beds. She slipped inside, the moist heat stifling after the dry cold. She wasn't ready to return to the house to humour Aunt Alice or be pestered by Daisy or the twins, or, heaven forbid, Petunia.

She paced the length of floor, avoiding the small puddles sitting in the narrow spaces between the stones. Neither the blooming plants nor their scent brought her any pleasure. All she could focus on were the red poinsettias and the image of Gregor standing across the bright leaves from her, trying and failing to tell her of France and to apologise. He'd been so open and honest with her, and this time it was she who'd refused to acknowledge him. In her grudge, she'd failed to see the wonderful man he'd become and had thrown away any chance they might ever be real friends, or possibly more.

The door swung open and Laurus entered with a cold draught. 'What are you doing in here? Father is looking for you. He needs you to oversee the decorations for the ball.'

She moved one poinsettia so its pot was in line with the one beside it. 'I needed some time away from all the noise, a chance to be alone before all our guests arrive.'

'Why? What's wrong?'

'What makes you think there's anything wrong?' Lily straightened her shoulders, trying to conjure up an air of indifference and failing.

'Because you were lit up like the Yule log last night with Marbrook and today you look as dour as if it were Ash Wednesday.'

Lily shifted on her feet, trying to think of some flippant response to send him away, but instead she sank down on to the bench beneath the window and buried her face in her hands. 'I've made a mess of things with Gregor.'

'Gregor?'

She looked up as her brother approached with one eyebrow arched with interest.

'I mean Lord Marbrook,' Lily nervously corrected. 'Do you know the real reason he wanted to come here for Christmas?'

'I do.' Laurus sat down beside her. 'He told me when he asked if he could join us.'

'Then you knew he'd come here to apologise to me?'

'I did. Otherwise I wouldn't have let him come. He might be my friend, but I remember what happened. It's why I haven't brought him around before.' He gently pressed against her with humour. 'Some of us in this family do have a regard for your feelings.'

She wished she had as much regard for the feelings of others, especially Gregor. 'Did he tell you what happened to him in France?'

Laurus shrugged. 'He said he was shot and spent some time in the hospital there, but nothing more.'

'He told me what happened and it was awful.' So was the way she'd treated him today. Just as she'd sensed his suffering four years ago, she should have guessed it yesterday and let it and not her own fears guide her.

'I think it's good Marbrook trusted you with such a thing.'

Lily shook her head. 'He didn't tell me out of trust but anger. He flung it at me as if it was the greatest insult he could imagine and it was because of how I'd insulted him.'

She explained to her brother the aspersions she'd cast on Gregor. 'He came here to make amends and I made a muddle of it. It would have been better if you'd refused his request to come.'

'I'm glad I didn't, dear sister, because I can see he has as deep a regard for you as you do for him.'

'We hardly know one another.' And what she'd learned of him she'd tossed aside because of her own fears.

'Look at Mother and Father. They barely knew one another before they married, yet two people couldn't be more perfectly matched.'

It was true, but at the present, Lily wasn't as trusting in providence as her parents. 'Petunia doesn't think Lord Marbrook and I are suited.'

'Petunia thinks too much of herself, while Rose thinks too well of everyone. Daisy doesn't act as she should, Mother and Father are too involved in their plants to check her. I take nothing seriously while you take everything much too seriously. It's part of your charm.' He cuffed her under the chin and she knocked his hand away.

'Try to be serious, Laurus. What am I going to do? He surely hates me now.'

'There you go, imagining the worst again.' Laurus knelt down in front of her. 'After coming all this way to see you, after four years of thinking about you when he might have easily forgotten you, I don't think he'll be so easily put off by this misunderstanding.'

'I'm not so sure.' She wanted to believe him, but whatever image of her Gregor had held on to in France, she'd surely shattered it with her aspersions today.

'Then it might be time to swallow your pride and find out. Apologise to him like he did to you.'

It couldn't be so simple. 'I don't think it will make a difference.'

'There's only one way to find out. Now come inside and get ready for the ball.' He rose, taking her hand and pulling her up with him, something of the Lord of Misrule coming into his face. 'You'll see there's Christmas magic to be worked yet.'

Chapter Five

A multitude of guests crowded the ballroom, their jewels and bright silks glittering with the many candles set in nearly every candlestick and candelabrum the Rutherfords owned. A small group of musicians from the village sat at the far end of the long room, their violins and flutes playing a lively tune to accompany the dancers going up and down in rows in the centre. Every family in the county was here, for there were very few who wanted to miss the Rutherford Christmas ball. Green garlands were draped in arches along the walls, rising to grace the tops of the windows before dropping back down between them. The last one had been hung by the servants under Lily's direction less than an hour ago. Through the windows, the falling snowflakes caught the light and began to pile up in the corners of the sills. To the pleasure of all, it hadn't started snowing until almost every guest had arrived.

A magnificent selection of treats was spread out on the table at the opposite end of the room from the musicians. The older people stood around them, enjoying Sir Timothy's hearty rum punch while the dowagers and aged wives nibbled at the delicate mincemeat pies. The younger people had no interest in the sweets or drinks, but only the endless reels sending the gentlemen in black coats and breeches and the ladies in deep green or red dresses up and down the dance floor in time to the clapping of their fellow dancers.

Lily didn't dance tonight, or share in the festivities. She stood near the refreshment table, at the back of a crowd of older folks, forgotten by both them and everyone enjoying the merriment. Across the dance floor, near the wall on the opposite side of the room, Lord Marbrook stood just as removed from the merry society as her. The many preparations for the ball had kept Lily occupied through the entire afternoon, leaving no time for her to seek Gregor out or to speak to him about this morning, though Lily wasn't sure if she should regret the lack of opportunity or be glad for it.

On the dance floor, Laurus made a sweeping turn with Sir Walter's granddaughter, catching Lily's attention as he moved. With a jerk of his head in the direction of Gregor, he silently encouraged her to cross the divide, but she couldn't. It was one thing to risk his rejection in the privacy of the house, amongst family. It was quite another to do so in public where more than one person was regarding both of them with curiosity, making it clear they hadn't forgotten the wedding ball any more than either Lily or Gregor.

Lily cursed her lack of resolve, realising Lord Marbrook was right about her. She wasn't the brave girl he remembered, just a self-absorbed spinster determined to hang on to the past. She loathed to think of him leaving Helkirk Place with such a low impression of her, but she didn't know how to begin to rectify her mistakes.

The dancers parted, opening up a space between Lily and Gregor. He stared at her, more sadness than distaste in his hooded eyes. Then at once something he'd said at dinner last night came rushing back.

I don't know where else to start. I've regretted what I did from the moment my father escorted me from the ball.

He hadn't known where to begin with his apology any more than she did, but at least he'd possessed the courage to make it. The couples came back together with the music, blocking him from her view.

'Miss Rutherford, what are you doing hiding here, you should be on the dance floor impressing us with your accomplished dancing skills,' Sir Walter called out as he came down the refreshment table towards her, his breeches making his sticklike legs even leaner. 'I'm sure Lord Marbrook would love to see your graceful steps again.'

Lily braced herself as the old man's white hair bobbed around his ears as he laughed, quite pleased with himself and his tiresome joke.

'Oh, be quiet, Sir Walter, no one wants to hear that rusty old barb any more,' Aunt Alice said sharply, wiping the smile from his face as she came to stand beside Lily.

Sir Walter set down his punch on the table, indignantly fluffed the lace of his stained cravat, then shuffled away.

'Thank you, Aunt Alice, for putting an end to his ribbing.'

'It's about time someone in this family did.' She held Toddy in one hand against her ample side and restrained Pygmalion on a leash with the other. The dog strained at the length of ribbon, eager to get away and do who knew what damage. 'Now, girl, what are you doing here instead of dancing with your young man?'

'He isn't my young man,' Lily corrected, trying to keep her voice steady so as not to reveal any of the turmoil plaguing her. 'He's Laurus's friend.'

'And I'm the Queen of France. Don't think I didn't see you two last night plucking the last berry from the mistletoe.' Lily gaped at her aunt, who remained unruffled. 'Now you two are standing across the room as if you don't know each other. Come and I'll reintroduce you and get things off on the right foot again.'

'No, I don't need any assistance with Lord Marbrook.' She caught her aunt's arm before she could set off. 'Besides, even if I did approach him, he isn't likely to take too kindly to me tonight.'

'You won't know unless you speak to him. Believe me when I say, my dear, you must take a risk or two if you don't want to find yourself one day with nothing but your wealth and a pack of dogs who don't even appreciate you.'

She jerked Pygmalion's leash and pulled him back to her side.

'I appreciate you, Aunt Alice.' Lily dropped a kiss on her aunt's wrinkled cheek. 'I appreciate all of my family.'

It was then Lily noticed the other Rutherfords watching her from different places around the room. Rose and Edgar, Petunia and Charles stood in a group near the large fireplace, casting more than one concerned glance her way. Even Mother and Father, gathered with their botanist friends, kept turning to take her in as did Laurus, despite his being cornered by one country girl after another. Gregor was right; they loved her. Despite their faults and silly ways, she loved them. They were her family and they cared about her. She'd been wrong to think they didn't.

Aunt Alice patted Lily's hand. 'But you need a family and a house of your own, dear.'

'Such a thing isn't likely to happen with Lord Marbrook.'

'It won't if you keep lingering here like some wall-flower. Be brave, girl, and go to him. He looks like the devil and needs a little Christmas cheer. After all, what are you afraid of? Tripping and falling in front of him again?' Aunt Alice elbowed her in the side.

'Your tact is extraordinary,' Lily chided, more amused than upset.

Aunt Alice rubbed Toddy's back, unaware of the dog fur clinging to her black glove. 'You'll find, dear, when you reach my age, you care little for what people think.'

Lily stared at Lord Marbrook, a new determination welling inside her. It was time to face him and her past and conquer them both.

She wrapped her arms around her aunt's shoulders and gave her a hug. 'I think I've reached such a realisation much sooner.'

'Good, then be off with you, otherwise I might never get Pygmalion back.' Aunt Alice gave her a wink and a playful push in Gregor's direction.

Lily strode off, following the perimeter of the dance floor, her heart pounding in her chest like the feet of the dancers against the floor. She was about to take another chance with Lord Marbrook, not in the late-night darkness of the hall, but here in the ballroom for all to see. Whatever happened next, it would be discussed for ages amongst everyone who saw it. Whether the results were good or bad, it didn't matter. Lily was tired of worrying about their opinions, of not living her life because she was afraid of what others might say or think. Tonight she would be brave and take a chance.

Rounding the floor, she made for the wall some distance from him, sliding up to him so he didn't notice her until at last she stepped in front of him.

'Good evening, Gregor.'

His attention snapped to her, his eyes widening with surprise before settling into the reserved aloofness which had marked them all evening.

All around them the conversation stilled as people began to watch while trying to appear as though they weren't. Let them see her, she no longer cared about their opinions, only Gregor's.

'Miss Rutherford.' He bowed to her, his formal greeting nearly scaring away her confidence. He'd used her formal name, not her given one. Maybe he wasn't waiting here for her to come to him, but hoping she wouldn't, eager for the night and his visit to be over so he could hurry home and forget this folly and the friendship he'd once wanted.

Whispers began to wick through the crowd around her like the silk dresses of the young ladies twirling on the dance floor. Lily moved one foot behind her, ready to flee before she pulled it back and fixed it beside the other one, then stood up straight. 'I'm sorry for this morning and the things I said. I treated poorly someone who deserved my kindness.'

His eyebrow rose a touch as he recognised his own words repeated back to him. He said nothing, lacing his fingers behind his back as he continued to regard her with a lack of expression meant to conceal from her whatever he thought of this exchange.

Lily wavered on her feet, worry rising like the applause from the dancers as the music drew to an end. 'I don't know if my apology is sufficient to make amends for my mistake, but I don't know what else to do.'

His stoic mask dropped a touch, his piercing green eyes softening as he let go of his hands and allowed them to fall at his sides. It was the subtlest of changes, but enough to give Lily the courage she need to carry on.

She held out her hand to him. 'Will you dance with me?'

More than one surprised gasp filled the air around them, but it was only Gregor's reaction which mattered to Lily now.

'Are you sure you wish to stand up with me?' he asked, not in disgust, but with a hope as frail as the small patterns of ice clinging to the windows.

'I'd consider it an honour to stand up with such a dear friend, someone who deserves my respect because he is one of the most genuine, caring and honest people I know.'

A long moment stretched out as she waited for him to take her hand. Around her the whispers increased, but she remained steady, willing to face whatever consequences her boldness brought down on her.

She was rewarded with Gregor's solid grip as he took her hand. She curled her fingers around his and not even her gloves could prevent the heat of his touch from wicking through her. He hadn't walked away, but accepted her apology and her, faults and all.

The people parted to let them pass as he escorted her to the dance floor, gaping at them as they had four years ago when Gregor had stood up with her.

'We're creating quite a stir,' he observed as they headed for the top of the line.

'Good. I'd like this to be as memorable a Christmas for them as for me.'

'I'm most happy to assist you in the endeavour.' His lips curled up at the corners with a mischievous grin as he let go of her and backed into his place at the top of the line.

The weight of his hand lingered in hers as they waited for the other couples to take their places. There was a scramble to secure positions close to Gregor and Lily with no one wanting to be too far away from this curious sight. Even the older guests who'd cared little for the dancing before now crowded around the edges of the dance floor. Aunt Alice stood amongst them, tossing Lily an encouraging wink as she pulled Pygmalion back to her side.

The musician struck up a tune, not a Scotch reel, but a country dance so similar in energy Lily nearly skipped as she moved forwards to link elbows with Gregor. As they spun around, the room disappeared in a blur with only his smile remaining. His hair fell over his forehead as he danced, his smile as wide as hers as they twirled and chasséd in time to the music, the clasp of his hands as sure as his regard for her. Once again he was her Lord of Misrule and she his Queen of Folly.

When it came time to sashay down the line, he took both her hands in his and they set off, eyes locked on one another, oblivious to everything, including Pygmalion, who bolted away from Aunt Alice, his leash trailing behind him as he hurried out to meet them.

It was too late by the time Lily caught the flash of brown at her feet. The dog became entangled in her skirts, knocking her off balance and sending her hurtling towards the floor. In an instant Gregor's arm went around her waist and she curled back against it as though he'd purposely dipped her in time to the tune.

The violinist scraped his bow against the strings and the flutist blew an off note as the musicians went silent, watching her and Gregor as intently as the crowd.

He continued to hold her, breathing as fast as she did, his hand firm against her back. Above him the candles shimmered in the darkness of his hair. She held on to his arms, unaware of anything except the closeness of his body to hers and the laughter making his eyes dance. He shifted and she braced herself, ready to rise with him and resume the dance, but he didn't set her on her feet. Instead, he leaned down and joined his lips to hers.

She closed her eyes, savouring the strong heat of him and not caring a fig about anyone else in the room. There was a promise in his kiss, a Christmas one made to her in front of everyone here. He loved her and she loved him, and this would be the first of many glorious Christmas balls during which they'd dance together.

* * * * *

Wallflower, Widow...Wife!

Ann Lethbridge

I would like to dedicate this book to someone who has been my greatest supporter over the years, who has served as my inspiration for the love you will find between the covers and who has played a major part in making so many of my Christmases a joyful occasion.

This story is for you, my husband, Keith.

Dear Reader,

I admit it. I am one of those people who adores all things Christmas: the season, the food, the singing, the gifts, the decorations. For me, it is all about gathering together with family, and that is what I wanted to reflect within these pages. While the story is fiction, I could not help but put a few of my own happy Christmas memories within these chapters, in particular the gathering of Christmas greenery and the singing out of doors.

If you would like to know more about me and my stories, you will find me at annlethbridge.com.

In closing, I would like to wish you and your family a very happy and loving Christmas.

Ann Lethbridge

Chapter One

December 1813

Adam Royston St Vire, Viscount Graystone and heir to the Earl of Portmaine, squeezed the bridge of his nose and once more applied himself to the column of figures in the dusty old ledger. Again his vision blurred. The linenfold panelling darkened by age, the dingy carpet and old oak furniture seemed to swallow what little winter sunshine filtered through the library's mullioned window. Perhaps another candle would help.

Stiff from the lack of warmth in this benighted old manor house, despite the blazing fire he'd lit, he arched his back and stretched his cramped hand. The ledgers told a sorry tale. Old Cousin Josiah had neglected Thornton for years. A large investment was needed to bring it up to scratch and even then… Portmaine had no need of such a drain on its coffers. A quick sale was what he would recommend to his father.

He rubbed at his nape. Paperwork. He hated it.

The old restlessness seized him. He eyed the brandy bottle he'd picked up with other supplies on his way through the local village the previous day. Brandy would not help him complete his task more quickly, even if it did dull his urge to move on. His duty, to his father and to the estate, required that he finish this up before going home for Christmas.

The thought of home, of being the subject of sympathetic eyes and concerned faces, made his stomach curl in on itself. Worse yet would be the matchmaking efforts made by his mother. She'd written, warning him of the young lady and her family invited for the holidays. He didn't blame his mother for her stratagems to see him leg-shackled once more. She didn't understand that he was perfectly content to leave the business of providing the next Portmaine heir to one of his younger brothers. Marriage was out of the question.

Damn it all, he did not want to think about his dead wife. It hurt too much. Especially at this time of year. Marion had loved Christmas. She'd loved life. And had he been a better husband, paid attention to his duty, she would have lived to enjoy this one.

Anger and regret churned vilely in his stomach. It always did when he allowed thoughts of Marion to slip into his mind. His fingers clenched around his pen. The urge to hurl it across the room had his hand trembling. He dipped it in the inkwell instead, forcing his mind back to Sir Josiah's account books.

Figures never let him down. They always did exactly as required. If they weren't right, they could be fixed. Unlike people. He peered at the crabbed line of explanations beside each number and grimaced. At least the mess Cousin Josiah had left him provided a reasonable excuse to put off his return to Portmaine for a few days longer. He began tallying the column again.

'You do it,' a high-pitched voice said right outside the window that looked over the sweep of drive.

'No, you. It was your idea. And you are the oldest.'

Female voices of the cultured sort. Too young to pose any sort of matrimonial threat, thank the sweet heavens.

The doorbell clanged.

He ignored it. Since Josiah's servants had been pensioned off—all but the stable boy—and Adam had sent his own man home for the holidays, there was no one to answer the door. He certainly wasn't expecting visitors. The solicitor who had given him the key had asked if Adam wanted to hire a housekeeper or some such from the nearby village, but he'd declined, given the shortness of his planned stay.

The doorbell pealed again. Not deterred, then. He sighed, rose to his feet and headed into the chilly cave of the entrance hall. He pulled the door open at the same moment the taller of two young females reached for the bell. She lurched into his belly with a cry of alarm.

He steadied her, set her back on her feet and glared down. 'What do you want?'

The smaller child disappeared behind her elder, peeping out and up at him with large blue eyes framed by pale lashes.

The elder, a rosy-cheeked brunette with her chin lost in a blue knitted scarf, whom he judged to be about the age of ten, put mittened hands on small hips. 'We want to see his lordship.' Her breath puffed out from her lips in a frosty mist.

How had they discovered his presence at Thornton House? He glared harder. 'And who is it who wants to see his lordship?' he growled.

The little one disappeared again, but the older girl drew herself up straight like a soldier on parade. He couldn't help but admire her fortitude. There wasn't a groom in his stables who didn't falter when he was in what they called one of his moods.

'I am Miss Lucy Melford, and this is my sister, Diana.' She spoke carefully, as if she had learned the words by rote yet needed to think about them. 'We wish to see Lord Graystone on a very important matter, if you would be pleased to announce us.'

An odd feeling rose in his throat. His lips twitched with the urge to smile at this small package of self-importance. She reminded him of his sisters at that age, appearing as brave as lions when they were terrified. He hunkered down, bringing himself to eye level with the imperious little baggage. 'His lordship isn't at home.'

Miss Melford turned to her sibling. 'They say that when they don't want to see anyone.'

Miss Diana whispered from her place of safety, 'I told you we shouldn't come.'

Adam couldn't resist. 'Why did you?'

The elder young lady regarded him thoughtfully, probably trying to decide if he was an ally or a foe. 'We have an important question to ask.'

'Lucy! Diana!' a breathless female voice called out.

Adam rose to his six foot four inches and regarded the third female hurrying up his drive towards him. An adult female in a drab-looking pelisse of some indeterminate brown colour and a faded black bonnet, which was about all he could see of her as she watched where she placed her feet on the snow-covered drive. Amusement fled. Gads, he should have known little girls would come accompanied by older versions. Governesses and mothers and such. Dangerous territory for a man alone, single and planning to stay that way.

He began to close the door as she arrived alongside the children.

The governess, or whatever she was, looked up, a frown on her face. 'Girls. I told you not to bother his lordship.'

Adam's breath caught in his throat. Because she was… so unexpectedly young. No one would describe her face, with cheeks deliciously flushed by the chill December air, as pretty. Her nose was too aquiline, her mouth too generously wide, for ordinary beauty. But she had the most remarkably luminous hazel eyes he had ever seen. Wide set and intelligent and expressive, they took in the tableau at the door with dismay. Her frown deepened. Her lips pursed. A very prim and proper lady, then, whom others might call unfortunately tall. Not him. It was rare that he met a woman he topped by only a few inches. Statuesque with a lush bountiful figure, he found her utterly carnally tempting. Shocked by his ungentlemanly thoughts, he forced himself to fix his gaze upon her face.

'Girls, you were wrong to go against my wishes,' she said, her expression becoming severe. 'Come away this instant.'

'But, Mama, he is going to ask his lordship,' Miss Melford said. 'You were, weren't you?'

Mama? How was that possible? She could not possibly be old enough to be a mother to these children.

He looked from the mother to the small serious faces staring up at him. 'It depends on your question.' Devil take it, did he have to sound quite so surly?

'Please, do not trouble his lordship,' Mrs Melford said, breathing hard from her dash up the drive, a circumstance resulting in a most pleasing expansion and contraction of the brown pelisse in the region of her chest.

Again Adam dragged his gaze back to her face and saw consternation lurking in those beautiful eyes fringed with lashes the colour of guineas. Strands of the same coloured hair had managed to escape in little tendrils around her oval face.

'And you are?' she said with a lift of delicately arched brows.

For a moment he frowned, then he realised the import behind her question and its tone. She thought him a servant. As did the little girls. They had no idea to whom they spoke. And no wonder. He had answered the door in his shirtsleeves and waistcoat. Something no gentleman would do. But then he wasn't much of a gentleman these days.

'Royston.' Almost without thinking, he gave his mother's maiden name as he often did when he travelled on estate business. Self-defence against toadies and matchmaking mamas.

The woman hesitated. 'Cassandra Melford. Please give my apologies to Lord Graystone for the disturbance.'

A proud woman despite her air of genteel poverty. The unexpected spark of interest deep inside him flared higher. 'Why don't I ask his lordship your question, so he can decide if it is a trouble or not?'

'We wanted to ask if his lordship would permit us to cut some Christmas boughs in his woods.' Miss Lucy spoke quickly, before her mama could forbid another word, sly little puss. She waved an arm off to the right where Adam had noticed a formidable expanse of deciduous forest. 'And perhaps, if we just happened to find a log—by chance, you understand—we could bring it home for the holidays.' She smiled and he could see a gap where an incisor used to be.

Miss Diana peeped around her sister and removed a finger from between rosebud lips. 'There is—'

'Hush,' Miss Lucy said.

Clearly the child had already located the log of her choice.

'Girls, it is not right for us to trespass in his lordship's woods,' their mama said softly, as if to ease the blow of her words. 'I am sure we can find some greenery in the hedgerows. I promised you we would go tomorrow. And Mr Harkness might have a log left at the end of the day we can…purchase.' How telling was that little stumble. Money was a problem. She smiled apologetically, a smile that transformed her face from stern to warmly charming. 'I am so sorry we bothered you, Mr Royston.'

The sadness in her eyes, despite her brave smile, was painful to see. Adam did his best not to see it. He was no knight in shining armour.

'Wait here, while I ask.' Blazes, now what was he doing?

Mrs Melford looked ready to refuse.

'I'll be but a moment.' He closed the door, castigating himself for his deceit. Yet, strangely, he found it pleasant to converse with a woman who was not *my lording* him all over the place. Or sympathising. Or simpering and batting her eyelashes.

'He said to wait,' Miss Lucy said, her high voice piercing.

A small silence.

'He just closed the door. He didn't go anywhere,' little Miss Diana announced, clearly hard up against the other side of the door. Listening.

Another odd twitch of his mouth he recognised as the beginnings of a rusty smile on lips tight from lack of practice.

He crept a few feet up the hall, not quite believing his idiocy, and stomped back to open the door, only to discover Mrs Melford in the throes of dragging her daughters away.

He followed them a few steps down the snow-covered drive and raised his voice. 'His lordship has one condition. I must go with you. He can spare me tomorrow afternoon.' He should be done with his paperwork by then, but it would be too late to set out for Portmaine Court and arrive before dark. Though why he was even thinking of doing this—perhaps because the girls reminded him of his younger sisters whom he rarely saw. Or perhaps it was his curiosity about the woman.

'No, thank you,' Mrs Melford said stiffly.

'Mama,' Miss Lucy pleaded, her eyes big and sad.

'I meant you also, Mrs Melford,' Adam said, at once realising the difficulty of a stranger accompanying two little girls anywhere. 'And Mr Melford, too, of course.'

The woman tensed. 'There is no Mr Melford.'

A widow. Now why did that lift his spirits when he should be expressing regret?

'Bring whomsoever you wish,' he said. 'But his lordship insists I accompany you.'

'We won't steal anything,' Miss Lucy said indignantly.

Adam shrugged, feigning surly indifference, when he felt anything but indifferent. 'Won't you need help with the log? Unless you have a servant to assist?' Which from the condition of their patched and worn clothing he very much doubted.

Clearly torn, Mrs Melford gazed at the hopeful faces of her children. She heaved the small sigh of the beleaguered parent; he'd heard enough from his own to recognise it as defeat. 'Tomorrow, then. At two.'

'Where do I find you?' he asked.

She looked surprised and then flustered. 'Ivy Cottage. We are his lordship's tenants.'

'Ivy Cottage?'

'A little way along the lane between here and the village.' She took her daughters' hands and walked away. For all its mud-coloured ugliness, the skirts of her pelisse swayed from her generous hips in a most pleasing manner. He stilled. His blood hadn't warmed to the back view of a woman in years. And nor should it be doing so now. The woman was his father's tenant. She deserved more respect. And clearly, she was not that sort of woman. While she might be a widow, she was also most definitely a lady.

He closed the door. Ivy Cottage? He didn't recall any rent-paying tenants anywhere on this blasted benighted property.

Twenty-five beeswax candles. Cassie stepped back to admire the fruits of her labours hanging from their racks. Hers and those of the wonderful little creatures who had also given them jars and jars of honey. Who would have thought a childhood interest could have kept them from the brink of disaster? Her throat felt a little too full. The prickle at the back of her eyes just a little too painful.

Sir Josiah St Vire had been a kindly old man and had professed a love of honey in his tea, her particular honey. The white clover that grew so well in this area gave it its delicate flavour. If this new landlord would also take honey and candles in lieu of rent as his predecessor had, they might survive another twelve months. His servant, Mr Royston, was certainly not a friendly sort. He'd practically frightened poor little Diana out of her shoes. He'd regarded Cassie herself as if he was Red Riding Hood's big bad wolf ready to gobble her up.

Her face heated. Oh, no. Not another blush. As she had told herself the previous afternoon, the look in his eyes had not been appreciation. Young men never gave her a second glance once they'd taken in her towering height and homely features. The heat in Mr Royston's expression had been annoyance at being thwarted.

When it came to women, it was her experience that men wanted everything their own way. Women were simply bargaining chips in their games of power. And when things did not go as planned, they turned unpleasant and vindictive. As her brother had, when she refused her first offer of marriage. He'd painted a pretty ugly picture of her future as his dependant. And as her husband had, when he discovered that even an earl could not guarantee his precious son the entry into polite society he wanted. No woman should trust a man to use his power wisely.

As a widow, she had the freedom to make her own decisions, to choose her own course of action. And she had managed very nicely, too.

She peered into the bottom of the tin pot standing in hot water over the fire in the little lean-to stable the girls had come to call her potting shed. Enough wax remained for a few small moulded candles and then her supply would be finished.

'Good afternoon,' a beautifully modulated male voice said.

She jumped and turned around. 'Mr Royston?'

Looming. Over her. Her recollections had not played her false. In this small space, the man was disconcertingly tall and uncomfortably wide across the shoulders. He made her feel small, almost dainty. A most disconcerting sensation. He stared around him with obvious curiosity. While his face was too rugged to be called handsome in the common way, she was once again struck silly by his fierce manly beauty. She was also surprised to discover that the eyes she'd thought dark were a striking shade of emerald. Her stomach gave a jolt.

She bristled against the strange reaction. 'Why are you here?'

'Are you ready?'

Her glance flew to the clock on the mantel. It wanted two minutes to two. Dash it, she had lost track of the hours. She had promised the girls she would return to the cottage well before the appointed time of their outing. 'I won't be but a moment. We will meet you in the lane.' Not exactly polite, but she was a single female and did not want any misunderstandings.

He ignored her hint, strolling around like a predator looking for prey, or the representative of a landlord looking for signs of neglect. Hands behind his back, he stared at the racks of candles suspended above his head. 'So those are your hives in the lower meadow.'

Not a question. 'Sir Josiah gave me permission.' Oh, dear sweet periwinkles, if the new owner refused permission to use the field, she would need a new home for her bees. No easy matter, when he owned all of the land within walking distance. 'I paid for the privilege in candles and honey. He thought the bees helpful for his orchards.'

Royston met her gaze with a frown. 'Are these for your own use?'

As if she could afford such luxury. She lifted her chin. 'Mr Driver sells the remainder of the candles and honey at the market in town.'

'Hmm.' He gave her a considering look. 'Should we be going?'

She blinked at his rapid change of topic and brusque tone. 'First I must remove the pot from the hearth and bank the fire.'

'Allow me.'

Before she could protest, he had intruded himself between her and the fire and swung the crane clear of the dying embers.

Silently she handed him the rag she used as a pot holder.

'Where do you want it?' he asked, lifting the container with ease.

'Outside to cool. I will deal with it later.'

He despatched the task quickly, while she untied her apron. Only to discover the tapes had become knotted somewhere in the small of her back.

After a moment's hesitation, he stepped closer and once again she was aware of his impressive height and breadth. 'Can I help?' He pulled off his gloves to reveal large male hands, elegant hands, and not at all work roughened, like hers. A gentleman's gentleman did not engage in rough work like gardening and candle-making.

She must either give him her permission or she must cut the ties and be forced to mend them later. She turned her back. 'Thank you.'

Warmth radiated from him as his fingers busied at her back. Her insides fluttered each time his hands brushed against her gown. She forced herself to stand passively while he teased at the knot.

'There,' he said, stepping back.

She turned with a smile. 'Thank you.' Her breath caught in her throat at the intensity of his gaze. A veiled glance that took in not only her face, but her full length. Most men were usually intimidated by her height, but not this one apparently and her skin tingled with female awareness.

Brilliant green eyes sparkled with amusement. 'Do you need help taking it off?'

Oh, mercy, she was standing here like some besotted schoolgirl instead of a widowed lady of a certain age. She slipped the apron strings over her head, only to have him take it from her hand.

He leaned forward and brushed his lips across hers. A whisper of a kiss that had fire racing up her face to her hair line and her feet stumbling backwards.

He caught her upper arms in those strong capable hands with a smile that dazzled.

Her heart fluttered wildly. Her hand went to her throat.

'Steady, Mrs Melford,' he said, his voice deep and rich with laughter. 'We don't want you tumbling into the fire.' He released her the moment he ascertained she had her feet firmly beneath her.

As firm as they were going to be around this man, since her knees were still misbehaving after his kiss. 'Mr Royston…' she began severely. 'You are not to take such liberties with my person. Indeed—'

He glanced upwards and she followed his gaze.

Saints preserve her, she'd been standing beneath a beribboned bouquet of mistletoe. So that was why the girls had been giggling when she caught them coming out of her shed this morning. Lucy must have climbed on a chair to tie it to the beam. Naughty girl.

He reached up and plucked a berry as tradition demanded, tucking it into his inside breast pocket.

Heavens, the man was wonderfully tall. The wind taken quite from her sails, she fought for words. 'You will await me outside, sir,' she said in her best reproving-the-children voice.

He bowed. 'Certainly, ma'am.'

The moment he closed the door she sank down onto the stool and propped her forehead on her hand. What was wrong with her? Was she really so lonely, so needful of male company she would fall for the first man to give her so winsome a smile? She should never have accepted his offer to escort them.

She took a deep breath, damped down the fire and went outside. He wasn't, thank heavens, standing outside her back door expecting her to invite him into her cottage. It would only need a villager passing by on the way to Padminton, their nearest town, for the same sort of gossip that had occurred when someone spotted Sir Josiah leaving her cottage to spring up all over again. She hurried indoors.

Adam swallowed a rueful laugh. Those little girls had caught him nicely when he knocked on the front door. He should have known the prim and starchy Mrs Melford would not have been part of a game to extract a kiss under the mistletoe. She hadn't even known it was there. And yet he couldn't regret the sweet contact of his lips with hers, the lovely scent of her, warm beeswax and roses. It was like summer on a wintery day.

He should apologise, but likely it would only make things worse. Besides, he did not feel sorry. Not the least little bit. He felt more aroused than he had for a very long time. Still, he had no business flirting with a respectable widow. One slip and he'd find himself being marched to the altar by her or by some ambitious relative.

Not that he suspected Mrs Melford of being some scheming chit on the hunt for a husband. Quite the opposite. She wasn't worldly enough to have deliberately stood beneath a sprig of mistletoe expecting to be kissed. The woman blushed every time he spoke.

No, she was sweet and innocent and practically penniless. A charity case according to old Sir Josiah's ledgers.

A darker thought intruded, one that had a pulse beating at his temple. Perhaps Mrs Melford was not an innocent after all. Perhaps it was another sort of payment her previous landlord had accepted in lieu of rent. Perhaps that was why she had blushed and looked uncomfortable.

If so, it was a good thing old Josiah had gone to his maker. He glowered at the cottage, contemplating men who took advantage of poverty-stricken gentlewomen.

The front door opened and Mrs Melford and her daughters emerged. Once again his gaze feasted on her gorgeously generous figure. The elegant turn of her neck beneath her ugly bonnet had him longing to taste that sliver of creamy skin. To feel the beat of her pulse against his tongue.

The devil! Had it been so long since taking a woman to his bed that he had lost all sense of decency? The woman deserved better. He forced himself to turn away, fiddling with Soldier's bridle as if making an adjustment.

The little girls ran out of the garden gate and stopped when they saw the horse and cart. They gazed in puzzlement. 'Are we going in that?' Diana said. 'We usually walk.'

'It occurred to me that we might need help transporting the log.'

'That's Sir Josiah's dog cart,' Lucy said.

'What a pretty horse,' Diana said. 'Can I drive?'

The pretty horse was his own mount. Sir Josiah's carriage horses, while nice beasts, were likely to consider such a lowly task beneath them.

'Not this time,' he said. 'There is only enough room for two up front. You and your sister must ride in the back and give directions. You will find a cushion or two back there for your comfort.'

'It seems you have thought of everything,' Mrs Melford said, helping Lucy up while he lifted Diana in.

Was she pleased about his perspicacity? Or not? It wasn't easy to tell with Mrs Melford. He helped her in and climbed up beside her, clicking his tongue for Soldier to walk.

'I did not mean to disturb your work this morning,' he said by way of a peace offering, both for disturbing her work and perhaps just a little bit for the kiss. Only a very little.

'I was finished.'

Taking him literally. As she should. No lady would acknowledge his teasing not-quite kiss. Though she perhaps should have slapped his face. Which made him think of something troubling, both to him as a man and as a brother. 'Do you have family nearby?' Some male relative responsible for the welfare of the ladies of this household.

'Not that I think it is your business, Mr Royston, but I have no family to speak of.'

Not speaking of family did not mean one did not have any, it simply meant one didn't intend to admit to them. 'I am sorry,' he said and meant it, because the likelihood of the next owner of Thornton keeping a tenant who paid no rent was highly doubtful.

'Perhaps there is a suitor among the local gentlemen?' A man who might rightly call him out for his wicked behaviour.

'Marriage is the last thing I want. Never again will I put myself beneath a man's thumb.'

He winced at her vehemence. Her marriage must have been unpleasant indeed. Stifling the urge to press her further, he brought the horse to the stand and handed off the reins to her. Soldier being the perfect gentleman, unlike the only other male present, waited patiently for him to open the gate to the field that gave way to the woods beyond. Adam leaped up and set the horse in motion once more.

'Is your employer of a mind to reside at Thornton?' she

asked, as if sensing the direction of his earlier thoughts. He liked that about her. The way she reasoned and contemplated, even if it did lead to uncomfortable questions.

Part of him, the landlord part, wished he had given her his real name yesterday and closed the door. The other part, the male-on-the-prowl part, was glad she had looked adorably flustered and deliciously feminine on his doorstep—so unlike his usual female company—and had tempted him to fall in with her mistaken impression.

'He won't,' he said.

'You are very certain,' she said doubtfully. 'Perhaps he might offer it for lease?'

A case of straw-clutching if ever he'd heard one. He could try to let the house and the land, but who would be fool enough to rent Josiah's mess of an estate when it required a significant investment to put it right? It would be unkind to get her hopes up only to dash them again. 'He won't.'

'You are in his confidence, then?'

He hated how disappointed she sounded. 'As the Earl of Portmaine's land steward I am party to all such decisions.' An accurate description of his duties on behalf of his father these past five years, so not exactly a lie even if it felt like one.

'Mr Royston,' Miss Lucy called out.

He turned in his seat. 'How may I be of service, Miss Melford?'

She giggled at his formality. 'Can you put me and Diana down so we can show you the way to the lovely holly tree we found? And the ivy.'

Perhaps there would also be mistletoe. He decided not to ask.

He jumped down and walked around the back. 'Out you come, ladies.'

Once on the ground the girls set off at a trot while Soldier flicked his ears back and forth as if trying to decide if he was displeased by this new turn of events.

'This way, Mr Royston,' Miss Lucy called over her shoulder.

Fortunately, the path she chose was wide enough and the snow hardened enough by the cold these past few days to accommodate the horse and cart.

'In view of Lord Graystone's intent to sell, it is kind of him to allow us to raid his woods,' Mrs Melford said, sounding disappointed.

Kind was not the correct word. Lustful. Deceitful. All of those suited the case much better.

'I should thank him,' she said. 'Don't you think? I would not be amiss in my courtesy.'

And then she would know what a deceitful lustful fellow he was.

'His lordship left for home first thing this morning.' Or he should have.

A frown furrowed her brow. 'And yet you remain?'

'Not for long. I have one more task to finish up and then I, too, will go.'

'And you are positive he plans to put Thornton up for sale in the New Year?'

For a moment he wished he could ignore his duty to his father and the estate and let her stay. To what end? To make her like him more? To take advantage of her sweet nature? Oh, he really didn't deserve her to look on him as any kind of saviour.

'I am sorry,' he said and was surprised by the genuine regret in his voice.

Chapter Two

Gazing at Mr Royston halfway up the tree, Cassie had trouble believing that a man who could kiss so tenderly beneath the mistletoe in her shed could hack down holly boughs with such ease and vigour. No doubt his thick leather gloves helped protect his hands from the worst of the prickles, but she was sure he had received more than a scratch or two.

'Stand clear,' he shouted from his perch.

She grabbed the girls by their hands and pulled them back. The branch hung on its neighbour for a second, then landed beside four other slender branches bearing clusters of vivid red berries amidst shiny dark green leaves.

Mr Royston landed beside the pile. He gave her an odd look. 'What is that tune?'

Oh, she must be humming, something she did without thinking when she was happy. Something that hadn't happened often beneath her husband's roof. And when it did, he'd found it annoying.

'It's a Christmas carol,' Lucy announced and promptly broke into song. *"The holly and the ivy..."*

To Cassie's surprise, Mr Royston joined in with a

beautiful baritone and the woods echoed with the first verse followed by the chorus.

'I suppose that is a hint for me to cut down the ivy next,' he said, pretending to grumble.

'This way,' Lucy said, dashing off.

Mr Royston winked. 'Her enthusiasm is catching.' He put his hands on his hips and looked down at the branches. 'Is this enough for your purpose?'

'For mine and half the village, too,' she said, then winced at how ungracious she sounded. 'Thank you. Our decorations will be the finest they have ever been.'

Diana reached for a twig. Mr Royston caught her hand. 'Careful, I have never seen so many prickles as there are on this tree. Or so many berries.'

'I think the two go hand in hand,' Cassie said.

He crouched down, cut off a small twig, denuded it of the prickly leaves at one end and handed it to Diana with a flourish. 'My lady's bouquet,' he said. 'Mind it does not bite you.'

She giggled and held it clear of her body.

'Say thank you,' Cassie said.

Diana grinned at him. 'Thank you, Mr Royston.' She lunged at him, gave him a hug and ran off in her sister's wake. 'Lucy, look what I have,' she called.

'You had better make another,' Cassie said, blinking back the stupidest tears at his kindness. 'For Lucy. If you don't mind, that is?'

It had been awfully sad when their older brother had competed with the girls for their papa's attention. Herbert had been a beastly tease, jealous of the daughters of his father's second marriage, though he had always managed to hide his nastiness beneath an innocent smile when his father was around. Herbert had hated that his father had married his housemaid. He thought it undignified.

Cassie guessed that Herbert was the reason his father had looked far higher for his third wife. The daughter of an earl no doubt seemed like a pretty good catch. Unfortunately, no matter what her brother had promised in regards to introducing Herbert to the *ton*, he had been unable to overcome the *beau monde*'s distaste for the vulgarity of the heir to Clifford Norton's fortune. None of the top-drawer gentlemen's clubs had accepted Herbert's nomination and he'd had to settle for third-best. Something that had left father and son less than pleased. They'd got their own back by finding a legal way out of providing the settlement arranged upon her marriage, because her family had failed to live up to their half of the bargain, leaving her penniless except for her jewellery.

'I don't mind in the least,' Mr Royston said, smiling, his gaze following the little girl with true warmth. 'You are doing a fine job with your daughters, Mrs Melford.'

Heat rushed all the way to her hairline. When was the last time anyone had offered her a compliment? Her husband had deemed her a disappointment when her family had not come through with their promises of advancement, and even more so when she had not produced the second son he wanted so badly, while Herbert had ridiculed her at every opportunity until Clifford was sure he had made a very bad bargain indeed. 'They are my stepdaughters. They missed their mama dreadfully when she died, but when I married their papa, we liked each other on sight.'

He held out an arm and she took it. They walked in the same direction the girls had gone. Cassie could hear their voices not too far ahead.

When she glanced up at Mr Royston, she saw curiosity on his face and discovered she welcomed his interest. During the past hour or so in his company, she had forgotten her worries about money and was actually enjoying herself. 'What did you want to ask?'

He looked surprised and then pleased. 'You are very young to be a widow and already responsible for two half-grown daughters.'

A polite enquiry as well as an observation. 'I was young when I married, barely eighteen. I was my husband's third wife.'

His expression became grim.

She turned her face away, not wishing to see either sympathy or disgust. She had made her choice knowingly. It was either that or reconcile herself to being a spinster aunt to her brother's children for the rest of her life, consigned to serving as a drudge for her family as needed. By marrying Clifford she'd had her own home to manage and her girls to love. After Clifford died, she'd been almost glad she had no children of her own to fall under Herbert's repressive thumb. Except she wasn't glad. Not one bit. Children would have been the only good thing to have come out of her marriage.

'My husband needed a female influence for the girls. He also hoped—' To say more about his other ambitions might not be wise. 'And I was in need of a husband. The girls mean a great deal to me.' The thought of losing them... The lump in her throat made speaking impossible.

He put a hand over hers. Warmth permeated her glove. Surely not possible, not through two thicknesses of leather. They walked into a clearing where the girls were tugging at vines wrapped tightly round a tree. She let go of his arm, ostensibly to help, but also for distance. The man made her heart race too fast. Made her want things she'd given up on long ago.

The fault lay with her. She liked his gentle gruffness

with the girls. And she liked the rare smile that showed another softer side of his nature. And, truth be told, no man had ever given her such undivided attention before. Her knees weakened every time he offered her one of his little courtesies. And despite his wicked kiss, his manners were those of a gentleman. Perhaps he was some distant cousin to the noble Portmaine family for whom he worked.

'Come help me, Mama,' Diana asked from amidst a tangle of ivy. She tugged on a trailing vine. As Cassie lifted her gaze to follow the vine's length up the tree trunk, she noticed it wasn't the only plant life in residence.

Naughty excitement rippled through her.

To redirect her thoughts, she wound one end of Diana's vines over her elbow like a skein of wool. Mr Royston helped Lucy do the same with her untidy bundle until they had two nice neat rings that each girl could carry over one arm.

'Why don't you girls take these back to the cart?' Cassie said, repressing the shocking urge to giggle. Women built on her proportions never giggled. 'Mr Royston and I will bring the holly. Lucy, please make sure your sister doesn't trip along the way.'

'Yes, Mama.' Clearly proud of her responsibility, Lucy put her bundle of ivy over one arm and took her sister's hand. Cassie watched them walk along the winding path until they were out of sight. She smiled *up* at Mr Royston, feeling surprisingly feminine and small compared to his bulk. 'Thank you. The girls haven't had an outing like this in a very long time.'

'It is I who should thank you for your invitation.' He bowed slightly. When she didn't move he walked towards her, a puzzled look on his face. 'Is everything all right?'

She held out a hand as if waiting for him to offer his

arm in support. When he came close enough, she put a hand on his shoulder and went up on her toes and kissed him on the mouth, not a simple brush of lips, but the soft pressure of mouths melding. Sandalwood, earthy forest and warm man filled her nostrils. She touched her tongue to the seam of his lips and he parted them on a small sound deep in his throat. His strong arms enfolded her, drew her close and he deepened the kiss. His tongue tangling with hers in a lovely silky slide of tenderness.

She leaned into him, curling her fingers into the silky soft hair at his nape. Her body hummed with pleasure and desire. Her limbs softened. She arched against his body, felt the press of his wide chest against her tingling breasts and sighed her contentment.

He broke their kiss, resting his forehead against hers as if to regain his balance. 'Mrs Melford, what is the meaning of this?' His voice was low and deep and deliciously wickedly teasing, but it also held hope for more of the same.

She leaned back a little and with a smile directed her gaze upwards, some twenty feet or so above their heads. 'Tit for tat, Mr Royston.' She held her breath. A bolt of nerves held her in thrall. Had she gone too far?

Glancing up at the mistletoe ball high in the branches, a boyish grin lit up his face. 'Tit for tat, then, Mrs Melford.'

Gruff, yes, but that smile warmed her through and through. The dawning sensual expression on his face, as if he found her attractive, made her heart stumble. 'Please feel free to call me Cassie, when we are private.'

His eyes widened. No doubt he wondered just how private she was planning they would be. 'Agreed, if you will call me Adam.'

A wicked shiver fluttered low in her belly. A breath

caught in her throat. Too far. Far too far. Clearly, she was getting out of her depth. She stepped away. 'We should go, or the children will come looking for us.'

By offering her name, this deliciously lush but prim and proper woman hinted at wanting him for more than friendship or aid. There was no other explanation possible.

She wanted him. Adam. Not heir to an earldom Adam, but lowly steward Adam. The man who sang Christmas carols with unfettered abandon. For once, the offer did not come with strings attached, financial or marital, though of necessity it could be nothing more than a very short dalliance should he let it go even that far.

He tossed the last of the holly cuttings into the wagon bed. 'Stay well clear of those,' he warned the two little girls.

'We will,' they chorused.

If there was to be dallying, how was it to be accomplished? He certainly did not intend an indiscretion to ruin her reputation with her neighbours, since once she left Ivy Cottage, she would likely rent something nearby.

Unless this was her way of seeking his aid to convince her landlord to let her stay. A cold hand fisted in his chest. She would have to know before they proceeded that it was not possible for him to grant such a favour. A sane man did not let every pretty female that crossed his path influence good financial decisions, no matter his lustful inclinations to the contrary.

The elation he'd felt, the anticipation, seeped away. He climbed aboard the wagon and set Soldier in motion.

Mrs Melford gave him a shy smile. She glanced at the sky. 'I think there is more snow on the way.'

The clouds were darker than they had been before.

Glowering. And the wind had picked up. It was as raw a December day as he could recall.

'Snow for Christmas?' Lucy said, looking between their shoulders.

'Possibly,' her mother answered.

The girl turned to her sister. 'Snow for Christmas, Diana.'

The little girl squealed her excitement.

Charmed by their youthful enthusiasm, Adam grinned over his shoulder. 'Then we must soon find this Yule log of yours, so you will be all toasty and warm at Ivy Cottage over the holiday.'

'It is at the edge of the wood, that way,' Lucy said, pointing towards Thornton House.

Soldier plodded patiently on.

'There,' Lucy directed.

'Oh,' Mrs Melford said, looking at a tree trunk which had been carefully sawn into large logs ready for transport. 'I think Sir Josiah must have intended them to be taken to the manor house, Lucy. That is not the old fallen log you described.'

'It is fallen.'

'It was cut deliberately.'

'Ladies,' Adam interrupted, partly amused by the sort of argument his sisters had so often engaged in when he had lived at home and partly worried about proposing a solution. 'I am sure Lord Graystone will not object to his tenant having a bit of Christmas cheer.'

'He should be asked first,' Cassie said firmly.

He had been. But she wasn't to know that. How the devil to get around the conundrum of this woman's pride without looking like a fool? 'When I mentioned we were to gather a Yule log before he left this morning, he had no objection.'

She looked doubtful. 'It was to be a windfall, Mr Royston. I would not like to take such a liberty.'

'Then I will take it on your behalf,' he said, jumping down. 'If his lordship proves not amenable to your foraging one of these logs, I will buy it as a gift.'

'I couldn't possibly accept.'

'A gift for Miss Lucy,' he said.

'Mama?' the little girl said, her eyes large and appealing. The child had clearly perfected the art of wheedling.

Her mama took a deep breath. 'Mr Royston, should his lordship require payment, then you will tell me and I will pay for it as we pay for our firewood. This is no different. You will let me know his lordship's answer, if you please.'

And so her pride was satisfied while he was left uncomfortable in his wallow of lies. He must end this now and not see her again once he left her at her front door. Dallying with a respectable woman was not an option for a man who considered himself a gentleman.

He wrestled the log onto the cart and glared at it, hands on hips. It was decided. He'd deliver them, their log and bits of foolish greenery back to Ivy Cottage and that would be it. Lord Graystone would write to them from wherever he arrived next and inform them they had six months to vacate his property. A stay of execution was the best he could do and only because she was a woman alone.

Much as he tried on the way back to the cottage, he could not keep his distance from this happy little family. They simply did not allow it. When Lucy sang 'Here We Come A-Waissailing' and Cassie and Diana joined in, silence wasn't an option. When they moved on to 'I Saw Three Ships' and ended with a spirited chorus of

'Deck the Halls', the recollection of St Vire Christmases, his wife singing those same songs, threatened his composure. He both regretted and was glad when he drew Soldier to a halt in front of the cottage as they sang the last rousing *fa-la-la.*

He carried the log into the house and placed it by the hearth in the parlour ready for lighting on Christmas morning and then helped the girls with their hoard of evergreens. Once the children had their coats off, Cassie set them to work at the kitchen table cutting the ivy into manageable lengths.

'May I offer you a cup of tea?' she said to Adam.

'We have shortbread,' Diana announced.

'Thank you, but, no,' he forced himself to say. 'I have work waiting at Thornton.' He was surprised at how hard it was to refuse in the face of her obvious disappointment and that of the girls, but he managed a smile. 'Soldier needs his stable and his oats after his sterling efforts, too.' A plausible excuse that seemed to lighten the mood as she walked him to the front door.

She handed him the hat he had removed on entry. Her smile was shy, and hellishly tempting, and her gaze flickered upwards, above his head. 'Thank you for your escort this afternoon.'

Mistletoe made a fool of a man bent on doing the right thing. She placed her hands upon his shoulders lightly, rose up on her toes.

A kiss. A friendly kiss was surely all she intended.

He took her mouth with his, felt warmth and softness and pliancy. He wrapped an arm around her shoulders, to steady her, to bring her close. She melted against him with a soft sigh as their lips fit together perfectly. Common sense flew away.

A giggle came from the kitchen and she broke away,

smiling regretfully. 'Will you come for dinner tomorrow evening, if you are still here?'

'I will.' Blast, he should have said no. He stepped back, clutching his hat before him like a shield. 'If it should so happen that I am.' He would not be.

'Let me know in the morning if you are not coming. We eat at five.' She closed the door.

In his head, he cursed his weakness, yet somehow couldn't stop himself from wondering if it really would be so bad to remain one more day.

Chapter Three

The stew was ready, the dumplings almost cooked and Cassie's mind was going around and around in circles. What had she been thinking, inviting a strange man for dinner? What on earth would the villagers say if they discovered that little titbit? It did not do to be the subject of wagging tongues in such a small place. Hopefully, given the weather, it was unlikely for anyone to be passing her cottage after dark.

In her heart, she'd known all of that and yet still she'd issued her invitation. There was something about him that made her think the man was lonelier than he would care to admit. After his kindness to the girls, it was only right that she should make him welcome.

She eyed the table Lucy and Diana had decorated with sprigs of holly. It looked cheerful. Cosy. She had even decided to use two of her beeswax candles in the candelabra for the occasion. She glanced at the clock and saw it was almost five. If she did not want to be caught in her apron again, she must make haste.

She ran up the stairs to her small chamber at the front of the cottage where she washed and changed into her Sunday-best gown. A glance at herself in the small cracked glass she had purchased in the market reminded her of her shortcomings, her dowdy appearance, her fulsome-to-overflowing figure. She heaved a short sigh. She was fooling herself if she thought he found her more than passably attractive. Likely his kisses had been spur of the moment, brought on by the spirit of the holiday season. They meant nothing. She touched a finger to her mouth, remembering the feel of his lips on hers.

So pleasurably shocking.

Would he kiss her again this evening? And if so, what would she do? Her heart raced. Dare she take what she wanted from this man before he went on his way? She wanted to. Widows were known to take lovers. To be bold and wanton. Was that why he had accepted her invitation tonight, when yesterday she thought he might not?

Was it really only the day before yesterday she had met him for the first time? She felt as if she had known him all her life, yet she knew nothing about him. Settling her cap upon hair drawn back in a neat tight bun, she crossed the small landing to the other chamber where the girls slept and did their lessons.

'You look lovely, Mama,' Lucy said.

Cassie hugged her daughter. 'So do you.'

Diana raised her arms and Cassie picked her up and bussed her on the cheek. 'Thank you for helping Diana dress, Lucy.' With the ease of long practice, for Clifford had not believed in spending coin on a lady's maid or governess when he had a wife to make herself useful, she tightened their lacings and brushed their pretty hair until it shone. 'Red or blue ribbons?' she asked.

'Red,' Lucy decided. 'To match the holly.'

Cassie smiled at Diana. 'Dearest?' Cassie did not make the mistake of taking her youngest child's choice for granted.

'Red,' Diana said, as usual following her sister's lead.

'Will the church in the village be full of candles, the way the one at home was?' Lucy asked as Cassie tied a bow over her left ear.

'I would expect so, but, dear heart, walking a mile in the depths of winter with no one to accompany us is not a good idea. Instead, we shall light our log and sing our carols here.'

'Will we have to go home?' Diana asked, a quiver in her voice.

Cassie hugged her tight. 'I don't know.' Not if she could possibly avoid it. 'Shall we go down and await our guest?'

The girls clattered down the wooden staircase ahead of her. Flutters invaded her stomach. It seemed no matter how she tried to remind herself that Mr Royston was no more than a guest for dinner, her body had other ideas. No doubt she wasn't the first widow, or yet the last, to consider entertaining a gentleman with more than her company, but she feared she might be making a dreadful mistake.

The girls had barely perched themselves on the chairs in the parlour when a sharp knock came at the front door. Heart fluttering madly, Cassie went in answer.

And there he stood, his chocolate-brown hair dusted by snowflakes, his smile hesitant, his green eyes dark with caution, as if he, too, harboured doubts about the wisdom of this evening. And yet he looked so handsome with the light from the parlour spilling over him, so large, so very male, her mind went blank as her body hummed with pleasure. 'It is snowing.'

He bowed. 'It is. Good evening, Mrs Melford.' He tilted his head in question.

Heat scalded her cheeks. 'Please, come in.' Once inside, she took his coat, hat and gloves.

He bowed in the direction of the girls. 'Good evening, Miss Melford. Miss Diana.'

Such lovely manners.

The girls, bless them, inclined their heads and dipped their knees as she had taught them. 'Good evening, Mr Royston,' they chorused.

Diana shot across the room and grabbed his hand. 'Come and see the table. It has holly and everything.'

Cassie couldn't quite believe her eyes. Shy Diana had decided he was safe, which said a great deal about Adam Royston.

The man made a great laughing show of allowing himself to be pulled into the kitchen and was assiduous in his praise of the table decorations. 'Something smells delicious,' he said, his eyes twinkling at Cassie.

'Dinner,' Lucy announced. 'We are to have vegetable soup and beef stew and custard tart.'

'That sounds positively wonderful,' he said. 'I have to admit I am sharp set after my walk in the snow.'

'Is it snowing hard?' Cassie asked to fill a pause.

'A few flakes on the wind. Not settling.' His eyes crinkled at the corners in amusement. 'Except on me.'

She smiled at his teasing. 'Please, everyone be seated. Mr Royston, if you would take the place of honour at that end.'

Adam held out a chair for each lady in turn and they sat.

'Lucy,' Cassie said. 'Please say grace.'

Replete beyond words, Adam stretched his legs before the hearth. Simple it might have been, but he could not remember when he had enjoyed a meal more. His contentment had nothing to do with the food, which had been plain, hearty and tasty, thank you very much, Mrs Melford. Above all, he had enjoyed the company of a warm-hearted woman and her two lively daughters.

Cassie was a treasure. Loving. Gentle. Kind. Yet full of fun. And her body, so magnificently lush he had trouble keeping his hands to himself.

He frowned at the flames in the hearth. This afternoon, for the first time in a long while, something inside him had come alive. He had actually enjoyed himself. Forgotten duty, forgotten responsibility and felt happier than he had in years. Without knowing it, he'd missed that feeling. Badly. Perhaps his parents were right, it was time to move on with his life.

What, and forget Marion? He could not. Would not.

The sounds above his head, the sounds of children readying for bed, the sounds of a mother caring for those children, slowly diminished. Sounds that should have been his, but were not. That was part of the reason he'd avoided Portmaine Court and his family. It reminded him too much of what he had so carelessly thrown away. Instead, he wandered from property to property on Portmaine business. Keeping himself busy. Keeping himself marginally sane by being useful.

Footsteps tripped lightly down the narrow staircase, followed by a view of a pair of prettily turned ankles and finally Cassie's sweetly smiling face.

He rose to his feet and his body tightened as that particular smile struck him low in his gut. It was a long time since a decent woman's smile had made his body stir with such enthusiasm. He was usually too busy thinking of ways to avoid their company in case they decided to pursue him in earnest. A proper gentleman would kiss her cheek, compliment her cooking, thank her for her kindness and trek out in the wind and the snow. But this evening he wasn't feeling much like a gentleman. Not even close. He wanted more.

She gestured for him to sit, but instead he took her trembling hand and gazed down into her extraordinarily expressive eyes. 'The girls are settled?'

She released a long breath. 'Yes. Diana is already asleep.' Her expression became serious. 'I had a wonderful time this evening. You are so kind to the girls.'

Only one reason would get a red-blooded male to play spillikins with a couple of schoolgirls after dinner. Getting closer to their mama. He wouldn't be merely *not good*, he would be a thoroughgoing scoundrel if he took advantage. 'Thank you for a most delicious dinner. I enjoyed myself immensely.' He spoke the truth, when a dalliance required innuendo and lies. 'I will treasure the memory.'

He saw when she realised he was saying goodbye. And the disappointment in her face wrenched sharply at something in his chest.

'Of the singing, no doubt,' she said, her voice teasing, but her gaze suspiciously bright.

Inexplicably, his throat tightened. 'Especially the singing.'

Fingertips on her cheeks, aware of the softness of her skin, the delicate warmth and the scent of roses, he turned her face up. Waited one heartbeat and yet another, for the smallest sign of protest, then touched his lips to her full luscious mouth. She melted into his kiss, encircled his shoulders with her arms and returned his gift with undeniable enthusiasm.

A pang caused his breath to hitch.

Regret that there would not be more than kisses if he was indeed still a gentleman.

Slowly, carefully, he put his arms around her, drawing her inward, caressing her back, learning the length of her spine, the dip of her waist, the way her ribs expanded and contracted, pressing her lovely full breasts against his chest. She was a bundle of feminine charm, this woman in his arms. Enthusiastic and...lacking in any sort of female wiles or defences. She was all that was good and wholesome in the world, like beeswax candles and the honey she had put in his tea after dinner. And for a man whose recent interactions with women rarely involved kissing, the feel of her lips on his was blissfully erotic.

Whatever gentlemanly inclinations he might aspire to slipped from his grasp.

Cassie loved his heavenly kisses. A feast for the senses. Dizzying.

Never before had she been so much as tempted by a man. The thought of where such temptation might actually lead had her going hot and cold in terror mingled with longing. Certainly there had been none of this heady passion in her marriage.

Did he sense her fear? He held her carefully against him, tenderly, giving her not the slightest alarm. Letting her know she could break free any time she wished. She should wish. A kiss under the mistletoe was one thing, but this was very different. This was the opening move in a dance of which she had little knowledge, except to recognise the tune.

She pressed a hand flat against his chest, feeling the steady beat of his heart beneath her fingers and his strength. He could crush her if he had a mind to do so, but she had no fear of that. Nor would he decimate her with cruel or disdainful words.

Intimacy with this man would be a memory to cherish, since she had decided for the girls' sake she would never wed again. How could she exchange them for the doubtful privilege of becoming a man's chattel, to be tolerated only as long as she was of use?

Slowly, reluctantly, he broke their kiss and gazed into her eyes. An unspoken question. Her face heated. Training warring with temptation. Inside she trembled, knowing he would not do anything without her permission. He began to withdraw.

Fingers shaking, she pressed her hand against his cheek. The delightful warmth of him infused her with courage. She leaned into him, kissed him back, tentatively at first, brushing his lovely mouth lightly with her lips. His guttural growl of approval gave her the courage to taste him with her tongue. His lips parted and, heart thumping, she delved deeper. He tasted of wine and honeyed tea. The scent of him, something darkly spicy, sandalwood, filled her nostrils and she inhaled deeply, savouring a perfume she would remember all of her days.

He encircled her in his arms, tangling his tongue with hers, until she could no longer think of anything, only feel the blood humming in her veins, the tingling in her fingers and toes, the heaviness in her breasts.

The hand on her back moved in circles, comforting and caressing. The other caressed the dip of her waist, the curve of her hip, in respectful delicious strokes. Never had she felt so female, so womanly, so sensually alive. So desirable.

He drew back with the slightest of sighs. Resignation. Regret. He gave her a small half smile. 'As pleasurable as this is, you strike me as a woman not in need of added complication. You deserve far more than I have to offer. I'm sorry.'

Idiot. He was too kind to hurt her feelings with the

truth. He didn't want her in that way. A well-set-up man like him no doubt had all sorts of women with whom he could choose to be intimate. He'd come to dinner out of politeness and she, an ungainly lonely widow, had thrown herself into his arms. He must think her so pathetic. The cold chill of shame spread outwards.

She pinned a bright smile to her lips. 'I will bid you goodnight, then.'

She bustled about, fetching his hat and gloves from the peg behind the door. 'You must be looking forward to seeing your family. It is always good to be with loved ones during the holidays,' she babbled, urging him towards the door. 'I don't expect I will see you again, before you leave,' she said briskly, 'so I would wish you a safe and pleasant journey.' She risked a glance at his face. His expression gave nothing away.

He took her hand and bowed low. 'Thoughts of you and your kind welcome into your home will keep me warm on the journey, Mrs Melford,' he murmured as he brought her hand to his mouth. He brushed her knuckles with warm dry lips. She drew in a quick startled breath and he let her hand go.

'Mrs Melford. Cassie—' He shook his head. 'Please, give my best wishes to Miss Lucy and Miss Diana.' He stepped out into the night. Snowflakes whirled around him. And then he was gone, nothing left to show his presence but large bootprints in the snow. Those, too, disappeared quickly.

Her heart thundered in her ears with embarrassment at how forward she'd been. She had shocked him with her wanton behaviour. By seeking more, she had lost his friendship.

Regret was an aching sadness.

Chapter Four

Overnight, the countryside had turned pillowy and white while the skies continued to threaten more snow. Cassie picked her way to the potting shed after spending the morning with the girls on their lessons. Forcing herself to think of nothing but the task at hand, she took down the candle racks, avoiding a glance at the mistletoe hanging from the beam. She separated each pair of candles by cutting the wicks in the middle. Against her will, her mind wandered back to the one person she should not be thinking about. The sweetness of his kisses. His honourable behaviour in light of her brazenness.

Any woman would count herself lucky to be married to Adam Royston. She suffered a pang at the thought of him taking a wife. She had no right to think that way. No reason, either.

She glanced out of the window at Diana and Lucy scampering about in ankle-deep snow making what they had ambitiously named a snow dame.

She heaved a sigh. Had Adam—no, she really should think of him as Mr Royston—got away to an early start? The ache of longing in the centre of her chest was sadness at knowing their paths would never cross again, but she

did not blame him for not calling in this morning. Their
parting the previous evening had been strained to say the
least. Still, she could not help hoping he'd arrived home
safely. During the long hours of the night she'd come
to terms with his rejection and her respect for him had
grown. A scoundrel would have taken advantage of her
loneliness. And yet she had the feeling he, too, was lonely.

She shook off her fit of the doldrums and carefully
wrapped a pair of candles in brown paper and tied them
with string. The batch must be ready for Mr Driver when
he came at the first of the year. Hopefully he would get a
good price for them, since she and the girls would need
a new place to live.

She didn't want to leave. But Adam's warning must
not be ignored.

'Mama!' Lucy came running into the potting shed.
'There's a man coming up the garden path.'

Adam? Her heart clenched. Joy sparkled through her
veins. He had come to bid her farewell after all. Oh,
how could she face him? How could she not, when seeing him one last time would give her so much pleasure?
A painful pleasure.

Lucy clenched her hands together in front of her chest,
her eyes wide. 'I think it's Herbert.'

Cassie's heart stopped, then staggered to life with an
unsteady rhythm. 'Herbert?'

Lucy made a face of distaste. 'I think so.'

'Take your sister indoors and remain upstairs.'

Lucy dashed off.

Heart pounding in her ears, Cassie removed her apron
and strode for the door. As she opened it, she almost collided with the stocky man standing on the threshold. The
brown scarf wrapped around his neck and pulled up over
his chin, exposed only the skin of his wind-reddened

cheeks, drawn-down sandy eyebrows and his distinctive retroussé nose.

Her stomach fell away. She took a breath. Squared her shoulders. 'Herbert,' she said coldly. 'To what do I owe this pleasure?'

Herbert slowly unwound his scarf, looking about him. He gave her a rueful smile. 'Is that any way to greet your only stepson? How are you, dear Lady Cassandra? At last I find you.' He wagged a reproving finger with a teasing smile. 'Good wheeze that, changing your name. Took me for ever to track you down.'

Too bad he had succeeded. 'Why are you here?'

'Come now. I know you were on the outs with me and Bridget over a trifle, but there's no need to cut up so stiff.'

He sounded so placatory, it gave her a sensation of dread in her stomach. 'I don't call your wife locking Diana in her bedroom and threatening to beat Lucy a trifle, Herbert.'

He gave a sorrowful shake of his head. 'Bad form. Bridget should not have flown into a temper. It won't happen again. I promise.' He gave her a blinding smile. 'Now, pack up their things and come along. We'll rent a carriage, be off in the shake of a cat's tail and all be comfortable at home in a trice. What do you say?'

Comfortable was not how she would describe the Norton household beneath Bridget's autocratic rule. But Herbert seemed genuinely sorry for his wife's behaviour.

While he waited for her answer, Herbert strolled around her little shed, poking a finger among the things on the table. He picked up a pair of candles ready for wrapping and tossed them from hand to hand. 'Did you make these yourself?'

'It is how we have been supporting ourselves this past year.'

'Very industrious, dear Stepmama. Not the sort of thing one generally expects of a lady.' He tossed them again. Fumbled.

She gasped.

He managed to catch them before they fell to the granite floor. 'Oops,' he said with a smile that bordered on sly. He put the candles down with exaggerated care. 'Wouldn't want to break them.'

Wouldn't he? Her nape prickled.

He turned to face her full on. 'Ready to go? Tally ho, what?'

He thought he was a gentleman, but compared to Lord Portmaine's steward, Adam Royston, he was nothing but a caricature.

'I should have thought you would be glad to be rid of the expense of keeping us,' she said, holding her ground. 'You were always grumbling about the cost.'

His shoulders stiffened. He hated resistance. 'I am their brother. Their legal guardian. Of course I am not glad they've run off. How do you think that makes me look? The Vicar...'

Understanding dawned. 'Old Mr Pettigrew wants to know what became of us, doesn't he? Poor Herbert.' Vicar Pettigrew had been a friend of his father's and not backward in his criticisms of Herbert's wild behaviour. He would see it as his duty to haul Herbert over the coals if he thought he'd neglected his duty to his sisters.

'Nosy old buzzard,' Herbert said. He gave her a wheedling smile. 'What do you say, old thing? Bury the hatchet and come home?'

With Ivy Cottage no longer available, it almost seemed like the best thing they could do. Almost.

'And you promise Bridget will leave me fully in charge

of your sisters?' In addition to being their unpaid house-keeper. 'No more punishments?'

'Promise.'

Cassie glimpsed a hint of triumph his expression, though he quickly hid it. Unease slid down her spine. 'Why now, Herbert? After more than a year? What has happened to set you haring off after us now? You receive the allowance your father arranged for the girls. Surely you are better off without them.'

'Better off?' His smile faltered, though he tried hard to hang on to it. 'We miss you.'

She did not believe him.

He must have seen it on her face. 'Pettigrew wrote to the solicitor Papa used in London about not seeing the girls. He's travelling to Nottingham, despite my assurances all is well. Wants to see them for himself before he hands over any more blunt next quarter-day.'

Finally, the truth. 'Why do you care? It's a pittance compared to your income from the mills.'

He glared at her, picked up the knife she used to cut her wicks and turned the blade so it caught the light. 'The factories are not doing too well. No demand for cloth now the war is over.' He grimaced. 'I had a run of bad luck at the tables.' He put the knife down with a lift of one shoulder. 'Debts of honour. A gentleman always pays his debts.'

A true gentleman looked after his womenfolk. But Herbert wouldn't see it that way. His concern had always been for himself. For his standing with the men he called friends. He didn't give sixpence for the welfare of his sisters. 'I'm sorry for your troubles, Herbert, but I think we are better off here.'

He lunged for her. Quick as a snake. Grabbed her

arm. 'You will tell my sisters to come with me now if you know what is good for you.'

She pulled her arm free. Backed away. 'What are you talking about?'

Cheeks red, he glowered. 'If you don't, I'll be swearing out a warrant for your arrest.'

Her heart thundered. 'For what crime? Stealing your sisters? I am sure the solicitor will be interested to hear how you misappropriated their funds.'

He waved off her accusation as if it was nothing. 'For stealing the family jewels.'

She gasped. Stared at him. 'I took nothing that was not mine.'

'The jewels you sold were my mother's. I have a hundred witnesses to say they were. Including old Pettigrew.'

'They were my bride gift from your father to me personally.'

'Prove it.'

She couldn't. The jewels had not been mentioned in her husband's will. Nor had Pettigrew known Clifford's first wife.

Triumph beamed from Herbert's face. 'And then of course there is the money you took from my desk in the study.'

Throat suddenly dry, she swallowed. Her shoulders sagged. She could see from his expression that he knew he had her in a cleft stick. She had no proof the jewels were hers to sell. Or that she had not taken his money. She'd have to let him take the girls or risk prison.

He stepped closer, his smile triumphant. 'Well, Lady High and Mighty. If you care for your liberty and your life, stop this nonsense and come home with me now.'

Hot fury coursed through her veins. She snatched up the broom leaning against the wall. 'Out! Get out.'

It wouldn't be the first time she had given Herbert a trouncing. He also clearly recalled the occasion he'd attempted a slobbery kiss and she'd slapped his face. He backed away. He narrowed his eyes, while maintaining a safe distance.

'You leave me no choice, then. I will be back with the authorities and we will see who has the upper hand.' His smile widened. 'Oh, and what it this I hear in the village, dear Stepmama, about the friendly widow and her landlord? Not a good example to set two young girls, is it? Or to impress the courts.'

She stared at him, mouth agape. 'Sir Josiah was an octogenarian.'

'My father was not much younger. That is your method, is it not? Marry an old man and pilfer his money.' He waved an airy hand. 'It is all a great heifer like you could possibly hope for. Too bad this one died before you had a chance to get him to the altar.'

Her face flamed. Herbert really knew how to twist a knife in an opponent's breast. 'Leave before I do something you will regret.'

'With pleasure. But make no mistake, I shall return.' He bowed. 'I wish you good day, dearest Stepmama.'

He swaggered off.

Rage mingled with fear blocked her throat. Blood roared in her ears. She couldn't breathe. Couldn't think. She put down the broom and walked out to the lane to be sure Herbert was gone. He would be back with the magistrate. No doubt about it, if he was that desperate for funds. But not today. Sir Josiah's death meant there wasn't a magistrate closer than fifteen miles.

She swallowed. Thank heaven Mr Royston had departed before her stepson's arrival. The shame of him hearing those terrible accusations of theft would have nigh killed her.

She ran back into the house. 'Girls,' she called out. 'Start packing. We leave first thing in the morning.'

'But tomorrow is Christmas Eve,' Diana wailed from the top of the stairs.

Standing at the bottom, watching her, Lucy's face showed sadness and understanding. Emotions far too old for such a young child. 'I'll help you, Diana. It will be fun. We'll sing carols while we fold.'

Curse the unfairness of it all. Damn Herbert, she would not let him win.

The snow had stopped. Adam stared out into the darkness, looking across the lawns he could not see, staring in the direction of Ivy Cottage, wondering what Cassie was doing. Tomorrow he'd go. He was packed and ready to leave at first light. He wouldn't let another day pass and risk his father sending out a search party. Hopefully it would stop snowing by morning. He unbuttoned his jacket with a sigh.

He should have left that morning, but after a night of dreams, some bad, some ridiculously erotic involving a certain woman whose gorgeous body he adored and whose feelings he'd hurt, he had finally dropped deep asleep near dawn. Naturally, he'd woken at noon, far too late to think of setting out. He'd also recalled that he hadn't finished going through the last of old Sir Josiah's ledgers.

Excuses.

He'd spent the balance of the day arguing with himself about whether he should or should not pay one more visit to Ivy Cottage. So why had he walked away last night? Going to bed alone, when he could have been in the arms of a warm and willing woman, made little sense. She wasn't after a husband. He liked her, perhaps more than he'd liked any woman, even—

Shocked, he stilled. Guilt swamped him.

He clenched his fist and pressed the side of it against the cold glass. How could he think of liking any woman better than Marion? It wasn't possible he could be so disloyal.

A twinkle of light flickered through the trees.

He frowned. Usually he could see nothing of the cottage from this window at night. Only in daylight did the smoke rising above the trees from its chimney give its presence away. Perhaps it was some sort of trick of the light, reflection on snow.

The light seemed to grow brighter. And it was flickering in an odd… Fire!

He raced downstairs, grabbed up his overcoat and gloves and was outside in minutes. He ploughed through drifts that in some places were shin deep. His heart thumped painfully in his chest. The cold stung his ears and his cheeks. His frosty breath was whipped away by the wind. A wind that would fan flames.

Blast. He had to be in time. He would not let it be otherwise.

He turned up the narrow lane to the cottage. Flames had already engulfed the interior of the lean-to shed and were now licking up through its thatched roof. A thick oily smoke filled the air. Sparks flew about on the wind and landed on the roof of the cottage. Thank God for the layer of snow. Where the hell was Cassie? And the girls?

He banged on the door. 'Cassie,' he yelled.

No answer. One of the upstairs casements was ajar. The smoke from the fire would have trickled inside, stunning the occupants or worse. His heart lurched. Fear set his heart thumping and his brain racing. He ran to what was left of the woodpile, found the axe, broke open the kitchen door, horrified to see flames eating through the parlour wall. He tore upstairs.

At the top he found Cassie, coughing and struggling on the landing with a girl on each arm. He swept the girls up and carried them downstairs, depositing them in the kitchen. Smoke billowed through the room. He closed the parlour door as Cassie arrived, still coughing with her arms full of coats. 'Boots by the back door,' she gasped.

Together they got the bleary-eyed shivering girls into their outerwear and outside into the lane. The girls clung to each other.

'Wait here,' Adam said. 'I'll see if I can put out the fire.' He ran to the back of the house. The shed was little more than a pile of collapsing timber, but only one wall of the parlour was affected, the one adjoining the shed. Someone must have boarded up a window in that wall when the shed was added.

Cassie rounded the corner. 'Heaven help us.'

'Buckets,' Adam said.

'In the kitchen. I'll get them. You work the pump.' She dived through the back door hanging precariously off its hinges.

Adam pumped a steady stream of water into the two buckets Cassie brought. Without words they worked together. While he took one bucket to the fire, she filled the next.

Slowly, slowly the smoke lessened and he became aware of the two little girls standing in the corner of the yard shivering and cold with tears running down their faces.

'I think we are done here,' he said to Cassie. 'Take the girls into the kitchen and get them out of the wind.'

She stopped pumping and blinked as if the words made no sense.

He gave her a little push towards the back door. 'Take the girls inside and pass me a lantern so I can make sure there are no lingering embers.'

She nodded and led the girls back into the house, returning seconds later with a lamp. She patted his arm in thanks, but also as if to reassure herself he was real before going indoors.

He crossed the yard and peered inside the shed. It was little more than a burnt-out shell. Nothing left but scorched beams overhead and on the floor, ashes, burnt bits of wood and lumps of melted metal.

Something glittered in the lamplight. He gazed down, then crouched to get a better look. Now, what were bits of glass from a broken lamp doing outside when the fire had started within? He forced himself not to think of what might have happened if he hadn't arrived to help. With the parlour also catching fire, Cassie might not have got the girls out in time.

He glanced around the little courtyard. There were footprints in the snow, small ones, his larger ones, and some he could not identify. Lamp held high, he walked out of the back gate. He could see where he had run into the yard. And he could see where the other prints came and went from the direction of the village, not from Thornton House. They'd appeared since it stopped snowing some time after dusk. He'd bet his now-ruined best boots that this fire was no accident.

Mrs Melford had an enemy.

Perhaps he would not be leaving in the morning after all.

He doused the remains of the shed and the burnt part

of the parlour wall with several more buckets of water before returning to the chilly comfort of the smoky kitchen.

Cassie glanced up, her eyes full of despair.

'Is it out?' Diana asked, her eyes huge.

'Yes.'

'It stinks in here,' Lucy said.

'I know,' Adam said. 'You are all going to come with me to Thornton House.'

Cassie stared at him. 'We couldn't possibly trespass—'

'You cannot stay here.' He didn't want to scare her, but he would if he had to make her see reason. 'What if the fire starts up again?' Or whoever set the fire came back.

She blanched. 'Very well. We will stay at Thornton until the morning. At which time we will be leaving as planned.'

It was then he noticed the valises on the floor in the corner. He narrowed his eyes. 'You never mentioned you were leaving so soon?'

Her gaze slid away. 'I decided we should go after you informed me Thornton is to be sold.'

A lie. She was afraid for some reason. That settled it, he was going to get to the bottom of the fire and find out exactly what Cassie feared.

Realisation swept through him. For the first time in years he felt tenderness, the need to protect, the longing to care for someone.

Something he'd never expected to feel again.

Not that he expected or deserved that she should care about him. He didn't. But he would do everything in his power to make sure she was safe.

Chapter Five

While she'd made the beds in Thornton's guest chambers and put the girls to bed, Adam had lit fires in the bedrooms and the kitchen. And now he had tea sitting ready for her when she came downstairs to bid him goodnight. She sank onto a chair with a sigh.

He put the teapot in the middle of the table with an understanding smile. 'Your daughters are as courageous as their mother.'

He was trying to bolster her spirits and she could not help but once again be struck by his kindness. 'They are good girls,' she said, hoping he would put the roughness in her voice down to the smoke from the fire and not her overwrought emotions. It wasn't until she had put the girls to bed moments ago that she had realised how few choices remained. The fire had destroyed any hope she might have had of supporting herself and the girls until the bees were ready to give up their honey once more.

The sharp glance he gave her let her know her hope was in vain, but at least he left her with her dignity by not commenting. He sat down beside her on the bench far closer than a man who was not a relation should sit and she took comfort from his large warm presence. It wasn't as if they were strangers. They had kissed after all.

'Is there someone who might seek to injure you and the girls?' he asked, pouring tea into their mugs.

Her breathing hitched. She tried to hold his searching gaze. 'Why would you say such a thing?'

He added cream and sugar and stirred for them both, pushing a mug at her. 'Cassie, the fire was no accident.'

She closed her eyes briefly, fighting for composure, for calm. If she told him the truth, that she had stolen two little girls from their legal guardian, he would likely be horrified. Any man would. 'Why would you think so? I must have spilled some wax. Or burning soot fell from the chimney after I damped down the fire.'

His lips thinned and he shot her a disbelieving glance. 'Someone deliberately tossed a lit lamp through the window. I found glass outside and footsteps in the snow.'

A feeling of panic threatened to swamp her. Herbert could have burned them in their beds. She could not believe that had been his intention. He'd merely meant to frighten her into going back. But with Herbert's accusations of theft, did she dare tell Adam the whole story? She had no proof of her innocence and everything she had done since leaving Nottingham spoke to her guilt. 'It might have been lads from the village playing a prank. A group of them let Mr Driver's bull in with his cows this summer.'

He sipped at his tea thoughtfully. 'If so, it was a prank that could have had far more serious consequences than a few gravid cows.'

She wanted to sip at her tea, too, but feared her hands were trembling too much. 'Boys are extremely foolish when they get together in a gang.'

'Then I will have a word with the local magistrate first thing in the morning.'

She swallowed. The local authorities were the last thing she needed at her door. 'I can do it if you wish.'

He looked angry, but also sad. 'I think not. The cottage is my responsibility.'

She ducked her head, avoiding that penetrating emerald gaze. 'I beg your pardon. I am used to looking after my own affairs...it is kind of you to care.'

'Strange you had already decided to leave though, hmm?' His voice was a low growl.

Her heart stumbled. He suspected her of something. 'A coincidence.'

Scepticism coloured his expression. 'Where do you go from here?' He took a breath. 'I know it is not my business, but I need to know you and the girls are not wandering the highways and byways in the middle of winter without a destination in mind.'

He was not going to let her go without assurances she would be all right and something like tenderness stole through her at his caring. While she could give him nothing else, she should at least give him the assurances he seemed to need.

'I have friends not far distant who will give me shelter until I can find a new property to rent.' Lies upon lies. But it was the best she could do right now.

His fingers tightened around his mug and then relaxed. 'What friends?'

She shook her head. 'Adam, we have to end this. Now.'

His face shuttered. 'Then there is no more to be said.'

'I would ask you for something,' she said softly. 'I would request that you ask Lord Graystone to have someone care for my bees in the spring.' Her voice broke. 'I am more than sorry to have to leave them. They have been good to me.'

'I will do what I can,' he said, his voice gruff, diffident, perhaps even disappointed.

Having given his word, he would do his very best, she knew. He was that sort of man.

Adam hated the idea someone trying to harm Cassie and her daughters. He also hated the idea of her travelling alone to these vague friends she had mentioned, but there was little he could do if she refused his offer of aid.

He put his arm around her shoulders, drew her close against his side. And thank all the heavenly beings she leaned against him as if drawing from his strength. Warmth flooded his deepest reaches, gratitude that she would accept this small token of support.

'What about money?' he asked. 'Do you have enough?'

She winced. She tried to hide it, but he was beginning to understand these little reactions of hers. 'You don't, do you?'

'I would have been fine, once the rest of my candles were sold. But...' Bleakness coloured her voice. Resignation. As if she'd come to an unpleasant decision.

'I have money put aside.' More than he'd need in several lifetimes, not counting what he would later inherit.

'I can't take your money.'

'A loan, then, to be repaid when you are settled.'

'Why? Why do you want to help me? We barely know each other.' She was clearly as bewildered as he was himself.

And yet he did understand, somewhat. 'Because I was taught that a man with honour should always help a lady in distress. And...' Honesty won out over platitudes. 'Because I find you attractive. I like you and it would haunt me if I thought I should have done more to help.'

'You are a good man, Adam Royston,' she whispered. 'If we had met at some other time…'

She cupped his jaw in her hand. A capable hand, work-roughened, yet small in comparison to his large paws. A gentle touch. Something lacking from his life as a rule. A siren's call to his lonely soul. He could not stop himself from gazing at her plush pink lips, from recalling the delicious feel of them beneath his own.

Her eyelids fluttered, as if she, too, recalled their last delicious melding. Her hand slipped around his neck, her body twisting towards him so her breasts brushed against his chest, her spine arching, her fingers combing through his hair. She kissed him.

Considerations of honour made a swift if weak appearance. And yet she had made it quite clear she would not accept any sort of permanent liaison. A gentleman should not argue with a lady, not one he desired and respected as much as he did this one, and who so obviously desired him. Not with regard to a kiss at least.

She was a widow with knowledge and experience, not an *ingénue*. A warm generous woman whom, to his great surprise, he'd become inordinately fond of in a very short space of time. More than fond. Much more than fond. And for reasons that went far beyond her outward appeal.

On her lips he tasted sweetness, despite the lingering odour of the fire, and beneath that was her scent, the earthiness of beeswax, the sweetness of honey mingled with the perfume of roses. No matter how long he lived, those scents would remind him of this moment, this kiss and this woman. He let himself enjoy it to the full, let it sweep all thoughts from his mind.

* * *

Kissing Adam was like drinking too much champagne. He made her feel warm all the way to her toes. And fluttery inside. She'd expected another refusal, but he deepened the kiss, sending pleasure rippling to the very tips of her fingers. Along with deep sensual longing.

She drew back and gazed into his eyes, smoothing his hair back from his face, enjoying the silky feel beneath her hand and the warmth of his gaze. 'I kept thinking of you yesterday. Imagining you on the road far from here.'

His expression became rueful. 'I was thinking about you, too.'

Perhaps he regretted their parting after all? 'You must have thought me dreadfully bold,' she said diffidently.

'Not dreadful. Lovely.' He kissed the tip of her nose. 'The timing was...wrong.'

'Because you have to leave.'

He nodded slowly. 'Partly.'

'And now I, too, am leaving.' An ache pierced her heart. 'Even though we have known each other such a very short time, I will miss you.'

He inhaled. A deep indrawn breath. 'Gads,' he said, 'we both smell of smoke.'

A change of topic. A man avoiding uncomfortable emotion.

'We do.' She pulled back, embarrassed by her boldness. 'I'll bathe the girls in the morning. They were too exhausted tonight. I fear your sheets will need laundering. I will do them before I go.'

'You will not. I will make arrangements.' He hesitated. 'No doubt you are terribly tired also.'

'I am, but I fear I shall not sleep given all that has happened.'

'Worry does that to a person.' For a man he was very

understanding. Sweet. Caring. The kind of man who would make a wonderful husband. She repressed a surge of longing. She could not marry anyone, not with all the complications of her life.

'Will you let me show you something?' he asked.

'If you wish.'

He put an arm about her waist and they left the kitchen with its gleaming rows of pots reflecting the glowing fire in the hearth, traversed a passage beyond a scullery and entered a large square chamber with whitewashed walls and a trestle table beside an enamelled sink.

'My, it is warm in here,' she said.

He let go her hand and lifted the lid of a large tin-lined wooden tub. 'What do you think?'

'This is where I am to do the laundry?'

He grinned. 'Guess again.' He pulled out several large linen sheets from a cupboard and lined the tub. He turned a lever on a pipe running up the wall. Water began to flow. Steaming hot water. 'As long as the fire in the kitchen is alight, the water in the cistern behind it is hot. Sir Josiah liked his bath and his servants were too old to carry water up to his room so he had this installed.' He turned a second lever and adjusted the flow of both. 'This water comes from the well.'

She peered over the edge of the tub. A wooden ledge ran around its circumference about a third of the way up the sides. 'A seat?'

'Mmm,' he said, stirring in a deliciously scented oil and adjusting the levers. The water continued to fill the tub, creeping upwards until it was more than half full. He turned off the water.

The idea of soaking in a tub of hot water was just too irresistible. 'This is marvellous. Are you saying I may use it?'

'Of course. There is soap on the shelf back there. Not very feminine, I'm afraid, but better than the scent of smoke.' He went to another cupboard. 'Dash it. No towels. I must have used the last one earlier this evening. I know where there are more.' He strode off.

Cassie dipped her fingertips in the water. Perfect. And the scent was lovely. Sandalwood. An earthy manly scent that reminded her of him. She stared at the water. Dare she? It would be terribly wicked. But what had being good ever got her? An old irascible husband. A stepson who hated her. It had brought her the girls she loved as if they were her own, though. If she could only find a way to keep them.

Again, her mind began whirling with thoughts, options, plans and, worst of all, worries. Adam was right, a bath would help her relax, perhaps even help her to sleep. Trying to deal with two girls on a long journey while bone tired was not something to contemplate with equanimity.

And travelling with the smell of smoke tainting her every breath would only make it worse. She pulled the pins from her hair and set to work on removing her gown. Before leaving the cottage, she'd exchanged her nightgown for the only thing left unpacked, the comfortable old-fashioned sack dress she had planned to wear on the journey. It fastened with a bow at the neck and a tie under the bust. It took her no more than a moment to step out of the gown and fold it. Next she stripped off her stockings. She hadn't bothered with stays when she had dressed so quickly, but should she keep her shift on? If she did, it would never dry by morning. She didn't have enough clothes to be leaving any behind. Hearing no sound of Adam returning, she whipped it off over her head. She climbed up the steps and threw one leg over the rim of the tub. The water was just hot enough to make her toes tingle.

A moment later, her foot stopped complaining about the heat and she brought the other leg over. Using the seat to step down, she immersed herself to her neck, the deliciously scented steam rising around her. Blissful. Sir Josiah had known a thing or two about pleasure. The warm twinkle in his eye had given him away. The old rogue. A kindly old rogue. He had been good to her, though he might not have been so kind if he had known she had told him nothing but lies.

Adam breezed through the door. His gaze sought her and when he found her already ensconced in the tub, he stilled. His face sported a grin. 'Is it to your liking, my lady?'

Her heart stopped beating. How did he know?

His smile fled. 'What is wrong?'

Oh, merciful saints, he was teasing her, not using her title. 'Nothing is wrong. It is perfect. Heavenly.' Only one thing would make it better. Her heart beat a rapid tattoo at the boldness of the thought that popped into her mind. 'Why don't you join me? You smell as bad as I did.'

Gah! That was hardly inviting or seductive. The shock on his face made her squirm. 'We will have to be up early in the morning,' she added in a rush. 'I thought you might prefer not to wait, since you must be as tired as I am.'

Dash it, she was babbling. Making things worse. 'I'll be as quick as I can,' she mumbled and grabbed for the soap.

All his erotic fantasies, every single one of them, had taken on lush female form. The skin on her face and shoulders had a lovely rosy glow, from embarrassment and the heat from the water. The arm rising above the rim of the tub was the most graceful limb he had ever seen and the thought of the rest of her naked below the surface of the water had him as hard as a rock. And... she was naked. It hadn't taken him a second to spot the fine lawn chemise folded with her gown or to understand the meaning of those bare, elegantly sloped shoulders.

And now she was inviting him to join her.

He'd managed to walk away the previous evening, but tonight he did not have the strength and not just because the offer would never come again. Indeed, he was surprised she was giving him a second chance. He certainly wouldn't have been so generous.

She had given him so much joy these past few days, far more than he deserved and she deserved that he return the favour, if she would allow it. 'I would love to join you.'

He turned his back and stripped off, very much aware of her interested gaze. It reminded him of the first time he had undressed after his wedding. Only then there had been a whole lot of blushing by both parties and giggles. They'd been so young and innocent. Heedless.

The recollection seemed more like a distant memory than usual. Less painful. Something to be thought of fondly rather than avoided. He turned around.

Her gaze took him in with obvious interest. She licked her lips as if they'd dried, or, given the flush on her face and the intensity of her gaze, as if she'd seen something she might like to taste. He strode across tiles cold beneath the soles of his feet.

She shifted along the seat to give him room to step down, her gaze rising to his face, her lips curving in a smile of welcome. He blushed like a damned schoolboy and sank into the water. Their thighs touched beneath the water. This close, he could see the rise of her gloriously full breasts and the darker rose of their peaks. He had either landed in heaven or hell. It would be up to her to decide which.

With a sigh she leaned back, her head resting on the edge of the tub. 'This is wonderful. One would never expect such decadency from the oldest knight in the county. I wonder how it works?'

A prosaic topic, likely deliberate so as to hide her modest blushes, though her use of the word *decadent* was inspiring all kinds of wicked thoughts in his head. 'I haven't quite worked out its exact workings, but gravity seems to have some part to play with the help of valves in strategic places and a constant supply of water from an underground stream.'

'Fascinating.'

Whereas a débutante might have yawned the word to ensure no one took her for a bluestocking, Cassie appeared genuinely interested.

'A local fellow put it together,' he said. 'I found his name and the bill for his services amidst Sir Josiah's papers. I am thinking of asking him to come to Portmaine Court and investigate the feasibility of something similar there.' He realised his error. 'If the earl approves, that is.'

She didn't seem to notice his hastily added amendment; lazily opening her eyes, she gave him a blindingly beautiful smile. 'He needs only to try it to approve. He might even decide to move in here.'

He wanted her to move in. With him. He stretched out a hand and laced his fingers with hers, brought her hand to his lips. 'It is too bad neither of us can stay.'

Her smile dimmed a fraction. 'Then we should make the most of the time we have.'

Thank you, all the gods on Mount Olympus. 'We should wash your hair.' Her hair was a glorious golden mass, the ends floating on the top of the water like the trailing fronds of an exotic water plant. He loved the way it flowed around her in silky waves.

She cast him a glance aslant. 'We?'

He leaned over the edge of the tub and held up a bucket. 'If I fill this with clean warm water, I can tip it over you once you have lathered.'

'Hence the "we".' She reached for the soap and sniffed at it. 'Nice.'

He leaned over and inhaled. 'Sir Josiah's. I'm sorry it is all we have.'

'I like it.'

It was what he had used on his hair and body earlier. And would again now. The idea of sharing something so personal was both arousing and endearing. A sweetly painful pull in the region of his chest made his breath catch.

She quickly worked up a lather in her palms before she handed him the sliver of soap and worked the suds into her hair.

'Let me,' he said, seeing she already needed more soap. He used the piece of soap directly on her hair, working it in, splashing up more water as needed.

'You have done this before.'

'I was married, once.' And until now he had forgotten the pleasure of such intimate moments marriage brought with it. Or he hadn't wanted to recall.

He used the tips of his fingers to massage in the soap, firmly enough to cause her to turn her back and give him better access. She sighed and leaned back languidly against his shoulder as he continue to work at her scalp. A small moan of bliss arrowed straight to his groin. His member gave a little pulse. Happy because she was pleased and more than happy because this was only the start. Or so he hoped.

An idea formed in his mind. Tenuous. Likely something which would not put him in good stead with the earl, but it made sense. It would solve his problem. At least he hoped she would agree, but he must not rush matters. He didn't want to ruin his chances.

'Lean back,' he said softly in her ear, holding one arm beneath her shoulders. 'Let us rinse off the worst of the soap.'

Without hesitation she complied and her magnificent breasts made a spectacular appearance, rising amid the bubbles now covering the surface of the water, causing him to become painfully hard. He forced himself to focus only on her hair, on running his fingers through the floating strands until they began to squeak. He lifted her back to sit on the ledge.

She beamed at him. 'Oh, my. That was simply lovely.'

'Let me finish the task, if you will.'

He picked up a small rag from the ledge and lathered it up. 'You know, in the old days washing a guest was often the duty of the daughter of the house.'

She cast him a look askance, though there was a teasing smile on her lips. 'Are you proposing I wash you?'

He raised his brows. 'You may if you wish, but I was thinking of it the other way around, since I am your host.'

'In the absence of your employer.'

His *employer* was very much in favour of the idea. He passed the cloth down her arm. Her eyes widened when he started at her throat and then worked down her chest and over her breasts. As he stroked the flannel across her delectable curves, he deliberately kept his mind blank. This was not about his pleasure, but about her enjoyment. She worked hard, looking after her daughters. She deserved pampering.

Chapter Six

This medieval form of bathing, Cassie thought dreamily as the cloth stroked down her inner arm and down the side of her torso, ought to be illegal, but she wouldn't have missed it for the world. The man excelled at the sensual seduction of the mind and the body, and that was before he had begun washing her.

'Other arm,' he said close to her ear.

The deep enticing murmur sent a shiver down her spine. A shiver of pleasure and anticipation that took up residence in places no lady acknowledged. And yet, as a married woman, she had heard talk of there being more delight to copulation than simply the begetting of children. For some women.

The care he took with his kisses gave her the sense that he was a man who would ensure his partner experienced more. She turned her body and held out her other hand, peering at him from beneath lowered lashes. The expression on his face was one of intense concentration, but, oh, his mouth, his lovely mouth, it had such a sensual cast as his gaze followed the motion of his hands down her arm, all the way to her fingertips and then upwards along the most sensitive skin of her inner arm, across her breasts and down her ribs to her stomach.

She couldn't move for the sheer unadulterated bliss of sensation, her skin dancing and prickling in anticipation of his touch and then sighing with pleasure as he soothed and stroked.

Would he go lower?

She tensed and he reached deeper into the water.

His hand wrapped around her ankle, drew it up and out of the water and rested her heel on his chest. Rough hair tickled the sole of her foot, the beat of his heart an erotic reminder of his nakedness. She let herself relax, her nape resting against the edge of the tub as he repeated his caresses on first one leg and then the other. She sank into the pleasure of the moment. Relaxed. Drifting on a river of delicious touches and strokes. Boneless. Mindless.

And when the cloth gently pressed between her thighs, she parted her legs and let his touch soothe her there, too. Soothe and arouse.

A moan escaped her lips.

He stroked again and parted her with his fingers, and his touch became firmer, more insistent, driving her somewhere she wasn't quite sure she wanted to go. She tensed, opening her eyes to discover he was watching her face, gauging her reaction. Her body seized. Her heart raced. 'Too much,' she gasped.

'Relax. Let it happen,' he said.

And then it did. Whatever it was, it shuddered through her, a shattering loss of self and then a rush of heat, leaving her breathless and limp. He caught her around the waist, pulled her close to his side, kissed her temple, her jaw, her lips.

'My sainted aunt,' she said when she finally had breath to speak at all. 'What on earth...?'

He gazed down at her, looking very pleased. 'Liked that, did you?'

'You are a wicked, wicked man.' And she was a very wicked woman, because she was very pleased, too. It was all she could do to prevent herself from sliding beneath the water, she felt so completely lax. And yet he had not... 'What about you? You did not...'

He smiled lazily. 'Watching you is all the pleasure I require.'

And yet there was something else in his voice. A sort of distance. As if he was intent on keeping himself apart, even as he gave her the greatest pleasure she'd ever experienced. It hurt, but she didn't know how to breach the wall he'd built to keep her out. Perhaps he did not find her equally desirable. Why had she even fooled herself into thinking he might?

While she debated just what she should say to fill the silence, he tossed the cloth over the side of the tub and slid under the water, washing his hair and body in quick efficient strokes. When he had finished his ablutions, he looked at her with lifted brows. 'I think it is time to rinse you off and get you out of here before the water cools and you catch a chill.'

So protective and thoughtful, her whole body sighed with contentment. She caught the thought midstream. Thoughtfulness in a man was to be encouraged, but not to the point where they believed they were indispensable. She'd proved she could manage perfectly well on her own. Yet, if she was honest, there was a great deal of loneliness in being independent. 'Good idea,' she said.

He retrieved the bucket and filled it from the tap, testing the temperature. 'Stand up.'

She froze. Him exploring her body beneath the water was one thing, but to expose what her mother had despairingly called her voluptuous proportions was quite another.

'Please,' he added, proving he was a man who saw that which she wished to hide. Her fear.

To prove him wrong, she rose to her feet. Seemingly unfazed by the sight of all of her, he tipped three buckets of warm water over her head and a couple over his own, then helped her out of the tub when she could have easily managed to step down. It seemed to give him pleasure to wrap first her body in a towel and then another around her hair. It also gave her a great deal of pleasure watching the muscles ripple beneath his skin as he patted and fussed over each inch of hers. It gave her a chance to admire the definition of his chest and abdomen, with its scattering of dark male hair and his magnificent arousal.

Why hadn't he wanted her to give him pleasure?

It was not the sort of thing one could ask. She picked up another large bath sheet and draped it over his shoulders, using the moment to hide her confusion. 'You need to dry off, too.'

She rubbed briskly at his back and he arched into her hand with a soft groan.

'Nice,' he said in a low belly-clenching growl.

So she moved on to his shoulders and his chest, trying not to notice his continuing state of arousal, yet secretly thrilled that even if *he* wasn't exactly willing, his body was interested. The man was certainly well endowed, though she had little experience by which to judge. Her husband had done his duty in the least possible time in the dark under the covers.

To her disappointment Adam stepped away. 'Your hair needs to dry before you go to bed.'

So much for his interest, though if she wasn't mistaken he was breathing faster than before.

He bent and fiddled with something around the back

of the tub. Water gurgled. The level in the tub slowly sank. 'It won't take long to empty.'

If he wanted to appear indifferent, she could play the same game. 'If this catches on, it is going to put a lot of footmen out of work.'

He looked at her thoughtfully, his lips tilting up at the corners. The merest hint of a smile appeared. 'I can see it now. Instead of weavers breaking machines, we will have footmen taking axes to bathtubs.' He picked up their clothes, looped his arm around her waist and led her back to the kitchen. He dropped the pile of clothes on a stool and gestured to the rug before the fire. 'Do you have a comb?'

She sank cross-legged to the floor, careful to keep her towel tidy. 'In my valise.' Which he'd carried upstairs to her chamber.

He reached for his coat and pulled one from his pocket. 'You can use mine, since it is handy.'

She unwrapped her hair and ran her fingers through the tangles, trying to separate the worst of them, then dragged the comb through.

'Let me,' he said, kneeling behind her and then sitting so his legs were each side of her hips. He gently pulled the comb through the ends of a clump and worked his way up to the roots. He was so gentle she felt not one jot of pain.

'You really would make an excellent lady's maid,' she said, smiling over her shoulder.

'My father does this for my mother. Sometimes I braided my wife's hair before bed.' His hands stilled.

She glanced back to catch an expression of longing on his face. And sadness.

'You miss her.'

His expression froze.

Her stomach dropped. 'I beg your pardon. I should not have—'

'It is all right,' he said harshly.

Clearly it was not all right. The man looked haunted. 'I am sorry, I should not have said what I did.'

'No. It really is all right. I don't know what brought it to mind. I haven't thought of it for years.'

Adam could not believe he had forgotten how much simple pleasure a man could find combing a woman's hair. Especially when she was sitting between his legs and was as gorgeous and voluptuous as this one. He'd missed the easy companionship of a wife. The fact that he could enjoy it with someone other than Marion should feel like a betrayal, but somehow it did not. It felt right. And good.

Too bad he'd only have this one chance to play maid for Cassie. He'd clearly reacted in a way that made her uncomfortable. He'd been surprised. And, yes, a bit sad at the thought that perhaps he was finally leaving Marion in the past. It had shocked him, too.

He lifted a strand of Cassie's hair to his nose and breathed in the clean scent of his personal soap. His blood tingled with pleasure at the idea of his scent on her body.

No matter their good intentions, all men truly were primitive beasts at heart.

He teased away at the rest of the tangles, trying not to think or feel. Soon this pleasure would be over and he'd be sending her off to bed. 'All done,' he said regretfully.

She shifted, her beautiful rounded posterior wedging itself tighter against his groin, against his rock-hard arousal. She must know the effect she was having on him.

The sultry glance she cast over her shoulder at that moment said she likely did. As did her kiss when she leaned back and cupped his cheek, turning her face towards him. They kissed.

Lovely. Sweet. And hellishly erotic.

'Will you make love to me tonight?' she asked softly against is mouth. 'Properly.'

The words heated his blood to boiling. Temptation was a hard knot in his stomach. And why not when she asked so sweetly?

'When are your menses due next?'

Heat washed along her cheek where their skin touched. A blush. Had her husband not talked to her about these things?

'In two days' time,' she said quietly.

'You are regular?'

A shy smile. 'Like a clock.'

'Then it should be safe.' *Thank all the stars shining in the heavens.* He let go a breath. 'There are no guarantees, though. You must promise me that if a child should result, you will come to me.'

He'd reveal his real name tomorrow. Regret filled him. When she knew who he was the easiness they'd found in each other's company would no doubt be lost. And that would be a shame. A piercing ache in his chest at the idea he might never see her again shocked him. Could he be... smitten? Surely not. That was the last thing he wanted. Another grand passion.

Still he would regret their parting. Perhaps rather than confess like a schoolboy, he would tuck his calling card in her pocket where she would find it later, along with her purse. He could not bear the thought of spoiling this moment by seeing her regard for him change to awe or, worse yet, cold calculation of his worth. He certainly did not want her to know he was the man who had decided to evict her. Better she discover that after he left.

He lifted her onto his lap and kissed her deeply. She sighed into his mouth and kissed him back far more confidently than before. What a delight she was. What an undeserved gift. With her still in his arms, he pushed to his feet. 'We are going to do this,' he whispered in her ear, 'in a soft feather bed and not on a cold hard floor.'

He carried her up the stairs to his chamber.

The man was immensely strong. She knew it intellectually, having observed him carry the Yule log, but this was entirely a more personal experience. Never in her wildest dreams had Cassie imagined being carried so effortlessly in a man's arms. Never dreamed such a thing would melt her from the inside out. She felt deliciously feminine. Sensual. Beloved? She squeezed her eyes shut for a moment, an effort to recapture reality.

Sensual would do perfectly well. It, too, was a novel experience.

'I can walk,' she said, hoping she did not sound as breathless as she felt. Or as regretful at the thought he might take her up on her offer.

'You will not trot about in chilly corridors wearing only a towel; not to mention you have bare feet, madam.'

She pressed her face into his shoulder to hide her smile. His tone might be brusque, but really, how long had it been since anyone cared so much as a jot for her comfort?

The door he stopped at was not her chamber. 'Hold tight,' he said, shifting her weight.

While she clung to his neck, he opened the door, kicking it closed behind them. Only the glow from the fire lit their way, but it was easy to see this was a room of grand proportions, with a huge four-poster bed, its sheets in a messy tumble.

He set her down gently in a large armchair beside the fire which he promptly attacked with a poker, causing flames to flare up, before adding more coal.

He turned to look at her and then glanced at the bed. 'I left in somewhat of a hurry when I saw the fire.'

'I appreciate you not stopping to make the bed.'

He grinned, a piratical flash of white teeth in the gloom. 'Give me a moment to warm the sheets.'

The pleasure of watching him work with brisk efficiency came as a surprise. What would it be like to be entitled to watch a young virile male go about his daily tasks? A privilege indeed.

And then he was sweeping her up in his arms again. He deposited her gently in the centre of the bed and pulled the sheet over her. Warm sheets. How luxurious.

'You should probably be rid of your towel before the sheets become damp.'

She wiggled out of the towel and dropped it over the side of the bed. 'Damp sheets would never do.'

As giddy as a schoolgirl, she watched him also divest himself of his bath towel. In the glow of the fire, he looked like a dark god of war, all carved muscle and flat planes outlined in shadow. A Zeus or an Atlas. He slipped beneath the covers, scooting right up along her length and lying on his side, his head propped on one hand. Delicious warmth rolled off him. He toyed with her hair where it spread out on the pillows, gazing into her face, his mouth a terrible temptation to her own.

'Comfortable?' he asked.

Comfortable, no. What woman could be comfortable in such a situation? But she was excited. Nervous. And happy, though it was tinged with the sadness of knowing they soon must part.

She stroked his hair back from his forehead and kissed his lips in answer to his question. He sighed deeply and kissed her back, coming up on his hand to bend over her. He took his time wooing her lips, causing her to rise up in impatience and better feel his hard warm chest against her breasts. Obligingly, he caressed first one breast, then the other, seemingly fascinated by their fullness, the way they filled his hand to overflowing. The tightness inside her body had her gasping for more. And when his mouth left hers and he kissed his way slowly across her face, lingering at her neck and moving on to the rise of her breast, she thought she might go mad with anticipation. She twisted her body to bring herself closer, to feel the sensation of skin against skin down the length of her body. The press of his hardness against her hip only served as further torture. Delightful torment.

Hot and wet, his mouth closed over her nipple and she moaned with the pleasure that arrowed low down as he suckled. His large warm hands roamed her body as if he would learn every contour. Too slow. The arousal he'd kindled in the tub and while combing her hair blazed out of control. Its heat scorched along her veins and settled deep in her vitals. Her core ached with need for him.

When his hand skimmed over the curls at the apex to her thighs, her hips rose in invitation. He cupped her and pressed down with the heel of his hand, shooting lightning bolts of heat to the very tips of her fingers. He eased first one finger, then another inside her, sending those same impossible, indescribable sensations rippling through her body. Wave after wave of pleasure. He rose over her, looking down into her face, nudging her thighs apart with one knee, then the other.

She wrapped her legs around his flanks and tilted her hips in overt welcome, pleased when his expression softened with a smile of gladness. Slowly, carefully, his gaze intent, watching her reaction, he penetrated her by gentle increments, pressing forwards and retreating until she could no longer focus on anything but the place where their bodies came together. Tension built to unimaginable proportions.

And yet he seemed to hold back some part of himself. Maintaining his control while she became a mindless creature of sensation and instinct. Something told her this was not how it was meant to be. She raised herself up and captured his mouth with hers, tasting and nibbling at his lips, exploring his mouth with her tongue, holding him close to her, until he sank down onto her with a groan that to her ears sounded like surrender, his weight pressing her deep into the mattress.

His thrusts became harder, stronger, faster, his breathing ragged gasps for air. She moved in unison, meeting each surge with arching hips until there was no separation of body or mind or spirit. A welling sense of wonder followed swiftly by deep affection brought tears to her eyes.

Why after all these years did she have to meet this particular man and fall in love? For there was no doubt in her mind that something deeper than pleasure had lodged in her heart.

The sensuality of the woman beneath him stole what was left of his brain and his control. Only instinct remained. A feral need to ensure she reached her climax before he let the urges gripping muscle, bone and sinew tear loose. The magnitude of his desire ached in every particle of his body.

'Come for me.' A hoarse whisper of desperation.

Unfocused, her gaze found his.

His heart stopped beating when he saw the glint of moisture at the corners of her eyes. Guilt tore a swathe through his chest.

'Sweetheart,' he croaked, barely reining in the need to move. 'What is wrong?' He rose up on one hand, determined to withdraw.

She looked bewildered. 'What?'

'You are crying.'

'Happy. Thrilled.' Her fingernails dug into his back. 'Don't you dare stop now.'

Relief rolled through him and pride that he'd brought her tears for such a reason. He buried himself to the hilt and reached the peak he had abandoned only seconds before. Her body tightened around him, sheathing him perfectly. And hot darkness beckoned. Beneath him she undulated, drawing him deeper. 'Adam?' Her eyes widened as a paroxysm shuddered through her body. He followed into the abyss of her lovely warmth.

'Cassie,' he groaned when he could breathe around the pounding of his heart. He collapsed to one side so as not to crush her, stroked her back and felt her snuggle against his shoulder. 'Everlasting saints, you have done for me.'

'And you for me,' she gasped, her body lax against him. 'I had no idea I could be so thoroughly undone. Shattered.'

Half dead as he was, he mustered a surge of anger against a husband who had never shown her pleasure. Anger tempered by satisfaction that he was her first real lover.

A comfortable silence existed between them. A satisfyingly comfortable silence. He kissed the point of her shoulder in gratitude for this cosy respite full of companionship and a tenderness deeper than anything he had known.

What he'd had with Marion had been larger than life. A grand passion, his mother had called it, looking troubled. A flame that had sparked instantly to life and, if he was brutally honest, had just as quickly burned itself out. What he felt for Cassie was an altogether different kind of affection, a banked fire that might well endure for aeons with enough care and attention.

If he was adequate to the task. He certainly had failed Marion in that regard.

'Thank you,' she said.

'For the kiss?'

'For everything. Your kindness. To the girls.' She patted his chest. 'Most especially your kindness to me,' she whispered shyly.

This was his *congé*, he realised with dismay.

'You deem this a kindness?' On his part it had been anything but kindness. Selfish lust was the best he could name it. Shame chilled him. 'Your husband neglected you.'

'My husband was an elderly gentleman when we married and his health was not good. And while he hoped for another son, he married me more as a caretaker of his daughters and his house than anything.'

'An unpaid caretaker, I assume.'

She stiffened slightly, subtly drew back.

He pulled her close again. 'I beg your pardon. Continue.'

The relief when she relaxed against him was wholly ridiculous, yet there it was.

'My hopes of marriage had dwindled after my first Season. Men do not like females built on gargantuan proportions, especially when they have no claim to beauty or fortune.'

'More fool them.' He kissed the top of her head while admiring the lush bounty barely hidden beneath the sheets. His body hardened. 'And if by beauty you mean the sort of insipidness women call pretty, that fades by the age of thirty, you should be glad. To me you are perfectly lovely.'

Her smile was a delight to behold, before she hid her face against his shoulder.

He waited for her to master her blushes and to continue her story, but he could not help smiling at her obvious pleasure.

Finally she glanced up at him. 'The offer from Clifford was my last hope of having a family of my own, but unfortunately I did not live up to expectations.'

'Expectations?'

'Things he hoped to gain from our union. More sons. Social connections for his heir. My family stuck to the letter of the settlements, barely, but…' she gave a small shrug '…vulgar is vulgar, and no one is *required* to welcome an outsider with open arms. When my husband died, I was not comfortable living with my stepson, so I took the girls and left.'

Something about her story stirred an understanding in his as yet soggy brain. 'Who is your family?'

She stilled as if realising she had given away something she preferred to keep secret. 'It doesn't matter.'

It mattered. A widow she might be, but, and the parts came together swiftly, she was also a woman from the nobility. 'What year did you come out?'

'I don't want to talk about it.' Her voice was barely above a whisper. 'It is all in the past. I married down. I am *persona non grata*.'

She spoke calmly, but there was bewilderment there,

too, and hurt. 'Why not go back to your family when your husband died?'

'My parents are gone. My brother might have taken *me* in, I suppose, but not the girls. I could not bear to leave them with Herbert and his wife. Their mother was a housemaid. Herbert's wife would have turned them into servants.'

Her loyalty to her stepdaughters deepened his admiration. 'The girls are fortunate to have you.'

'You don't have children, do you?'

To his endless sorrow.

'Adam? Do you have a child?'

Blast. He had hesitated a moment too long. 'My wife died while expecting our first child.' He spoke clinically, as he always did, though the pain of it was no less raw than it had been when it happened. That and the guilt.

'To lose a wife and baby is a terrible loss.'

A terrible sense of failure. 'I didn't know she was with child until after she died. I don't think she knew it, either, or I am sure she would not have risked...' He could not put into words the suspicion that had hung in his mind all these years.

'What happened to her?'

'I'd accepted an invitation to a house party in the country. For both of us. There was to be a boat race. I like to row. At the last minute, she decided she wanted to see a play in town with some friends. I was furious at the change of our plan.' He sighed. 'My plan. She insisted that if I loved her I would go to the play with her. I told her to stay in town and see her stupid play with her stupid friends. Did I tell you we were ridiculously young when we wed? Anyway, I went off in the closed carriage, thinking I would send it back for her and she could come when she wished. Or not.'

'Did you?'

He shook his head. 'Apparently, she changed her mind. Later that afternoon she had my phaeton put to, intending to surprise me. It was so like her to do something outrageous.' It had been her attraction from the very beginning. She'd infuriate him, then do something completely unexpected and make him mad for her all over again. 'She was an excellent whip, but the team was young and scarcely broken in. I told her not to attempt to take them out without me. I might as well have told her not to breathe. I wished to God I'd never bought them. She went off the road about ten miles from London. The fall broke her neck.'

He hadn't seen the accident scene. He'd been called to a nearby inn to identify her body. That was when the doctor had told him he suspected she'd been pregnant. It had been a bitter blow.

'You blame yourself.'

'I should have known better than to storm off that way. I should have guessed she'd come after me in some dramatic gesture.' He couldn't help his slight smile at the thought. Then he winced. 'Her father was pretty clear that I had failed in my husbandly duty to keep my young wife safe.'

She rose up on her elbow and looked down into his face. 'You feel guilty.'

'Hellishly guilty.'

'Oh, Adam. She also made choices that day.'

The sympathy in her voice made speech difficult. He didn't deserve sympathy. His hand curled into a fist.

'While she was railing at me for not loving her enough, I had this strange feeling she was right. That our marriage was a mistake. Afterwards I realised it was because I wanted my own way. Unforgivable selfishness.'

Nor did he ever again want direct responsibility for another person's welfare. His duty to the Portmaine estate was quite enough. 'So in answer to your question, no, I do not have children. And nor do I want them.'

She sighed and he knew he had disappointed her with his last statement. But at least he'd been truthful.

Reasonably truthful, because somehow these past few days with this woman made him want things he knew he didn't deserve. And for the first time in a long time, he didn't feel quite so angry. At himself. At Marion.

He swept her hair back from her face. 'You know, that is the first time I really talked about what happened. At least, how I felt about it. Thank you for being such a good listener.'

Chapter Seven

Surprised by the gratitude in his voice, Cassie smiled at him. He had listened to her, too. Yet she had not told him everything. He had asked her about who might mean her harm. Offered her aid. The longing to share her burdens was an ache in her chest. If she had learned one thing these past few days, she had learned Adam was an honourable man and not the sort to take advantage of his power. She would trust him with her life. He deserved the truth.

'My stepson found us yesterday. He is insisting I return the girls home.'

His breathing changed. His eyes became watchful. 'You think he set the fire.' His voice sounded harsh. 'I'll swear out a warrant against him for arson—'

'There is no proof. And he is the girls' only family.'

Adam glowered. 'You are their family.'

'Please, Adam. I do not want to involve the authorities. He is their legal guardian and I took them without permission. The authorities will take his part. If you drive us to catch a stagecoach tomorrow as you promised, we can go somewhere he cannot find us.'

'I can do better than that. Come home with me.' He

looked startled. As if he had surprised himself as well as her.

'You can't mean it.'

'I do. Indeed I do,' he said firmly. 'Cassie, there is something I must tell you—'

Loud banging echoed through the house. The doorbell clanged. Someone was at the front door.

'Oh, sweet periwinkles.' She sat up, clutching the sheet to her chest, her heart thundering. 'Can it be Herbert?'

Adam shot out of bed and looked out of the window. 'No carriage. You think it might be him?'

'I don't know. He went off to find a magistrate. I thought it would take him a couple of days at least. Time enough for us to be far away.'

The clanging came again. The banging louder.

Adam pulled on his shirt and breeches. 'Wait here.'

Her heart thundered as she listened to his footsteps on the stairs. If it was Herbert with a magistrate, what could Adam do? If he tried to stop them from searching the house, he might be charged with aiding a fugitive. At the very best, he would lose his position. Better she face the music than get Adam into serious trouble. All Herbert wanted was his sisters' money. It was nothing compared to a man's future.

She wrapped herself in the dressing gown she found cast over a chair and crept down the stairs to the sound of continued knocking. Why hadn't Adam opened the door? When she reached the bottom step, Adam emerged from the library. He shook his head at her. 'A man alone. Stay out of sight.'

She moved into the shadows.

He pulled open the door. 'What the devil do you mean, banging on my door at this time of night? It had better be something important.'

He sounded so autocratic she could almost believe he owned the house.

A red-faced Herbert shoved his way in. 'Where is she?' he shouted.

'Where is who?' Adam asked coolly. 'And who the devil are you?'

'Norton. Herbert Norton.' Herbert flourished his card. 'Be so good as to rouse Graystone at once. I know Lady Cassandra is here with my sisters. I followed their footprints from the cottage. I demand their return.'

Adam's shoulders stiffened. His back was all she could see of him in the light from the branch of candles he held, but she sensed his shock. 'Lady Cassandra?' Heard it in his voice.

Cassie stifled a groan. She hadn't given a thought to Herbert using her title, but then he liked to consider himself part of the nobility by association. It was another of the reasons he'd insisted she live under his roof. He liked trotting her out to impress his friends with important relations.

'My stepmother. Well, fellow! Are you going to take up my card?'

'No,' Adam said.

Cassie could not stifle her gasp.

Herbert must have heard her because his gaze sought her out. 'Ah, there you are, madam.' He curled his lip. 'I might have guessed you'd worm your way in to some chap's bed.'

Adam's fist crashed into his belly. Herbert's knees sagged. Adam struck him on the jaw. He sank to his knees cradling his face. 'Ouch.'

Fists clenched, Adam loomed over him and she feared he would strike again.

Cassie stepped forward and caught his arm. 'Adam, please.' She glanced up the stairs. 'The girls…'

'I'll thank you to keep a civil tongue in your head about a lady beneath my roof or face the consequences,' Adam said, breathing hard.

'The *lady* is wearing your—' Herbert put an arm up and cringed away when Adam clenched his fist. He shuffled back on his rear, until his back met the wall. 'You have no right to keep my sisters here,' he said truculently, pulling out a handkerchief and dabbing at his lip. 'I am their guardian. That…' He gave Adam a wary glance. 'That woman—' he pointed at Cassie '—stole them from under my roof, along with other valuable items. You will hand over my sisters if you know what is good for you.'

Cassie glared down at Herbert. 'Your wife threatened them with a beating.'

Adam clenched his fists again.

Herbert didn't seem to notice the effect of his words. 'Spare the rod and spoil the child. My father indulged those girls. Lucy was rude to my wife.'

'Bridget called Diana a good-for-nothing penniless orphan. Is it any wonder her sister responded as she did?'

'She needs to learn her place,' Herbert responded.

Cassie was glad Adam had knocked him down. But Herbert had the law on his side. If she did not allow the girls to go with him, he would not hesitate to bring the authorities down upon them. And she could not let them go alone.

'Very well. I will go with you. But I will have your word as a gentleman that there will no more beatings or deprivations for Lucy and Diana.'

'I agree.'

Adam gazed at her, his face bleak. 'You might have

died in that fire. How can you think of trusting the word of such a cur?'

Herbert flushed red. 'Fire? Nothing to do with me, old chap.'

'Liar.' Adam glanced down at Herbert's feet. 'Yours were the footprints I saw in the snow and if I'm not mistaken...' He bent and picked something from the leg of Herbert's breeches. 'Glass. From the lantern you broke.'

'I must have picked it up when I went to the cottage tonight.'

'Hardly likely. Glass cannot fly up from the ground and embed itself at the knee.'

'Who is going to take the word of a servant against that of a gentleman?' Herbert said, looking down his nose. 'Seems to me you would do better to go along with me, or risk losing your job.'

Cassie's stomach fell away. 'Adam, this is not your concern.'

'Oh, I think it is,' he said. 'Very much so. This man committed a crime. And I mean to see him punished.'

'You, sir?' Herbert spluttered. 'Just who do you think you are?'

'I am Viscount Graystone. My father is the Earl of Portmaine. Should my father learn you burnt down a building on his property, he will demand justice.'

Graystone? He could not be... Why had he lied to her all this time? She backed away. 'Adam?'

But he was not looking at her; he was glaring at Herbert, who sagged back against the wall.

'I don't believe you,' Herbert said, eyes wide. 'The heir to an earldom doesn't open doors.'

'This one does.'

'Adam?' Cassie repeated.

'I'm sorry, Cassie. I was about to tell you right when

this idiot banged on the door.' He glared at Herbert. 'What do you have to say for yourself now?'

Herbert dabbed at his brow. 'I—I beg your lordship's pardon. Had I known, I would never have—'

'You, sir, are a bully and a coward and you will leave my house at once. Cassie, do you want me to have charges laid against this fellow?'

The brusque man was back. And for a moment it felt good to contemplate Herbert's punishment. But he was still a part of her family. Herbert was an idiot. Led around by the nose by his unpleasant wife and his overweening ambition to be more than he was.

'Lady Cassandra,' Herbert said, trying to smile ingratiatingly and failing miserably. He wrung his hands. 'It was all a misunderstanding. I'll do anything. Sign guardianship of my sisters over to you, if you wish.'

'I suppose I could be persuaded to ask Lord Graystone not to lay charges,' she said slowly, seeing a glimmer of hope. 'If you sign over guardianship of the girls and swear in writing that when I left your home I took nothing that did not belong to me.' She glanced at Adam. 'If you think Lord Portmaine would agree, my lord?'

'I'll do it,' Herbert said quickly.

'And you will sign over the girls' allowance into Lord Graystone's care,' she added.

'What?' Herbert's face blanched.

'Starting now, since I assume all that has come before is gone.'

He swallowed.

Adam tugged him up by the collar. 'Well?'

'All right. All right.'

He and Adam disappeared into the library. Cassie slumped into a hall chair. Adam was Graystone. It made sense. The story of his wife. Him owning two carriages.

She would have seen it if she hadn't felt his pain so much as he told his story. Why had he lied?

She recalled their first meeting. She'd assumed he was a servant and he hadn't denied it. But he had given a false name. Likely he was regularly importuned by women seeking to marry a well-heeled and titled widower, while he remained true to his dead wife. Poor Adam. Well she would not make one of their number. She cared for him too much.

A few moments later, a chastened Herbert left by the front door. He slid a glance in her direction as if he would speak, but one look at Adam's fierce expression had him scuttling out. Adam threw the bolts home. 'He won't give you any more trouble. I had him admit in writing to setting the fire. The girls' allowance will come to you, though it seems a paltry enough sum.'

'Thank you. It will be all we need. But, Adam—I mean, Lord Graystone, I must apologise—'

'None of that,' Adam said gruffly. 'Cassie, darling Cassie, I hope you don't think less of me, because of the title. Believe me, I was about to tell you—'

A sound on the stairs made her look up. Two little girls were peering over the balustrade. When they re-alised she'd seen them, they ran down and flung their arms around her. 'Do we have to go back and live with Herbert and Bridget?' Lucy asked, her eyes over-bright.

Cassie hugged the girls close. 'Not if you do not wish it.'

'We want to stay with you, Mama,' Lucy said.

'And you, Mr Royston,' Diana added.

Adam's expression changed. Tenderness altered his harsh face into endearing handsomeness. He looked so lovely standing there looking down at the girls and there was such longing in his face. He glanced over at Cassie.

'Would you, Cassie?' he asked. 'Would you consider staying with me after I lied to you?'

She made a helpless gesture as longing of her own filled her. He could not mean this. He had not thought it through. He was being too kind. 'You have done so much for us already—'

'I need you, Cassie. My life was an empty shell until these past few days. I thought work was enough, but it isn't. You made me see that.'

Her heart felt too large for her chest. 'Adam, I—'

He closed his eyes, moved away to gaze down into the fire. He shook his head slowly as if coming to a decision. 'It's all right, Cassie. Having misled you, I know I don't deserve your trust.' His voice thickened. 'I also know how much you value your independence, so I won't push you into something you do not want. I do insist you and the girls remain here at Thornton until I find you a decent place to live. You will allow me to help you.'

'Why did you lie about who you are?' she asked.

He turned back to face her, his expression set, his eyes bleak. 'I often travel incognito. With the title comes obligations. Doing the pretty. After Marion died—' He shrugged. 'I didn't have the heart for it. And later, when I got to know you, I wanted to tell you, but worried I'd cease to be a man to you and become nothing more than my title. I feared we'd lose what we had. The easy companionship. I'm sorry for ever believing such a thing of you.' He squared his shoulders. 'And now you will accept my aid.'

Diana was staring at him, her little nose wrinkled up. 'Are you going to cry, Mr Royston?'

'No,' Cassie said. 'Lord Graystone is simply being manly and honourable and giving us what he thinks we want.'

'I don't like Lord Graystone,' Diana said. 'I want Mr Royston.'

'And you shall have him, darling,' Cassie said. 'If he still wants us.'

Adam expression changed to careful neutrality, but hope shone in the emerald depths of his eyes. 'Cassie. Only if it is what you truly want.'

She went to him, put her arms around him. 'Oh, Adam, how could you even doubt it? I love you, you lovely man.'

'I love you so much I don't have the words—' He hugged her tight with one arm, put his other arm out to the girls and enclosed them within the circle of his embrace.

'Welcome home,' he said softly.

Christmas Day

Adam stood beside his mother in Portmaine's great hall, watching the rest of the family gather around the enormous Christmas tree that was a tradition started by his great-grandmother, who had come as a young bride from Prussia. While his father, still an imposing man despite the way he'd grown portly and lost most of his hair these past few years, chatted with Cassie, the two little girls played at their feet with the dolls his mother had found in the attic when they had arrived tired and overwhelmed on Christmas Eve.

'I thought never to see you wed again, Adam,' his diminutive but stately mother said, her green eyes a shade lighter than his own intent upon his face. To anyone else she would have appeared her usual calm self, but he felt her concern.

'Nor I,' he said cautiously. He wasn't exactly sure she approved his choice of a bride or the manner in which he had announced it upon his arrival. His father, though, had seemed more than pleased.

'She is not the woman I would have chosen for you.' Her gaze drifted from Cassie's statuesque blonde lushness to the slender dark beauty making sheep's eyes at his younger brother, Rad, who was sorting through music at the piano. A young woman very much like his first wife in appearance.

'My tastes have changed.'

'Matured,' his mother agreed. 'I am so very happy for you.'

He relaxed. 'Thank you.' He grimaced. 'I hope you don't mind if we don't do the whole St George's church thing. Neither of us wants a lot of fuss.'

His mother's eyes twinkled. 'Yet another departure from the past.' Her lips curved in a knowing smile. 'And I am sure you have no wish to wait for weeks while the banns are called.'

He grinned. 'You are a wicked woman, Mama. And I love you for it.' He gave her shoulders a quick squeeze.

'Really, Adam. Remember my dignity.' But her eyes glowed with quiet joy. 'All I want is for my children to be happy.' She wandered off to stand behind Rad, putting one hand on his shoulder. Rad looked up at her and gave her his devil-may-care grin. Adam's oldest sister, Mary, joined them. Soon all the family would gather to sing carols as they had done all of Adam's life.

He strolled over to collect his betrothed and his soon-to-be daughters. 'Father, it is time for carols.'

'Then it is time to make sure our glasses are full.' The earl bustled off.

Diana rose to her feet and slipped a warm little hand inside his palm. 'May we sing, too?' she asked, looking up.

'Of course. You are part of my family now.' He picked her up and set her on his hip.

Cassie smiled at him and slipped her arm through his, while gesturing to Lucy to join them. 'You, too, young lady.'

The four of them joined the rest of the family.

'Happy, my love?' he asked in a murmur in Cassie's ear as Rad played the opening notes of 'Deck the Halls'.

'More than I ever could have believed,' she whispered back. 'But only with you, my dear sweet man.'

He kissed her cheek. 'Likewise, heart of my heart,' he murmured.

* * * * *

COMING NEXT MONTH FROM

⊞ HARLEQUIN®

ℋISTORICAL

Available November 17, 2015

MORROW CREEK MARSHAL (Western)
by Lisa Plumley
Dancing girl Marielle Miller makes sure no cowboy steps his boots out
of line. But then, one night, she tumbles from the stage into the arms of
Dylan Coyle!

HIS CHRISTMAS COUNTESS (Regency)
Lords of Disgrace • by Louise Allen
When Grant Rivers, Earl of Allundale, stumbles upon Kate Harding having a
baby out of wedlock, he's compelled to help... Will she consent to marrying
a stranger on Christmas Day?

THE CAPTAIN'S CHRISTMAS BRIDE (Regency)
by Annie Burrows
Lady Julia Whitney has struck upon a plan to ensure her marriage by
Christmas. She soon finds herself fully compromised...by the wrong man!

WARRIOR OF FIRE (Medieval)
Warriors of Ireland • by Michelle Willingham
Fleeing an unwanted betrothal, Lady Carice knows her days are numbered.
So when she meets Norman soldier Raine de Garenne she longs to
experience one night of passion...

Available via Reader Service and online:

LORD LANSBURY'S CHRISTMAS WEDDING (Victorian)
by Helen Dickson
Lord Lansbury knows true love must come second to a suitable match. So *why* is
he so bewitched by the violet eyes of his sister's companion Jane Mortimer?

LADY ROWENA'S RUIN (Medieval)
Knights of Champagne • by Carol Townend
Kidnapped by a masked horseman, Lady Rowena fears for her reputation. Until
she discovers her abductor is her father's favored knight Sir Eric of Monfort...

**YOU CAN FIND MORE INFORMATION ON UPCOMING HARLEQUIN® TITLES,
FREE EXCERPTS AND MORE AT WWW.HARLEQUIN.COM.**

HHCNM1115

REQUEST YOUR FREE BOOKS!

ⓗ HARLEQUIN®

ℋISTORICAL

Where love is timeless

2 FREE NOVELS PLUS 2 FREE GIFTS!

YES! Please send me 2 FREE Harlequin® Historical novels and my 2 FREE gifts (gifts are worth about $10). After receiving them, if I don't wish to receive any more books, I can return the shipping statement marked "cancel." If I don't cancel, I will receive 6 brand-new novels every month and be billed just $5.69 per book in the U.S. or $5.99 per book in Canada. That's a savings of at least 12% off the cover price! It's quite a bargain! Shipping and handling is just 50¢ per book in the U.S. and 75¢ per book in Canada.* I understand that accepting the 2 free books and gifts places me under no obligation to buy anything. I can always return a shipment and cancel at any time. Even if I never buy another book, the two free books and gifts are mine to keep forever.

246/349 HDN GH2Z

Name	(PLEASE PRINT)

Address	Apt. #

City	State/Prov.	Zip/Postal Code

Signature (if under 18, a parent or guardian must sign)

Mail to the **Reader Service:**
IN U.S.A.: P.O. Box 1867, Buffalo, NY 14240-1867
IN CANADA: P.O. Box 609, Fort Erie, Ontario L2A 5X3

Want to try two free books from another line?
Call 1-800-873-8635 or visit www.ReaderService.com.

* Terms and prices subject to change without notice. Prices do not include applicable taxes. Sales tax applicable in N.Y. Canadian residents will be charged applicable taxes. Offer not valid in Quebec. This offer is limited to one order per household. Not valid for current subscribers to Harlequin Historical books. All orders subject to credit approval. Credit or debit balances in a customer's account(s) may be offset by any other outstanding balance owed by or to the customer. Please allow 4 to 6 weeks for delivery. Offer available while quantities last.

Your Privacy—The Reader Service is committed to protecting your privacy. Our Privacy Policy is available online at www.ReaderService.com or upon request from the Reader Service.

We make a portion of our mailing list available to reputable third parties that offer products we believe may interest you. If you prefer that we not exchange your name with third parties, or if you wish to clarify or modify your communication preferences, please visit us at www.ReaderService.com/consumerschoice or write to us at Reader Service Preference Service, P.O. Box 9062, Buffalo, NY 14240-9062. Include your complete name and address.

HHI5

SPECIAL EXCERPT FROM

♦ HARLEQUIN®
TM

ℋISTORICAL

Fleeing an unwanted betrothal, Lady Carice's days are numbered. So when she meets Norman soldier Raine de Garenne she longs to experience one night of passion...

Read on for a sneak preview of
WARRIOR OF FIRE, a powerful new book from
Michelle Willingham,
*the second in her **WARRIORS OF IRELAND** duet.*

In the darkness, she reached up to Raine's face, touching his cheek. She explored the smooth surface, fascinated by him. He caught her hand and drew her fingers back to her lips in a warning to be still and silent.

The risk of being discovered was far too high. She knew that—and yet, she was tempted to seize a moment to herself. He was only going to push her away as soon as they were out of hiding. She wanted to embrace every last chance to live, even if it was pushing beyond what was right. Raine would never understand her need to reach out for all the moments remaining.

This man intrigued her, for he was a living contradiction. He was both fierce and benevolent, like a warrior priest. And though he claimed to be a Norman loyal to King Henry, she knew he was a man of secrets.

His skin was warm beneath her fingertips, his face revealing hard planes. A sudden heat rushed through her as she explored his features. During her life, she'd never had the opportunity to be courted by a man, and her illness had shut her away from the world. Her father had isolated her until it seemed that only the hand of Death was waiting in her future.

Perhaps it was the lack of time that made her act with boldness. Or perhaps it was her sudden sense of unfairness. There was a handsome man beside her, one who attracted her in ways she didn't understand. Being so near to him was forbidden...and undeniably exciting. Why shouldn't she seize the opportunity that was before her?

Her pulse was racing, and the proximity of his body against hers was a very different kind of risk.

He leaned down and, against her lips, he murmured, "Don't move." The heat of his breath and the danger of discovery only heightened the blood racing through her. She was aware of every line of his body, of his warm hands around her, and the feeling of his hips pressed to her own.

Her imagination revelled in what it would be like to be kissed by this man. His mouth was so close to hers...and if she lifted her lips, they would be upon his.

Don't miss
WARRIOR OF FIRE by Michelle Willingham.
Available December 2015 wherever
Harlequin® Historical books and ebooks are sold.

www.Harlequin.com

Copyright © 2015 by Michelle Willingham

HHEXP1115

Turn your love of reading into rewards you'll love with
Harlequin My Rewards

Join for FREE today at
www.HarlequinMyRewards.com

Earn **FREE BOOKS** of your choice.

Experience **EXCLUSIVE OFFERS** and contests.

Enjoy **BOOK RECOMMENDATIONS**
selected just for you.

PLUS! Sign up now
and get **500** points
right away!

Earn
FREE
REWARDS
HarlequinMyRewards.com
Join
Today!

MYR16R